SHIELD OF JUSTICE

What Reviewers Say About BOLD STROKES' Authors

✍

KIM BALDWIN

"Her…crisply written action scenes, juxtaposition of plotlines, and smart dialogue make this a story the reader will absolutely enjoy and long remember." – **Arlene Germain**, book reviewer for the *Lambda Book Report* and the *Midwest Book Review*

✍

ROSE BEECHAM

"…a mystery writer with a delightful sense of humor, as well as an eye for an interesting array of characters…" – *MegaScene*

"…her characters seem fully capable of walking away from the particulars of whodunit and engaging the reader in other aspects of their lives." – *Lambda Book Report*

"…creates believable characters in compelling situations, with enough humor to provide effective counterpoint to the work of detecting." – *Bay Area Reporter*

✍

JANE FLETCHER

"…a natural gift for rich storytelling and world-building…one of the best fantasy writers at work today." – **Jean Stewart**, author of the *Isis* series

✍

RADCLYfFE

"Powerful characters, engrossing plot, and intelligent writing…" – **Cameron Abbott,** author of *To the Edge* and *An Inexpressible State of Grace*

"…well-honed storytelling skills…solid prose and sure-handedness of the narrative…" – **Elizabeth Flynn**, *Lambda Book Report*

"…well-plotted…lovely romance…I couldn't turn the pages fast enough!" – **Ann Bannon**, author of *The Beebo Brinker Chronicles.*

"…a consummate artist in crafting classic romance fiction…her numerous best selling works exemplify the splendor and power of Sapphic passion…" – **Yvette Murray, PhD**, *Reader's Raves*

SHIELD OF JUSTICE

by

RADCLY*f*FE

2005

ISBN 1-933110-19-8

THIS TRADE PAPERBACK ORIGINAL IS PUBLISHED BY
BOLD STROKES BOOKS, INC.,
PHILADELPHIA, PA, USA

FIRST EDITION: RENAISSANCE ALLIANCE 2002
SECOND PRINTING: MARCH, 2005 BOLD STROKES BOOKS, INC.

CREDITS
EDITORS: LANEY ROBERTS AND STACIA SEAMAN
PRODUCTION DESIGN: STACIA SEAMAN
COVER PHOTOS: LEE LIGON
COVER DESIGN BY SHERI (GRAPHICARTIST2020@HOTMAIL.COM)

By the Author

Romances

Safe Harbor

Beyond the Breakwater

Innocent Hearts

Love's Melody Lost

Love's Tender Warriors

Tomorrow's Promise

Passion's Bright Fury

Love's Masquerade

shadowland

Fated Love

Distant Shores, Silent Thunder

Honor Series

Above All, Honor

Honor Bound

Love & Honor

Honor Guards

Justice Series

A Matter of Trust (prequel)

Shield of Justice

In Pursuit of Justice

Justice in the Shadows

Justice Served

Change Of Pace: *Erotic Interludes*
(A Short Story Collection)

Acknowledgments

The second printing of *Shield* marks its entry into the Bold Strokes Books lineup in the same month that the fourth book in the Justice series (*Justice Served*) is released. I had no idea when I first wrote out this story with a black Flair pen on yellow legal paper that it would be the start of a series that would challenge me as a storyteller and author like no other. The plot surprises and unexpected character twists along the way have been well worth the sleepless nights I spent wondering how I would ever hold it all together.

My first beta readers remain trusted friends, selflessly donating their valuable time and expertise to read and critique the work as it develops, while offering sensitive support and endless encouragement when I have doubts and misgivings. I would not want to do this without them.

Athos, I rely on you for your quick, careful reading and many personal 'good's. JB, as always, you hear the heartbeat of the characters and keep me close to them. Jane, chapter by chapter, your detailed comments and fine eye for subtle points chart a course that I can trust. Tomboy, you can always be counted on for fine critique of both concept and construction.

In addition, I'd like to extend my appreciation to HS (P,TB) for initiating and nurturing the Radlist all these years, to the list members for constancy and inspiration, and to Laney Roberts and Stacia Seaman for fine editorial input.

Lee, of course, deserves more than mere words can express for making room in our life for all it takes to tell these stories. *Amo te.*

Radclyffe 2005

Dedication

For Lee
For Believing

CHAPTER ONE

Dr. Catherine Rawlings pushed the last patient file aside with a sigh and glanced at the clock on the wall opposite her desk. During a session, she could see the time without looking away from a patient regardless of whether they occupied one of the two leather swivel chairs in front of her desk or the sofa on the far side of the room.

Not too bad—9:20 p.m. Just enough time to head home for a hot bath, a cold drink, and an hour in bed with...who will it be tonight? Kellerman? Grafton? McDermid?

Smiling ruefully at the mundane plans that were fast becoming her nightly routine, she ran a slender hand through her shoulder-length auburn hair and tried to shake the fatigue out of her neck and back. She was halfway to the door when the interoffice line on her desk buzzed. With a frown of surprise, she turned at the sound. At this time of night with her office hours over, her secretary, Joyce, had usually left. Even if Joyce stayed to catch up on filing, she rarely put a call through that could wait until the next day, and almost all of them could—a consult at the hospital, a new patient referral, a current patient calling about a prescription renewal. Puzzled, she leaned across the wide teak desk to push the speaker button.

"Yes?"

"There's a police officer here to see you, Doctor," Joyce replied in the voice she reserved for professional exchanges.

Catherine noted her formal tone and didn't bother to ask for details. She frequently performed consultations for law enforcement agencies—evaluating officers for work-related stress or other forms of psychiatric disability—but she'd rarely been called for anything on an emergency basis. She tried not to speculate; things were rarely as one imagined them to be. "Show him in, Joyce."

A moment later, her secretary, a slight, dark-haired woman who had worked for the Department of Psychiatry before becoming her personal assistant, pushed open the heavy mahogany door separating Catherine's office from the outer waiting area. Joyce's expression was both curious and slightly perplexed. Before she could speak, however, a figure moved from behind her and strode briskly forward.

Catherine, private by nature and reserved by virtue of her training, knew that her face rarely revealed her inner feelings, and she was glad of that now. She would not have liked her surprise, or her subsequent chagrin, at assuming that *police* meant police*man* to be displayed to the woman who approached with one hand outstretched.

Quickly, Catherine took in the gold shield clipped to the pocket of the officer's navy blue blazer and noted the tailored fit of her pale shirt and gray gabardine trousers. Tall, blond-haired, and blue-eyed, the woman moved with a degree of assuredness that suggested she was rarely intimidated. She was slender, but there was a suggestion of power in the sleek lines of her shoulders and narrow hips. *Viking* was a term that flashed through Catherine's mind, and it certainly seemed appropriate. Surprisingly, she felt an instant surge of curiosity that went beyond the basic interest in people that had led her into the practice of psychiatry. Putting the distracting thought from her mind, she rose to accept the woman's outstretched hand. "Catherine Rawlings." The strong hand that took hers was smooth and surprisingly warm.

"Dr. Rawlings, I'm Detective Sergeant Rebecca Frye. I'm sorry to disturb you so late, but I need to ask you a few questions."

Her voice was as cool and even as Catherine had expected it to be, totally professional, and although her words were appropriately apologetic, her tone was not. There was a hint of impatience and something else—something just beneath the surface. Anger?

"Yes?" Catherine replied, settling into her high-backed leather chair, looking into the clear blue eyes that revealed nothing. "Is it Detective or…"

"Detective is fine," Rebecca said tersely, considering her next words carefully.

Interrogation was an art. Some people you befriended, some you manipulated, some you intimidated. Almost never did you reveal what you wanted, and you never gave up until you *got* what you wanted. What she wanted now, what she desperately *needed* now, was information, and Dr. Catherine Rawlings had it. The problem was that the legalities in this particular situation were cloudy. If they got bogged down in technicalities right off the bat, she might have to wait days for answers. And she didn't even have hours to spare. She took stock of the psychiatrist seated across from her, trying to get a quick fix on the best way to proceed.

Medium height and build. Eyes—gray-green; hair—reddish brown. Pale green silk suit. Expensive, not flashy, just like her. Confident carriage; intelligence behind the eyes. Intense, composed—cool. No anxiety, no irritation, no hostility. Solid, steady, strong. Bottom line—she's not going to be impressed by my badge or intimidated into divulging information. Let's try the direct approach.

Rebecca pulled a small black notebook from the inside of her jacket, flipped it open and gave it a cursory glance. *Maybe a little surprise will soften her up, make her lose a little of that composure, and she'll tell me what I need to know before she has a chance to think about it too much.*

"Dr. Rawlings, do you have a patient by the name of Janet Ryan?" Rebecca had hoped to catch the doctor off guard, but the eyes that regarded her were calm, almost gentle.

"Detective," Catherine said softly, leaning forward over her desk, her hands folded loosely on the top, "surely you know that I can't answer that question."

Oh, fuck. Not this again! Rebecca shifted almost imperceptibly in her chair, struggling to contain her intense irritation. God, how she hated dealing with these ethically rigorous types, when all she needed was a little assistance. People kept saying that the Special Crimes Unit—really the *Sex* Crimes Unit—wasn't responsive enough to the needs of the community. It was damn hard to be effective when no one, including the victims themselves sometimes, wanted to tell you anything.

"Believe me, Doctor, I wouldn't be here if this weren't serious. I understand that you have to protect your patients' privacy, but this is official police business."

"I do believe you, Detective, but, police business or not, it does not supersede my responsibility to my patients," Catherine replied quietly. "There are protocols for these situations."

Rebecca bit off a retort and settled back into the chair, reminding herself that she'd handled roadblocks like this before. Persistent to the point of belligerence, or so she'd been told, she was often effective where other investigators failed precisely because she wouldn't allow the resistance of professionals or even the fear of victims to deter her. She never harassed the victims, though. With them she took it slow, explaining as many times as necessary how she could help if given the chance. Most of the time, her sincerity and compassion won the needed cooperation, and she had been able to bring to trial many offenders who might otherwise have gone free. This time, the stakes were so high that her usual imperturbation was taxed to the limit, and she knew she would blow the whole interview if she didn't settle down.

"I don't want you to reveal confidences, Doctor," Rebecca tried again, forcing a conciliatory tone into her voice. "I need help with an identification, that's all." She was stretching the truth, but she was in the ballpark of veracity at least.

Catherine watched her carefully, sensing the detective struggle with her impatience. "Perhaps if you could tell me what this is about?"

"I presume you've heard of the recent attacks along River Drive?"

Catherine's face grew tense as she nodded.

Good, that got some reaction. "We have reason to believe that Janet Ryan witnessed an assault around six o'clock tonight near a turnoff on the Drive. There is evidence to suggest that this may be the third attack by the same perpetrator. I need to find out what she saw." *And I need it two hours ago. Every minute I sit here teasing information out of you, the trail gets colder.*

"Why don't you simply ask her?"

Rebecca's gaze never altered. She continued to stare directly into Catherine's eyes. "Because she's in the intensive care unit at University Central. She's been beaten; she's incoherent; and as far as we've been able to ascertain, she can't remember anything about what happened. Your business card was in her purse. It seemed like a place to start."

Oh, Lord, Janet! Catherine stood up and walked to the window that overlooked the downtown skyline. After a moment's deliberation, she returned her gaze to the detective, who sat silently watching her. "Would you mind stepping into the waiting room for a few moments? I need to make a phone call."

Rebecca rose immediately, hoping that the psychiatrist was going to meet her halfway. Before she broke eye contact, Rebecca said vehemently, "I want this bastard, Doctor. I want him off the streets before he touches one more woman." She thought she saw a flicker of rage that matched her own in the green eyes that held hers. "Right now, I can use any help you can give me."

Chapter Two

As soon as the door closed behind the tall detective, Catherine unlocked her active patient files and retrieved a pale blue folder. She glanced at the personal intake form and jotted down a number. Dialing quickly, she prayed she wouldn't get one of those infernal answering machines. To her relief, a human voice answered after only two rings.

"Hello?"

Sensitive to the slightest nuance of tone or expression, Catherine heard the anxiety and fear in the young woman's voice and began gently. "Barbara? This is Dr. Rawlings—"

"It's Janet, isn't it?" Barbara Kelly interrupted tremulously. "She should have been home hours ago, and she always calls if she's going to be late. What is it? What's happened?"

"She's alive and in no immediate danger," Catherine said immediately, knowing that the fear of death was what caused most people to panic in these situations. "I don't know all the details, but I do know that Janet is in the hospital. She's injured, but she's conscious. Do you understand that, Barbara? She's alive."

"Oh, God! Where is she?"

"University Central. I was afraid that you hadn't been notified." Inwardly, she cursed the system that ignored the most important relationship in a person's life when it most mattered. "I know you want to be with her, Barbara, but there's something I need to discuss with you first. The police are here at my office. They believe that Janet may have witnessed a crime, and they need some information. I'd like to help them as much as I can if you'll trust me to protect Janet's confidences."

She hated to do this to Barbara now; the young woman's anxiety was practically palpable over the phone. Still, she couldn't discuss Janet

Ryan with the police without the consent of Janet's designated medical power of attorney. She was stretching the definition as it was, but she knew Janet well and made the judgment that Janet herself would have given her permission had she been able.

"Yes, of course—we both trust you. Do what you think is best. Please, I need to go to her!"

"Wait. Do you have someone to drive you there?"

"I'll call my sister, Carol. She'll go with me. Thank you for calling me…"

Having been left with the dial tone sounding in her ear, Catherine set the receiver in its cradle and walked to her office door, opening it to scan the waiting area. Joyce had apparently gone home, as the lights had been turned down low and the room was still.

Detective Frye was slumped in a chair, her head tilted at what appeared to be an uncomfortable angle. For the first time, Catherine noted the deep circles under the detective's eyes and the lines of fatigue that marred her otherwise flawless face. The well-tailored clothes were also rumpled from hours of wear. *She looks like she hasn't been to bed for days.*

"Detective," Catherine said softly.

Rebecca Frye jolted upright, her eyes snapping open. She focused instantly on Catherine. "Yes?"

"Come in, please."

When they were once again seated, Catherine informed her, "Janet Ryan *is* my patient. I'm not sure how I can help you, however."

"I don't know either, but at this point any information is a start," Rebecca responded in obvious frustration. "We need a statement from her as to what happened tonight. We think she's a witness, but she *claims* she can't remember anything. Is she likely to lie to us?"

"I doubt it," Catherine answered with certainty, "but it would help if you could tell me the circumstances of the situation."

"Around six p.m. tonight, a twenty-year-old woman was savagely beaten and sexually assaulted. That makes a total of three similar sexual attacks in that area of the park in the last eleven months. This one and the last one were only six weeks apart. This rape victim is in a coma, Dr. Rawlings. She's one of the lucky ones. The other victims are dead." Rebecca was unable to keep the anger from her voice.

She and her partner had been working the cases since the

beginning, but they hadn't connected the first two assaults because of the long time interval between them. With the third attack, the pattern had become clear, and they realized that they were dealing with a serial rapist. Now, three victims too late, they had almost nothing to go on and no witnesses. She blew out a breath. She couldn't make up for the lost time, but she refused to lose any more.

"There were signs of a significant struggle, but the victim didn't look like she had a chance to fight back at all. Your patient was found wandering around not far from the scene just before 7:00 p.m., disoriented and clearly having been involved in an altercation. We need a break—and your patient may be that break."

"And she can't tell you what happened?"

Rebecca shook her head.

"Surely you've had the psychiatrist on call see her?"

Rebecca nodded and consulted her notes. "A Dr. Phillip Waters."

"I know Phil," Catherine remarked. "What did he say?"

"That it *might* be traumatic amnesia—shock induced by whatever she may have seen." Rebecca tried not to sound skeptical, but it wouldn't be the first time that she'd been stonewalled in an investigation by cautious health care personnel who didn't want to commit to a diagnosis.

Catherine nodded in agreement. "Very possibly. What about head trauma? You said that she'd been beaten." Her voice was steady, but she shuddered inwardly at the thought of the young woman she knew being violated that way.

"A CT scan was normal," Rebecca said, again consulting her notes. "Preliminary examination showed evidence of concussion and a...uh...nondisplaced fracture of the left orbit."

"That's a significant injury, Detective," Catherine said quietly. "It makes the possibility of traumatic amnesia even more likely."

"Is Janet Ryan a stable person?"

"What do you mean?" Catherine asked.

Rebecca was too tired to hide her annoyance. Why did these people insist on answering every question with another one? "I mean, Doctor, is Janet Ryan likely to fake this amnesia thing—for attention, or a thrill, or to fuck with the police? Until I know, my hands are tied." At Catherine's questioning look, she continued sharply, "If Janet Ryan is mentally impaired, any statement she makes will likely be inadmissible in court. At the moment, I'm more interested in an arrest, but I'll need her to testify when the time comes. I can't question her under less than optimal circumstances."

Catherine regarded Rebecca silently for a moment. She would have been irritated by her seemingly callous suspicions of Janet's condition, when Janet was clearly a victim herself, if she hadn't recognized the detective's frustration and fatigue. Everything about her, from the barely contained tension in her body to the rage simmering in her voice, made it obvious that this case affected her strongly.

"I have known Janet Ryan for several years," Catherine answered firmly. "She is a very reliable, responsible woman, and I would be very surprised if she didn't do everything in her power to assist you—when she's able."

Rebecca started to point out that people were capable of all types of subterfuge, given the right motivation, but she was interrupted by the sound of her pager. Grimacing at the intrusion, she flicked it off with her thumb and pointed to the phone. "May I?"

"Of course," Catherine replied, watching the detective, who had leaned one hip against the edge of the desk as she dialed. As she was facing the windows, her profile was to Catherine. If she was aware of any scrutiny, she didn't show it. Her eyes were fixed on the streets below, her expression distant, and Catherine doubted that she actually saw the life passing outside. She seemed impervious to distractions. Catherine wondered what price that kind of focus and control exacted, especially when the case was as high profile and emotionally charged as this one.

"Frye here," Rebecca said as the dispatcher picked up. She raised an eyebrow as she listened. "When?…Yes, I'm there now…All right, fifteen minutes." She replaced the receiver and turned to Catherine. "Janet Ryan is asking for you."

Catherine rose quickly. "I'll go right now."

Rebecca reached the door first, pulling it open. "I'll drive you."

Catherine understood that this was not a request and lengthened her stride to match that of the taller woman beside her. It was clear that Rebecca Frye was not used to giving up until she got what she wanted, and, unfortunately, she wanted something that Catherine knew she might not be able to give her. For some reason, that thought bothered her.

CHAPTER THREE

Detective Jeffrey Cruz found Rebecca in the visitor waiting area on the fifth floor of University Central, feeding nickels into the coffee machine. He thumped her lightly on the shoulder as he stepped up beside her.

"Hey, Reb. How's it hanging?"

She looked at her partner, noting the sallow color of his normally light brown skin, and shrugged tiredly. "Better than yours, probably. You get anything from the crime scene techs?"

He grimaced as he, too, pushed coins into the slot. "Not yet. Flanagan and her crew are still out there. It started to drizzle about thirty minutes ago, and they're running around like maniacs stringing tarps up between the trees, trying to preserve the scene."

"Fuck," Rebecca swore, cradling her cup and leaning against the dispenser. "Just what we need. Did they at least get the castings of the footprints done?"

"Some of them," Cruz replied, "but it's a real mess. The jogging path is right there, and even though the spot where he took her down is isolated, there's still a lot of foot traffic. And then there's the whole area where the witness was found. It's a big section to cover. They're going to lose a lot of trace evidence in the rain."

"Yeah." Rebecca sighed in disgust. "At least it's Flanagan. She'll have them straining the mud if it comes to that. If there's something there, she'll find it."

She walked to the row of plastic chairs and sat down with another sigh, this one of fatigue. She'd only caught a few hours of sleep the night before and would likely have even fewer tonight. "Anything from the lab yet on the physical evidence from the rape victim?"

"Not much we don't already know. Preliminary analysis points to the same perp. He's a secretor—blood type, A-positive. I tried to goose the lab guys for more, but they're complaining about being swamped with stuff from that apartment fire. They say it looks like it might be arson. The earliest they'll have the semen analysis will be sometime tomorrow morning. Emergency room docs confirm she was sodomized, though, just like with the first two."

Rebecca took a deep swallow of her coffee, wincing at the cardboard aftertaste. "Yeah, well, the rest of it fits our guy's pattern, too. A jogger again. Same time of day—early evening, not yet dark. The location's no help, though; there're miles of park along the river. Nothing stands out about this particular place."

Jeff slumped into the hard seat beside her, shaking his head. "Something's funny, Reb. The park is *always* crowded—kids on bikes, runners, not to mention cops—and nobody sees nothing. Nobody notices anyone just hanging around or in a hurry to get somewhere. He just comes and goes without a trace." He laughed sourly at his own joke.

Rebecca shook her head, as frustrated as her partner. "There's a lot of brush along those trails, Jeff. Once he grabs someone, he can just pull her off into the scrub. Then they're invisible. Christ, we didn't even find the first body for three days."

She had been to her captain twice in the last few weeks, pleading for extra patrols to stake out the dense parkland bordering River Drive, a six-mile stretch of twisting highway along the river that bisected the city. His answer had been the same each time—yes, this was a nasty crime; yes, he cared about catching the son of a bitch; and, no, he couldn't spare the people to beef up surveillance. They had to do the best they could with what they had, and Rebecca was haunted by the knowledge that it wasn't enough.

"Well, *he's* still got to get in and out," Jeff observed. "He probably parks somewhere and goes in on foot or maybe on a bicycle. Someone has to have seen him. With this warm weather, there's even more people around."

"Maybe somebody *did* see something—maybe it was Janet Ryan."

He sighed deeply, leaned his head back against the rim of the plastic seat, and closed his eyes. "Maybe."

"There's something we're missing, Jeff, I agree with you," Rebecca mused aloud, not even sure if Jeff was awake. "Serial criminals—

rapists, murderers—they follow a pattern. At least a pattern that makes sense to them. We just have to find it."

"You're probably right," Jeff answered, his eyes still closed. "But whatever it is, it isn't simple. Different days of the week, no set time interval, no physical resemblance between the victims, and nothing symbolic left behind."

"We should cross-check the victim profiles again. Resubmit the data to VICAP at the FBI, too," Rebecca said, knowing it had to be done but secretly doubting it would help. The crimes had a random feel to them. "We have three now; maybe we'll turn up an association we missed the first time. Maybe they all go to the same health club, or the same grocery store, or the same friggin' dry cleaners. Maybe he knows them. Maybe he stalks them."

"Maybe," Jeff murmured again, envisioning the next few days. *More canvassing, more interviews, re-interviews, more computer spreadsheets. Wonderful.* He sat up and checked his watch—almost the witching hour. *Jesus, I'm tired.* "Did you get anything out of the shrink?"

"Still waiting. She's in there with the witness now."

Jeff stood and walked to the double doors marked Hospital Personnel Only and craned his neck to see through the small windows. "That her by the first bed?"

Rebecca followed him and glanced inside. The psychiatrist was leaning down, holding the hand of the woman in the bed nearest to the doors. "Yes."

"Nice," Cruz remarked absently. "Who's the other one—blond, early twenties, good body?"

"The roommate, I think. I haven't had a chance to talk with her yet." Rebecca didn't add that she hadn't had the heart to question the young woman who had arrived to see Janet Ryan. She had been clearly distraught and probably didn't know anything anyway. There'd be time enough to talk to her once she'd had a chance to see her girlfriend.

Jeff looked at his watch again and groaned. "Shit. Shelley's gonna have my balls if I don't get home before dawn again tonight."

They'd officially been off duty six hours ago, even though neither of them watched the clock when they were working a fresh scene. Still, he knew if he waited for his partner to call it a night, he'd never get to bed. She didn't seem to notice how late they worked, and she never seemed to have anywhere else to be except at work. If he kept her kind of hours, his wife *would* kick his ass.

Rebecca stretched, trying to ignore how tired she was. "Why don't you go ahead? I want to see what the shrink gets, but there's no sense in us both sitting around. You can write up what we've got so far in the morning...deal?"

Jeff grinned happily, all vestiges of fatigue gone. He wished for the thousandth time that he was as tall as his good-looking partner. He never let on that it bothered him that she was an inch or two taller, and he couldn't help noticing the admiring glances she got, from men *and* women. She never seemed to notice, though. Oh, well, his wife thought his body was spectacular, so what the hell. He thumped her affectionately on the arm again and sprinted for the elevator before something else turned up to delay them. "I got the best part of this deal," he added over his shoulder.

Rebecca didn't doubt it. There was no one waiting for her at home, and there hadn't been for a long time. She had forgotten what it felt like to open her door to anything other than the cold welcome of her empty apartment, and she didn't want to remember now. She sat back down, closed her eyes on the thought, and adjusted her long frame into a more comfortable position for the inevitable wait. She fell asleep with the image of Janet Ryan's battered face in her mind.

Chapter Four

Catherine wearily pushed open the doors of the intensive care unit and stepped out into the quiet corridor. It took a moment for her eyes to adjust to the dimness after the bright lights inside, and when she could see again, she noted Rebecca Frye asleep on a visitor chair.

Even in repose, the detective didn't appear relaxed. Her right hand twitched slightly as it rested against her thigh. Her jacket lay abandoned on the chair beside her. The silk shirt she wore was stretched tight by the slash of a leather weapon harness encircling her shoulders, the muscles of her arms and the swell of firm breasts clearly outlined by the tautly drawn fabric. Catherine's pulse quickened as her eyes wandered from Rebecca's chiseled face down the sensuous planes of her body. She smiled slightly at the unbidden physical response, wondering yet again at the body's remarkable will of its own. She didn't need to remind herself why they were both there; she simply ignored the pull of her autonomic nervous system.

"Detective," she called gently as she approached.

Rebecca sat up immediately, rubbing her face briskly with both hands, and looked up at the psychiatrist, who somehow managed to look fresh despite the hour. Rebecca grinned a little sheepishly, taken off guard by the welcoming softness in Catherine's eyes. "Sorry."

"No, I'm sorry," Catherine said with a smile. "I seem to keep waking you up."

"No problem. I tend to fall asleep wherever I can."

Catherine laughed. "I know what you mean. When I was a resident, we had a saying, 'See a chair, sit in it; see a bed, lie in it; see food, eat it.' And we did exactly that."

Rebecca stood, stretching to her full six feet. "I'm sorry," she said again. "I know it's late, but I have to talk with you. It won't take too long, but if there's someone you need to call…"

"No, there isn't," Catherine replied without hesitation. She looked at her watch and was surprised to see that it was now officially tomorrow. "But I have no intention of saying one more word to you unless I'm fed first. I missed dinner, and it feels like my last meal was a week ago. Can you wait that long?"

Rebecca regarded the elegant woman before her, sensing the smile in her voice, and felt suddenly energized. She reached for her jacket and slung it over one shoulder.

"Why not? I'm on my own time now, anyhow."

"Excellent," Catherine responded, surprised at how much the prospect of dinner with the handsome detective pleased her. She was also surprised at the sudden warmth in the other woman's eyes that made her heart race. Again. She was rarely this susceptible to appearances, and yet there was something more than just good looks about this woman that attracted her. Perhaps it was the intensity with which the tall, blond detective seemed to do everything, even stride down the hall.

"There's a diner up the street," Rebecca offered as they walked toward the elevators.

"Arnie's? Not at this hour. My digestive system would never survive," Catherine exclaimed in mock horror. She hesitated for a moment and then said lightly, "My apartment isn't far. Could we finish up there? It will just take me a minute to fix something."

Rebecca was momentarily taken aback by the offer. Then to her surprise she realized that she would like nothing better than to have a late dinner with Catherine Rawlings. Hoping that she sounded casual, she replied, "Sounds fine. Don't think I could take one more burger anyhow."

The address to which Catherine directed her was in a gentrified section of the city bordering the university area, replete with the requisite coffee bars, small sidewalk cafés, and huge rents. It matched the image Rebecca was forming of this woman—refined but in no way staid.

"I'll just be a minute. I've been in these clothes all day," Catherine said as she let them in and tossed her briefcase on a small telephone table just inside the door. "The living room's to your right, and the kitchen is in the back. Help yourself to a drink if you like."

Catherine's large first-floor apartment was in a recently renovated brownstone, and the small but well-appointed kitchen opened onto a private rear garden. Rebecca couldn't see much of the patio through the sliding glass kitchen doors, but the high-ceilinged rooms she had glimpsed through partially open interior doors were tastefully decorated in soothing earth tones and elegant but functional furnishings. She decided she liked the doctor's style, although it would be hard not to appreciate the understated but obviously expensive surroundings. The atmosphere was warm and welcoming, and Rebecca finally began to unwind.

She wandered into the spacious living room and perused the titles—mostly recent novels and biographies—on the floor-to-ceiling bookcases that lined one wall, noting several she had been meaning to read but kept putting off. Something usually came up at the station that devoured any available spare time. She was reminding herself this was not a social engagement and that she still had work to do when the doctor came through the archway from the kitchen.

"Glass of wine?" Catherine had changed into a loose white cotton blouse over black brushed-silk trousers and carried a bottle in one hand.

"Just seltzer and lime, if you have it," Rebecca replied, suddenly aware of Catherine as more than just a subject in her case log. She was truly a beautiful woman. Her angular features and prominent cheekbones were softened by flawless skin, framed by wavy, richly highlighted auburn hair, and appeared very nearly perfect. Her wide set, gray-green eyes sparkled with intelligence, and her generous mouth bestowed a human quality that was far more appealing than any artist's classic rendition. Rebecca found herself really appreciating another woman for the first time in months. She didn't realize she was staring until Catherine's full lips parted in a soft, playful smile, breaking her reverie.

"No drinking on duty?"

"No drinking for me any time. At least not for the last four years," Rebecca said evenly. *Four years, three months, and two days.*

"Ah," Catherine said, hearing the tension in her voice. "I'll put this back, then."

"No," Rebecca countered quickly, allowing herself a genuine smile. "Most of the world still drinks, and honestly, it rarely bothers me now. It would be harder if you didn't drink just because of me."

"Well, then," Catherine responded graciously, "come into the dining room so I can at least feed you."

❖

Rebecca pushed back her chair with a sigh. She had forgotten how pleasant it was to sit down at a table and enjoy a meal. And to enjoy the company of a warm, intelligent woman. "Thank you," she said. "It was wonderful."

"Pasta and salad—my specialties," Catherine replied lightly, unaccountably pleased by the compliment. She felt almost rewarded by the detective's enjoyment and found that odd. Perhaps it was just a response to that brief flicker of pleasure that had softened the hard edges of Rebecca Frye's fatigue and given her a younger, carefree look for an instant. "I take it you don't cook much."

Rebecca shrugged ruefully. "Never did, and it's worse now that I live alone. I just don't think about eating as something to enjoy anymore." She stopped, suddenly embarrassed. *Christ, Frye, why don't you tell her all your problems?* "At any rate," she finished hurriedly, "it was great."

"You're welcome." Catherine recognized the detective's discomfort as well as her withdrawal. Neither surprised her. She generally found people in Rebecca's line of work reluctant to reveal intimate details and slow to trust. The police officers she had evaluated all seemed to expect the worst from any situation—or from any relationship. Suspicion and a basic wariness of surface appearances had saved many an officer's life, but it had destroyed many a marriage, too. She wasn't sure if it was the work that made them that way, or if those pre-existing traits were what made them so good at their jobs. And that question suddenly interested her very much.

Be honest, Catherine. Rebecca interests you. She had to admit that she wondered what lay beneath that cool, controlled exterior—for she was certain that there were depths to Rebecca of which the woman herself was unaware. She'd caught glimpses of tenderness when Rebecca smiled, but she remembered, too, the barely controlled rage in the detective's voice when she had described the rapist's last attack—and her passionate declaration to stop him. *Oh, yes, there's much more to this woman than she wants anyone to see.*

"So, what do you need to know, Detective?" Catherine asked as she refilled her half-empty wineglass and directed the conversation away from the personal. At the moment, they had other issues to deal with. She leaned back, watching her dinner companion, waiting.

"Probably more than you can tell me. I need to know what you learned from your evaluation of Janet Ryan. Does she have any memory of the last eight hours?"

"Not much. She remembers pulling into a drive-off on River Drive on her way home from work. She doesn't remember the time. The next thing she remembers is waking up in the ICU."

Rebecca frowned. "Does she recall seeing anyone else around when she pulled in? Can she recall anything out of the ordinary?"

"I don't know. I didn't specifically ask her. She was pretty disoriented and frightened. I was trying to establish the extent of her amnesia and get her calmed down."

"Of course," Rebecca said, trying not to let her aggravation show. She couldn't expect a psychiatrist to think like a cop. She'd planned to interview the woman in the morning anyhow. "Anything else? Anything at all?"

"I'm sorry, no. Her amnesia is total for the time in question."

"And you have no doubt that she's telling the truth?" Rebecca looked at her carefully, watching for some sign of uncertainty.

"None at all."

Satisfied, Rebecca nodded. Catherine Rawlings had a way of making you believe her. "How long will it last?"

"I don't know," Catherine said regretfully. "I wish I did."

Rebecca stood up, her jaw set with determination. "I can't wait for her to remember. The time between attacks is getting shorter. If she can't help us, I'll have to find some other way to get to him." She thanked Catherine absently, already preoccupied with planning her next move.

Catherine watched her as she walked to the door, wondering how long it would be before Rebecca Frye let herself rest again.

CHAPTER FIVE

Rebecca let herself into her apartment and tripped over the gym bag she had left lying on the floor several days earlier. The air had the musty, close smell of an unoccupied house, and when she switched on a floor lamp by the sagging sofa, she caught a shadow of the fine dust covering the sparse furnishings. She pushed open a window and stood looking out. Her second-floor, one-bedroom place was over a mom-and-pop grocery store in a neighborhood that straddled the narrow border between trendy and downtrodden.

She'd grown up a few blocks away and had walked the beat below her window as a rookie, ten years ago. She liked the casual comfort of living in a place where people knew her name, maybe because the people who waved to her as she carried sandwiches back from the deli or trudged wearily past the storefronts after two days on her feet were the only people in her life besides the other cops at the station house.

It was warm for early June, and the night air held just the hint of a breeze. She leaned against the window ledge, hoping to wash away the depression that had settled over her the moment she got home. The empty apartment was too clear a reminder of her own empty life, an aching barrenness she tried hard to ignore whenever she couldn't outrun it. Usually, she was successful. The demands of her work left her little time for reflection, and when she did have a spare moment, she spent it at the gym, lifting weights until she was too exhausted to think about anything at all. Days, weeks sometimes, passed before she was forced by some phrase or memory to remember that it hadn't always been this way—that *she* hadn't always been this way—solitary and withdrawn. Or maybe she had, and she had just never noticed.

The interlude with Catherine Rawlings had unsettled her. The quiet intimacy of the doctor's apartment, the shared meal, the soft but insistent strength she had sensed in the woman, touched some chord of emotion that she had thought long stilled. For a few brief moments, she had forgotten all about her case, and she had contented herself with just looking at Catherine, being soothed somehow by her gentle eyes and quiet laughter. She didn't want to think about the quick surge of loneliness she had felt as Catherine's door closed gently behind her.

She pushed back from the window and looked at her watch—3:00 a.m. She was tired but too restless to sleep. It was one of those times she longed for a drink. Or, she corrected herself, more than one drink, as had usually been the case. Something to deaden the edges of her isolation and ease her away from the horrors and pain she witnessed every day. She fought the urge, again, by turning her mind to her current case. There was something there, she knew, that she just wasn't getting. A missed connection. Some little thing she had heard, or seen, or *should* have seen, that would give her a handle on him. Whatever it was, it eluded her now.

Unbidden, her thoughts returned to Catherine Rawlings. She couldn't figure out just what it was that made the woman so compelling. Her integrity concerning her patients was unshakable, and Rebecca admired that resolve even though it was making her job more difficult. She was obviously beautiful, intelligent, and compassionate, but it was something deeper that had captured Rebecca's attention. Catherine Rawlings had, in the course of a few hours, awakened in her some long-buried yearning for the company and solace of a woman.

Rebecca wondered then if she hadn't merely imagined the warmth in the doctor's gaze when she had looked at her. With an irritated shrug, she shook off the memory of Catherine Rawling's smile. *It's what she does, you idiot. She's supposed to make people feel as if they're supported and really matter.*

She tossed her jacket on a chair and pulled off her shoulder holster, draping it on the back, before stretching out on the worn couch. She rarely slept in her bed; the empty space beside her only made sleep more elusive. What she couldn't know as she finally closed her eyes was that, across town, Catherine Rawlings turned in her sleep and smiled at the image of a tall, blond woman with lonely eyes.

It was not yet seven a.m. when Rebecca pulled her red Corvette convertible into the lot behind the Eighteenth Precinct, slotting it in between the police cruisers and vans. She knew Jeff would be upstairs already, typing out their report of last night's events. She smiled to herself at the thought of Jeff's face as he labored over the typewriter. She should probably take pity on him because she typed three times faster than he did, but a deal was a deal. As anticipated, she found him hunched over his rickety metal desk in the tiny squad room on the third floor, slowly two-finger typing a report in triplicate.

"Hi, Reb," he said without glancing up. "Anything from the shrink?"

"About what you'd expect," Rebecca answered, shedding her jacket to the back of her chair. "Nothing yet. Want some more coffee?"

"Yeah," he said, looking up long enough to toss her a lecherous grin. "I'm gonna need it. Late night. Shelley was still awake when I got home."

"Nice to know someone's making out," she grumbled good-naturedly as she headed for the table at the back of the room. She threaded her way between dilapidated chairs and dented desks haphazardly crowded together, nodding to the few people finishing up paperwork from the night shift.

She and Jeff Cruz were a two-man team within the Vice unit, specializing in one particular area—sex crimes. They pursued their allotment of battered spouses and child abuse call-outs, but, for most of those cases, they assessed the situation and then assigned the follow-up to uniforms or turfed the appropriate ones to the Youth and Family Services division. Their bread and butter was handling bigger, more organized problems—child pornography rings, prostitution as a subsidiary of organized crime, and, like now, the repeat sexual predator.

She filled two Styrofoam cups to the brim with the evil-looking black liquid that passed as coffee. She carried them at arm's length back to the desk that faced Jeff's and pushed a stack of files to one side with her elbow. After settling into her chair, she steeled herself for the first taste of the bitter brew.

"Ah," she murmured after her first swallow. "Nectar of the gods."

"You must still be asleep if you think that swill is good." Jeff reached for his own cup without taking his eyes off his typewriter.

She shrugged and snatched the first page of his report. As usual, it was neat and complete. "You could use the computer, you know," she remarked. "It would make corrections a lot easier."

He favored her with a dour look and said nothing.

"Nothing new, I take it," she continued, skimming the brief review of the latest assault.

"Still waiting on the lab reports, but I figured we could stop down there later and bug Dee Flanagan. See if her crime scene crew turned up anything after I left last night." Jeff stretched his legs and pushed his chair back from the cramped table. "I ran a background check on the shrink."

Rebecca looked up in surprise, instantly and unexplainably defensive. "Why? She's not a suspect."

"Yeah, I know," he acknowledged with a shrug, "but she's tied in with our only witness to date. She might be the one who can open that particular box for us. I figure it never hurts to have a little leverage."

The idea of strong-arming Catherine Rawlings was not a pleasant one, but as much as she hated to admit it, Rebecca had to agree. If they were going to get anything from Janet Ryan, she suspected they would need the lovely doctor's help. *And if we can't get her cooperation, we may have to try less-friendly tactics.*

"So, what did you find?" she asked, careful not to reveal her interest. Jeff might be her partner, but even with him, she rarely disclosed anything personal. She certainly wasn't about to tell him of the disturbing effect Catherine Rawlings had had on her.

"Professionally, above reproach—medical degree from Johns Hopkins; psychiatry residency at University Central. From there, she accepted a teaching position at the medical school and is now a…" he paused to check his notes, "clinical professor of psychiatry. Directs the residency program; busy private practice. A big shot as those things go. Personally though, it seems the lady is quite a mystery."

Rebecca listened intently. She wasn't surprised by the impressive list of credentials. It fit with the impeccable professional image she had formed the previous night. "So, what's the mystery?" she asked impatiently when Jeff suddenly stopped talking.

"I talked with a couple of the docs I know, and they all say the same thing. Or rather, they all *don't* say anything. No one knows word one about her personal life. She lives alone, apparently always has.

Everyone is happy to tell you about her professional accomplishments, but nobody will say squat about the rest of her life."

"Maybe there isn't anything to say," Rebecca countered, just a hint of irritation in her voice. "Some people are pretty consumed by their work, you know. Look at cops. They leave the station house, go have a few beers with other cops, check in at home for an hour or two, and come right back in. The job is their life."

Jeff looked at her thoughtfully, thinking if anyone should know about that, it was his solitary partner. "Yeah, well, that may be. But I did dig up something interesting about her private practice—she specializes in rape and incest cases. She's even done some work with us on that kind of thing. Sensitivity training or something."

"Huh." Rebecca thought of Janet Ryan and her amnesia. *Possibly a link?*

"And that's not all," he continued, "a lot of her private patients are dyk...uh, lesbians."

Rebecca slowly raised her eyes to his, fixed him with a steady stare, and waited for him to say something further. He looked away.

"Might be useful information," she said nonchalantly. She felt anything but nonchalant, her mind racing with questions about Catherine Rawlings. She forced herself to consider the information Jeff had gathered. "Maybe I should have another talk with Dr. Rawlings."

"Thought you might want to," Jeff replied dryly.

Catherine was nearly finished with morning rounds when her pager went off. After excusing herself, she left the group of residents and students, who were discussing the latest drug therapy for depression. She picked up a wall phone and dialed the extension registered on her beeper.

"Dr. Rawlings," she said as the call was picked up.

"Rebecca Frye, Doctor. I wonder if we could talk?"

Catherine glanced at her watch. She had an outpatient clinic to supervise in an hour. "I'm in-between right now. How about joining me in the cafeteria?"

"Fine."

"It's on the second floor."

"I'll find it," Rebecca replied.

Catherine picked up a chef's salad and seltzer and glanced around the cafeteria. She saw Rebecca Frye at once, looking slightly out of place in her gray jacket and black trousers amidst a sea of white coats. She made her way across the room to join her at a small table near the windows.

Rebecca watched the doctor approach, appreciating the fact that she did not wear a clinical lab coat but was dressed instead in a simple navy suit. Only the beeper clipped to the waistband of her trousers indicated she was a doctor. Rebecca tried not to notice her trim figure or the curve of her breasts under the softly tailored jacket. It wasn't easy, because Catherine Rawlings was stunning. Finally, she looked away, studying her coffee cup and waiting until the other woman was seated before speaking. "I have a few more questions, Dr. Rawlings."

"I gathered that, Detective Sergeant Frye," Catherine commented dryly, studying the other woman's face. She was glad to see that the circles under those clear blue eyes had faded slightly and that some of the tension had disappeared. She was also simply glad to see her.

"Is it true that you specialize in rape and incest cases?" Rebecca asked abruptly.

Catherine was a little taken aback, not with the directness of Rebecca's approach—she expected that of the forthright detective—but with the rapidity with which she gathered information. Catherine had known that this, among other things, might come up. She just hadn't expected it so soon. She answered steadily, "Not exactly *specialize*, but it is a particular interest of mine."

"Don't give me double talk, Doctor. I'm not the enemy," Rebecca said quietly.

Catherine sighed and pushed aside her unwanted salad. She met Rebecca's penetrating gaze. "Yes, it's true that the majority of my private practice involves treating sexual abuse survivors."

"Why didn't you tell me this last night?"

Catherine looked genuinely surprised. "I didn't think it was relevant."

"You didn't think it was *relevant*?" Rebecca asked incredulously. "We finally have a witness, we *hope*, to a brutal rape—a *series* of rapes we can't get a single lead on—and our only witness suddenly has amnesia. You happen to be an expert in such crimes, and you didn't think it was *relevant*." Rebecca didn't raise her voice, but her anger was evident. *God, save me from dealing with civilians!*

"Detective Frye," Catherine began in a reasonable tone, "I am not an expert on the *crimes*. I am an expert, if you will, on the *effects* of the crimes. That's a very big difference."

"And what about Janet Ryan? Is she a victim of the crime?"

"Don't ask me questions you know I can't answer," Catherine said quietly, her eyes holding Rebecca's. "Don't make this a contest."

Rebecca sighed slightly. "I have to try."

Catherine leaned forward, her face intent. "Rebecca, I will do anything I possibly can to assist in this case, but I cannot, and I *will* not, disclose patient confidences. Please try to understand."

"I do understand." The use of her first name did not escape Rebecca Frye. She tried to ignore the quickening of her heartbeat, reminding herself she was in the middle of a hospital cafeteria and in the middle of an investigation. "I appreciate your desire to protect your patients, and I respect you for it. I'm just grasping at straws here. I can't get a handle on this guy, and it's driving me nuts." That last was an uncharacteristic outburst. If she had personal feelings about a case, she rarely displayed them, not even to Jeff, and most certainly not to a subject she was in the process of interviewing.

As Catherine watched the torment play across Rebecca's fine features, she felt every shred of the detective's frustration and helplessness. "I'm seeing Janet at three this afternoon," she confided, her voice quiet with compassion. "She requested that I take over from Phil Waters. Perhaps she'll remember more—something I'll be able to tell you."

The concern was evident in the psychiatrist's voice, and so was her obvious desire to do what she could to assist the investigation. For that, Rebecca met her gaze gratefully. And for an instant, her awareness of the people seated nearby and the sound of many voices echoing in the cavernous space faded, and she surrendered to the comfort offered in those green eyes. It felt like a caress, so tangible her heart pounded almost painfully. Seconds, minutes passed—she didn't know. Flushing, she finally looked away and forced herself to remember why she was there, willing her pulse to still. When she spoke, her tone was cool and uninflected—a cop's voice again. "I'd like a report either way."

Acutely aware of the fleeting connection and the equally sudden distance between them, Catherine accepted Rebecca's withdrawal reluctantly. She pushed her chair back, replying formally, "Of course. You can call me around six tonight. I should be done here by then."

"Fine," Rebecca replied, except it wasn't. The psychiatrist's effect on her was almost addictive. Her skin actually tingled just from the memory of the warmth in Catherine's eyes. Impulsively, she added, "Why don't I pick you up here? We can talk over dinner. And you won't have to cook."

Surprised, Catherine nodded with pleasure. She would like nothing better than to spend more time with this intriguing woman.

CHAPTER SIX

Rebecca caught up with Cruz midafternoon at the station house. He was staring at a computer screen, muttering under his breath, a half-eaten burrito forgotten by his right hand. The soda next to the crumpled fast food bag had sweated through the cardboard container and looked in danger of flooding the desktop any second. She looked over his shoulder and sighed when she saw the list of license plate numbers and drivers' addresses scrolling down the page.

"Checking the summonses given out on the Drive yesterday?" she asked.

"Yeah," he snarled. "Talk about long shots."

"Has to be done," she remarked, shaking her head in sympathetic agreement. "Remember Son of Sam. We'd look like morons if it turns out our perp parked his car somewhere, got a ticket while he was beating and raping a woman, and we never noticed."

"There were twenty tickets written in that area in the two hours on either side of the time we figure it went down," he said, pushing back in the swivel chair and then rubbing his face.

Rebecca whistled softly. "Busy place."

"It's the regatta," Cruz remarked dispiritedly. "People end up parking anywhere to watch the boat races."

"Well, commandeer some uniforms from traffic and have them cross-check these with the names and numbers on tickets given out on the days of the first two assaults. Give them a general rundown of the working profile—you know—eliminate all women, kids under eighteen, men over fifty. The usual. You and I can screen the rest and maybe get one of the eager beavers from patrol to run down any possibles for us."

Cruz grinned up at her. "I suppose you were never one of them?"

When Rebecca cocked a questioning eyebrow, he clarified, "Eager beaver, dying for the gold shield?"

"Yeah, maybe," she said, her eyes shadowed for an instant. "Once."

He studied her, surprised that after almost five years he still didn't know what secrets she kept. He shrugged the thought away. It wasn't his business what ghosts haunted her, not unless it affected the job, and it never did. Not anymore. "Want to go start a fire under the crime team people?"

Rebecca shook her head. "Later. Let's walk the scene again first."

He didn't see what good that would do, but on the other hand, they didn't have anything else to do except wait for a break from the lab. And Frye had an uncanny way of piecing the scene together and coming up with a lead for them to follow. He'd seen it before—that cop sense that let her see or feel or somehow sense what had gone down. She had the instinct, and he hoped somehow it would rub off on him.

"Right," he said, as he scooped up the remains of his lunch and dumped it in the trash.

Twenty minutes later, they stood surveying the spot where the third assault had occurred. The site was a copse of trees that edged the riverbank, no different than a dozen other spots along River Drive. Thirty feet from the water's edge, running parallel to the river for miles, was a narrow, unpaved path bordered by trees and water on one side and a thicket of low shrubs and grass on the other. The road, which followed both the river and the path, was easily fifty yards away. Although the park and its many trails were frequented day and night by bicyclists, runners, and dog-walkers, this section of the trail was poorly maintained and densely overgrown, which tended to discourage all but the most serious joggers. The isolated location was similar to that of the previous two rapes, a fact that helped them not at all.

The most recent victim—Darla Myers, age twenty-two, a business graduate student—had been found by a middle-aged man chasing his errant golden retriever. He'd almost stumbled over her in the brush just off the path, and it was probably a chance encounter that saved her life. Had she lain on the ground unconscious all night, or longer, she probably would have died.

"So," Jeff Cruz said as they walked slowly under clear blue skies surveying the detritus left by the crime scene analysts the night before. Bits of yellow police tape, an occasional splatter of plaster of paris used to cast the few footprints left on the rocky ground after the rain, and one curled paper backing from a Polaroid print littered the area. "He pulls them off the trail, rapes them, and then beats them half to death. Then he waltzes away and nobody notices. Prick bastard."

"Yeah, he is," Rebecca said quietly, looking at the broken branches and trampled shrubbery in the spot where Darla Myers's body had been found. "But I don't think that's quite how it goes down. He beats them first, into unconsciousness, *then* he rapes them. The first two didn't fight back, remember—probably because they couldn't."

Cruz followed her gaze, looking at the obvious evidence of a struggle. "This one did."

"Yeah," Rebecca said softly, "*someone* did. And that's a change."

She walked a few feet off the trail; Jeff followed silently. She stood in the thickets, looking back up the path the way Darla Myers had probably come, judging from where her car had finally been found. She couldn't see more than ten feet.

"It doesn't quite work," she said almost to herself. "Even if he was hidden back here, invisible, he would have had to step out into plain view to get close enough to subdue her—and the others. They should have had some warning, a chance to run or to scream—something."

"Maybe he just looks innocent," Jeff offered. "Or maybe he's doing the Bundy thing. Pretending *he's* injured and asking for help like Bundy did when he faked having a broken arm."

"No weapon's been found," Rebecca countered. "The injuries sustained by the victims only indicate that some kind of blunt object was used. Damn. We need a witness. If Myers doesn't wake up, then the only chance we have to learn what really happened here is if Janet Ryan really *was* here, and that she remembers what she saw." *Soon, make it soon.*

The details of the crime continued to elude her, and she knew in her heart that the key to finding the attacker was in the specifics of what he did. She forced herself to imagine it all in slow motion, like reviewing a movie frame by frame. She tried to distance herself from the mental images she constructed. If she allowed herself to hear the victims' cries, feel their fear, experience their helplessness, her own anger and revulsion and pity would paralyze her. She would never be able to do her job, and she would never be able to help them. It was a lesson she had learned early in her career, and the emotional detachment came naturally to her now.

"Jeff," she mused, "how about this? Our guy waits in the trees until a lone jogger comes along. He steps out and strikes her...a rock, or a club of some kind."

"We didn't find *any* kind of weapon," Jeff pointed out.

"He must take it with him. I guess a guy with a baseball bat wouldn't seem that unusual. Still, he needs to get to *his* car. Or maybe he has a bicycle. That would make it very easy for him to come and go."

Cruz nodded, clearly frustrated. "God, though, you'd think someone would have seen something! It's been in all the papers. No one has even come forward with a *bad* tip."

"Yeah, it's hard to believe that no one has seen or heard anything. But then, perhaps someone finally has." She looked at her partner as they followed a progressively narrower path through the trees toward the water. "It keeps coming back to Janet Ryan. Did you get a report yet on the tissue under her fingernails?"

"Due later today," Jeff replied, pushing aside the shrubs that leaned out over the water on the edge of the riverbank. There was a narrow strip of sand a few feet below them and then the bottom fell steeply away. He could make out the shapes of the boathouses a few hundred yards down the river. There was nothing unusual about the place.

Rebecca led the way back toward their car. "I bet you find that the tissue type matches the semen analysis we have. Janet Ryan must have seen the rape in progress, or she heard something and went to investigate. My guess is that *she* tried to fight the guy off, not Darla Myers. Janet has scratches on her arms and legs as if she got tangled up in the brush. He probably beats her, too, then leaves her for dead, or just panics and runs."

"Could have gone down like that," Jeff agreed. "That makes Ryan one gutsy lady, or a crazy one. Most people would have run for help, don't you think?"

Rebecca shrugged. "Who knows? Maybe she didn't even think about it. She sees what's happening and just reacts."

"Then we really need to know what Janet Ryan saw," Jeff said with finality.

❖

Rebecca pulled into the no-parking zone in front of University Central Hospital at 5:45 p.m. She took out the notes she had made at the crime scene that afternoon and was soon absorbed in trying to find some angle that she hadn't considered.

Catherine felt a surge of pleasure when she spied Rebecca waiting in the car across the street, frowning over her notebook. The convertible top was down, and the detective looked attractively windblown. She was jacketless, and the thin leather strap that circled her shoulders, holding her holster against her side, was apparent as Catherine approached. She had no particular feelings about firearms, and she appreciated the necessity of them in Rebecca's line of work, but the sight of the gun under the detective's arm reminded her forcefully of the kind of life Rebecca led.

She admired her and yet, at the same time, wondered what the steady onslaught of danger and violence must do to her. The previous night at dinner, Detective Sergeant Rebecca Frye's capability and strength had been obvious, but it was the fleeting glimpse of compassion and vulnerability that had captivated Catherine. The complexity of the contrasts made the detective all the more appealing.

As she walked up to the passenger side of the car, Catherine tried not to think about how much she had enjoyed their few hours together, reminding herself firmly that this woman had been there on business. Still, she couldn't quite dismiss the excitement Rebecca's presence evoked. "Hi," she said.

Rebecca looked up, and in a rare unguarded moment, welcomed Catherine with a blazing smile. "Hi."

The doctor stood motionless, transfixed. *Lord, she's breathtaking.*

"You're very prompt." Rebecca leaned over to push the passenger door open.

"Don't be fooled. It doesn't happen often." Catherine laughed, settling into the contoured leather seat, and ignored the quick racing of her heart. She wasn't used to being so susceptible to a woman's mere smile. She waited until Rebecca maneuvered into the dense traffic crowding the street in front of the hospital before speaking. "Have you made any progress with the case?"

"Not much," Rebecca replied, frowning. "Everything points to what we first thought. Your patient interrupted him, probably physically intervened. That means she saw him. She might be able to give us a description." She gave Catherine a questioning, hopeful look.

Catherine shook her head. "Not yet. She's heavily sedated and still has only slim recall of last night's events. It could be a few days, perhaps a week even, before she has any clear recollections."

"Can I speak to her?"

"She already spoke with the officer who brought her to the hospital."

"I know that," Rebecca responded curtly, no longer smiling. "But that was just a preliminary interview, and she was incoherent then. I need to go over things in detail, and I know what to ask."

Catherine thought about Janet's fragile emotional state and tried not to consider her own ever-increasing desire to assist Rebecca Frye. Janet must remain her primary concern. "I have an hour scheduled with her tomorrow afternoon. If she's ready, I'll let you know. I'd like to be present when you question her. Do you mind?"

"Not at all," Rebecca said quickly, turning off the main city arterial onto a twisting two-lane road that led to one of the affluent suburbs. "In fact, I'd prefer it."

"Well, then, it would seem we don't have much to discuss over dinner," Catherine remarked with regret. She realized then just how much she had been looking forward to their time together. More, she had to admit, than she had looked forward to an evening with a woman in a very long time. *This is business, Catherine. That's all it is to her and all it should be for you.*

"Good," Rebecca replied, turning her eyes from the road to glance at Catherine expectantly. "I still want to take you to dinner." She didn't want to think about what it meant; she only knew she didn't want to say good night to Catherine Rawlings quite so soon.

"Good," Catherine answered softly, immediately forgetting her cautionary thoughts of an instant before. "I was hoping you'd say that."

CHAPTER SEVEN

Rebecca pulled into a tiny, tree-shaded parking lot behind a three-story, hundred-year-old mansion with a wide pillared porch, French doors, and leaded glass windows that looked as if it were someone's home. It was. Catherine glanced at Rebecca in surprise when she recognized the restaurant. DeCarlo's was exclusive, expensive, and renowned for its world-class chef and quiet, intimate décor.

"Do you happen to have a reservation?" Catherine asked as they walked up the flagstone path. She couldn't imagine they would be seated without one.

"No," Rebecca answered, apparently unconcerned.

Less than a minute after Rebecca gave her name to the maître d', who smiled at her with obvious pleasure, the owner, Anthony DeCarlo, approached.

"Ah, Rebecca," he said by way of greeting, taking her hand in both of his. "You stay away too long."

"Anthony," Rebecca responded quietly. "How are you?"

"I am fine. We are all fine."

"Good."

"Come. I have a nice little spot just for you." He showed them to a secluded table that afforded a view of the sweeping lawns and luxurious gardens. He left them to ponder the eclectic selections artistically displayed on fine parchment menus, promising to send the sommelier immediately.

"Do you come here often?" Catherine asked, more than curious about the special service they were receiving. They had been seated without delay, despite several parties waiting ahead of them.

Rebecca shrugged uncomfortably. "Not for a long time. But whenever I do, Anthony insists on waiting on me himself."

She's embarrassed, Catherine thought, intrigued. She waited, knowing there was more.

"His daughter disappeared a few years ago," Rebecca continued in a low voice, remembering the run-down rooming house and the frightened teenage girls inside. When she looked at Catherine, she couldn't quite disguise the pain of the memory. After so many girls in so many squalid squats, the sorrow had become a dark ache in her eyes. "She was fifteen years old, working on her back for a pimp who had promised her the excitement a girl her age longs for. What he gave her was a needle in the arm and a beating if she didn't earn enough."

She hesitated, wondering how to describe the rest. She didn't know how to explain what she felt when she found Anthony's youngest daughter strung out on smack and turning tricks for twenty dollars a pop—anger so intense that she forgot she was a cop. Her overwhelming need to stop the waste and the abuse blinded her to the consequences of what she was doing. She'd been on the verge of beating the young pimp with her bare hands and, if Jeff hadn't interceded, she probably would have done serious damage. She was grateful now that Jeff had stopped her, but the rage still seethed, fueled by her daily witness of the devastation of lives and the destruction of dreams.

"I brought her home," she finished, keeping the anguish to herself, refusing to acknowledge it. That was the price she paid to maintain her sanity, even though people who couldn't see past her cop's eyes had accused her of being cold and uncaring.

Catherine, though, so sensitive to the sounds of silence, caught glimpses of Rebecca's secret tears in the expressive planes of her face and the ever-changing depths of her dark blue eyes. She ached for the young girl who had nearly been lost but even more for the detective who had found her.

"You returned his child. To him, that would be life's greatest gift. He's trying to thank you without making you uncomfortable," Catherine said softly. Rebecca winced, and Catherine continued lightly, "You'll just have to tough it out, Detective. I don't imagine he's going to stop."

Rebecca heard the gentle mocking in Catherine's voice and caught the glimmer of a smile on her full lips. The knot of anger in her chest loosened, and her tension miraculously dissipated. She broke into a grin that brought a flash of brilliance to her eyes and a youthful energy to her face. "Well, Doctor...if that's your professional opinion..."

"It is," Catherine responded, rewarded by the light in Rebecca's eyes. *She's even more beautiful when she smiles.*

Never could Catherine remember being moved so deeply, so quickly, by anyone, and the force of her response was frightening. She listened to the pain of others every day, and although she cared, she could distance herself in order ultimately to help. But it had been different with Rebecca from the first moment she had seen her. *I hardly know her. Why do I want so badly to take the sadness from her eyes?*

Rebecca startled Catherine from her reverie with the words, "Then it's *my* professional opinion that we should enjoy dinner. No more business tonight."

Catherine agreed happily and, after following the detective's suggestion to try the house special, settled back contentedly with a glass of wine. Over the course of the delicious meal, she found herself telling Rebecca about her life.

"I'm an only child. My father was a college professor and my mother a doctor, also a psychiatrist," Catherine said, thinking about the estate on which she had grown up, not far from this very place. "I loved my parents, and I'm quite certain they loved me. I rarely saw them, however; at least that's how it seemed to me then. They had me later in life; I think I may have actually been an accident. They were both very active in their professions, and I lived away at school from the time I was ten."

Rebecca watched her while she spoke, hearing the distant tone creep into her voice as she remembered aloud. She heard the sadness, too. "Were you lonely?"

Catherine stared, surprised by the question, wondering how she knew. "I was," she admitted. "I always got the feeling that I was an interloper in their lives. They were madly in love, I know now, and I don't think that they really needed—or wanted—a child to make that complete."

Her parents had always maintained an emotional closeness with each other that sometimes made Catherine feel excluded. As a result, although this was something she didn't share with Rebecca, Catherine was reserved in her own personal life. She wasn't interested in casual relationships, and she'd never found anything to compare to the intensity of what she had witnessed between her parents.

She smiled at Rebecca, who was regarding her seriously. "Don't misunderstand. They were loving and supportive, and I wouldn't have traded them, now or then."

Rebecca nodded. "So noted." Realizing they had strayed into very personal terrain, she searched for more causal ground. "What do you do for entertainment?"

"I love to read and take long bike rides. I'm a sucker for old movies, and I have been known to spend several hours in a bookstore on more than one Sunday morning," Catherine answered. "How about you?"

Rebecca grinned ruefully. "Ah. I'm a pretty typical cop, I'm afraid. When I'm not working, I'm working out. I have on occasion been known to read a book, though."

"How did you decide on law enforcement?"

"I didn't decide," Rebecca said with a shrug. "I was born into it, like a lot of cops. My father was a beat cop for forty years, just like *his* father. I always knew I would be a cop, too. I took a slight detour and went to college first, but there was never any question I would be a street cop."

"And do you like it?" Catherine asked, interested professionally on one level but much more intrigued because she wanted to know the woman beneath the cop's armor.

Rebecca looked startled, as if the idea were new to her. "There's nothing to like or not like. It's what I do."

It's what I am. She didn't say that, but Catherine heard the words nevertheless. Rebecca's pride and satisfaction were evident in her voice. She looked more at ease now than Catherine had ever seen her, and Catherine found herself appreciating the handsome detective's quiet charm and attentive companionship.

"A family legacy, I see," Catherine commented lightly. "I'm sure your father is proud."

"He was," Rebecca admitted, her expression distant. Then she added, her voice steady, "He answered a domestic dispute call eight years ago. When the wife opened the door, her husband shot her and my father. He died at the scene."

"I'm so sorry," Catherine responded softly, appreciating the depth of the detective's loss.

"Thanks," Rebecca acknowledged. "It happens." She smiled faintly at Catherine and pushed back in her chair, letting the memory go. She didn't want to think about that now, not when she was enjoying the doctor's company so much. "I promised no shop talk," she added. "Tell me about the next movie on your list to see."

Catherine complied, and they lingered long after the other diners had departed, only leaving when neither of them could hide her weariness. They drove in companionable silence through the now quiet streets, and, for the first time in weeks, Rebecca didn't think about work. What she thought about was the hint of Catherine Rawlings's perfume that drifted to her on the night breeze. When she pulled up in front of Catherine's brownstone, she realized suddenly that she didn't want the evening to end.

"Catherine, I..." Rebecca began, turning to face her companion in the close confines of the front seat of the sports car. She faltered, wondering what in hell she was doing. She wanted to tell her how great the evening had been, and how much she wanted to see her again, but the very words felt foolish. Even if the timing weren't terrible, which it was, she couldn't imagine why a woman like Catherine Rawlings would be interested in her. *What could I possibly have to offer?*

"Yes?" Catherine's expression was warm and welcoming as she responded.

Rebecca flushed and looked away, her jaw tightening. She sensed Catherine waiting, but too many disappointments haunted her, holding her a silent hostage.

Catherine touched Rebecca's arm gently, causing her to look at her in surprise. "I had a wonderful time tonight."

"Me, too," Rebecca answered, amazed at how good it felt to say that. "A very good time." She hesitated, took a breath. "Maybe we could do it again?"

"I'd like that." Then Catherine added, hoping that her intuition wasn't way off base, "Rebecca, for the record...I'm a lesbian. If you didn't already know that, I'm sure you would soon. Also, not necessarily for the record, I find you very attractive."

Rebecca's pulse quickened. "I should say something suave right now, and I'll be damned if I can think of anything."

Catherine laughed, then continued seriously, "I have no idea what your situation is, or what your interests might be, or even if..." She stopped, realizing that she was in danger of babbling, which was completely unlike her. "I *do* want to see you again. I just want you to know that I have no intention of doing anything to make you uncomfortable."

Unable to hide the quick surge of pleasure, Rebecca grinned. "Catherine, there is *nothing* about you that makes me uncomfortable."

The doctor grinned back as she slipped from the car. "That, Detective Sergeant Frye, is very good news."

Rebecca waited until Catherine had unlocked and opened her door before pulling away. Catherine stood, her hand on the doorknob, watching Rebecca drive out of sight. They were both still smiling.

CHAPTER EIGHT

At 7:45 the next morning, Rebecca met Jeff in the squad room. It was their morning routine to review open cases and map out the day while they got jump-started with the high-octane dregs of the night shift's coffee.

"What's the plan?" he asked, regarding her across their file-strewn desktops. He deferred to her not so much because she outranked him but out of long habit. He'd worked with her since he was a rookie detective, and he was comfortable with her steering their investigations.

Rebecca grimaced. "I've got a court appearance at noon to give evidence in that racketeering trial. Until we get something from the crime scene techs, I thought we'd finish some of the paperwork on the cases heading for the dead files."

These were inactive investigations, cold trails abandoned for lack of leads after fruitless weeks of searching or, even more frustrating, cases where witnesses were unwilling to appear in court. She hated to abandon cases she knew she could get convictions on, but too often, people refused to cooperate, either from fear of exposure or retaliation. It was another disheartening part of working Vice she had learned to live with.

He scowled at the mountain of paperwork piled on his desk, muttering, "I can't face this today."

"Give me some," Rebecca said amiably, reaching out a hand. "I'm just filling time until court. I was going to drop by the lab just to make a little noise. See if I can shake anything out of Flanagan. It'll keep."

Jeff raised an eyebrow and took a good look at his partner. She was dressed as usual in well-fitting linen trousers and a tailored cotton shirt, but something was different. There was an aura of freshness and energy about her that he hadn't noticed in months. "Something happen?"

"What do you mean?" Rebecca asked absently, tossing a finished folder to one side.

"Well, you look like something good happened. Something break on the River Drive case?"

Rebecca blushed. After dropping Catherine off the night before, she'd found herself more restless than usual. Her normal antidotes hadn't seemed to work. She'd driven around, stopped at the gym for a late workout, even contemplated cleaning her apartment when she'd finally arrived home. Eventually, she'd stripped down and pulled on a tank top and pair of loose boxers, finally deciding to try to sleep.

She stretched out on the bed, something she hadn't done since her last lover left. Amazingly, when she shut her eyes, it wasn't the case she thought about, but Catherine—the astonishing warmth in her gaze, the tender tone of her voice, her gently curving smile. She remembered, too, the light scent of perfume and the outline of breasts under a sheer silk blouse. Heartbeat quickening, without intending it, she imagined the soft weight of breasts in her palm—nipples stiffening under her fingers—and the heat of pale, perfect skin under her lips.

She brushed her hand under the thin cotton of her tank top, gasping at the quick contraction of her nipples. She squeezed them firmly, her legs parting involuntarily as she began to harden and swell. She drifted, thought surrendering to sensation. Light teasing strokes down her abdomen made her shiver. Legs tensed as one hand trailed up the inside of her thigh, fingers finally slipping under the edge of the loose shorts. Breath rushing in and out—not thinking, just feeling—all her attention focused on the pressure between her legs. Moaning softly, spreading wetness over the hard prominence of her clitoris, circling, pressing from side to side, feeling it become impossibly larger. Legs twisting in the sheets as she clenched her teeth, denying herself as long as she could. When the distention became almost painful, she broke. Bearing down harder with her fingertips, she worked herself faster, pushing toward the edge. Groaning, her skin flushed with the heat of need and loneliness and desire, she hovered on the brink. So close, she tugged at the engorged base, arching her back, every muscle tensed to explode. She shouted when it hit, grabbing herself with her whole hand, squeezing out the last spasm as she jack-knifed on the bed from the force of the orgasm.

She looked at Jeff, her expression carefully blank. Something had happened all right, but she wasn't about to tell her partner that she had awakened, still wet from the night before, with Catherine Rawlings on her mind. She didn't want to think too much about wanting her last night...this morning...now. She didn't want to admit to herself just how much she had enjoyed her company. She knew only too well how devastating it could be to need a woman.

"No," she said, more harshly than she had intended. "There's nothing new. I might get to interview Janet Ryan this afternoon, though, if Catherine gives us the green light."

Jeff didn't miss the first-name reference, but he let it pass. They were as close as two partners could be, and he considered Rebecca his friend, but he knew better than to ask for details. He respected the distance she demanded in their relationship.

"Sounds good to me. Want me along?" he asked.

Rebecca thought about it for a moment, then shook her head. "Not this time. She might talk easier if it's just me. Then again, she might not talk at all."

Jeff loosened his tie a fraction of an inch, which was his only concession to the stifling heat in the room. He was always Brooks Brothers neat, unlike most of the other male detectives, who seemed to cultivate the disheveled look. "I agree. The two of us could put her off. I've got a meet with Jimmy Hogan later anyhow. He called this morning."

"Has he got something for us on Zamora?" she asked with interest.

Jimmy Hogan was an undercover narcotics agent who had infiltrated a multistate drug distribution network. He'd been under almost six months when he'd first contacted them with the news that the same organization was trafficking in kiddie porn and maybe in the kids themselves. He said he'd tip them to the details if he could do it without blowing his cover.

"Don't know," Jeff said as he drained his coffee cup and got up to get a refill. He motioned with the cup inquiringly to Rebecca, but she shook her head no. "He said he couldn't talk, but that he had something hot for us."

"Good," she said sharply. Like most cops, she hated anyone who preyed on children. "Let me know if you get anything we can roll on."

"Right," he said absently as he walked away, wondering if he'd be able to get home for an afternoon quickie with Shelley after the meet with Hogan.

Shortly after four p.m., Rebecca stepped off the elevator onto the inpatient psychiatry floor. Turning left toward the patient rooms, she saw Catherine leaning against the counter at the nurses' station, studying a chart. She slowed and took advantage of the opportunity to observe the psychiatrist unawares, noting the easy way she stood, her sleekly tailored skirt outlining shapely legs. Even the slight frown of concentration couldn't diminish the delicate allure of her features.

Rebecca knew what she was feeling as she looked at Catherine Rawlings, and it worried her. She didn't *want* to be stirred by her, but she was, and it wasn't just physical, despite her erotic fantasy the previous night. The swift rush of desire was bad enough, but what she *felt* when she saw her, the ache of longing—that more than worried her. It scared her. That was downright dangerous. To make matters worse, she was in the middle of an ugly case, and the last thing she needed was a personal complication. Rebecca had stopped walking without realizing it and was standing a few feet away, awash with conflicting reactions, when Catherine looked up.

"Hi," Catherine called as she pushed the chart aside, smiling in welcome. Not even thinking to hide her pleasure, she surveyed Rebecca's tall figure with appreciation. She knew very well that she had been distracted all morning, an unusual circumstance for her, and she also knew very well why. She'd been thinking about seeing the detective again, remembering the swift stab of excitement she'd experienced when she'd been favored with that brilliant grin the night before. There had been nothing ambiguous about *that* reaction. She'd been...aroused in a way she couldn't recall ever having been before. *Pheromones*, she thought, watching Rebecca Frye, long-limbed, lithe, and so commanding, and felt that tingle start again. *Whatever they are, she's got them.*

Rebecca forced herself to start moving again, ignoring the heat spreading through her as she noted Catherine's admiring glance. *It's probably all in my mind,* she chided herself. She deliberately kept her face impassive. "Hello. Is this a good time to talk?"

Catherine recognized something of Rebecca's uncertainty. Detective Sergeant Rebecca Frye might know exactly who she was in the world, on the streets, but it was plain to Catherine that the woman behind the badge was much less certain of what she wanted or needed. But some things could not be rushed. *Go slow. She doesn't trust you— or herself.*

"I've just finished speaking with Janet," she said. "I think she's ready to see you."

"Good. Does she know I'm coming?" Rebecca asked, grateful that she was able to focus on the case and pretend that the faint hint of Catherine's scent did not affect her.

"Yes. I thought it best to prepare her."

"How is she?"

Catherine shrugged, a small frown puckering the skin between her finely arched brows. "She's still quite disoriented and badly shaken. She knows there are things she can't remember, and the dread of what they might be is terrifying her. She wants to remember and is scared to death at the same time. She's very frightened, Rebecca."

Rebecca recognized the cautionary tone in Catherine's voice and responded defensively, "I'm not going to interrogate her, Catherine." She immediately regretted her flash of temper when she saw the surprise in Catherine's eyes. *Hell, I'm too sensitive around her. I can't run an interrogation being worried that I'll offend someone.*

Still, she placed her hand on Catherine's arm, leaning toward her slightly as she spoke. "I'm sorry. I just want to find out how much she can remember. I won't push her, I promise."

Catherine covered Rebecca's hand lightly with her own, very conscious of the pressure of Rebecca's fingers on her. Even that innocent touch sent her pulse racing.

"I trust you, Rebecca. If I didn't, I wouldn't let you see her." She pressed Rebecca's hand again and stepped away. "Come on, I'll take you to her."

❖

Janet Ryan, a twenty-five-year-old computer analyst, lay propped up on several pillows. The narrow, slatted hospital blinds were drawn against the afternoon sun, allowing stripes of light and shadow to fall across the bed like bars. The television, perched on the wall opposite the bed, was tuned to a TV talk show. The hostess raced up and down the aisles, thrusting her microphone at the members of the audience. There was no sound.

The left side of the young woman's face was swollen and discolored. Her eye was a mere slit, the lashes caked together with dried blood. Fine black sutures closed a series of lacerations on her forehead. She clutched the covers up to her breasts despite the heat. Her hands were covered with cuts and scratches. Looking at her, Rebecca thought she was probably very attractive. Her body under the light sheet appeared trim and her bare arms were muscled as if she worked out or had a passion for sports. Rebecca thought that she must have put up a hell of a fight, too.

Catherine went immediately to the bedside and took Janet's hand. "Detective Frye is here."

Janet nodded her head slightly, carefully, as if the small motion hurt. "Please stay with me."

"Of course," Catherine said, pulling a chair up to the left side of the bed.

Rebecca dragged a similar worn plastic chair next to Catherine's and sat down, opening her notebook as she did so. She leaned forward so Janet could see her face.

"Ms. Ryan, I'm Rebecca Frye. I'm a police officer. I'm trying to find out what happened the night you were injured." She watched the young woman carefully, looking for any unspoken reactions to her questions. "Can you tell me what you did that day, Tuesday, three days ago?"

Janet glanced at Catherine, who nodded encouragement. Then she began to speak in a slow, halting whisper. "I was…late…I missed the train. So, I drove…to work."

"Where is that?" Rebecca asked. She knew the answer, but she liked to get a witness comfortable with the interrogation process before she pressed them for more important details.

"Compton Building. I'm a software programmer…" She halted uncertainly, her grip on Catherine's hand tightening.

"Go on," Rebecca urged.

"It was a normal day. Barb…called at lunch…I told her I'd be home around seven." A single tear slipped from between her lashes and dampened her cheek.

Rebecca reached for a tissue and pressed it into Janet's free hand. She waited a moment, then asked, "What did you do after work?"

"It was beautiful outside. I…I decided to go home on the Drive, even though the traffic is slower…" She stopped again, a slight tremor noticeable in her hands. "If I hadn't…"

"It's all right, Janet," Catherine said quietly. "None of this is your fault."

"I remember," Rebecca said softly, wanting to draw Janet back to that day. "It was cool, there had been a shower—"

Yes! It had been so sticky all weekend. I stopped the car…oh…it's all so confusing. I can't remember where I stopped!" Her anxiety was more pronounced now. She glanced anxiously around the room, her fingers pulling on the sheet.

"That's okay, Janet, you're doing a great job," Rebecca soothed her. "You don't have to get everything straightened out now. Just tell me anything you can remember, even if it doesn't make sense right away."

Catherine gave Rebecca a startled look but remained silent. *Maybe I should take her on rounds with me. She's better at this than some of my residents.* Rebecca continued to surprise—and intrigue.

"Do you remember why you stopped? Did you see something from the road? Something that concerned you?" Rebecca probed. She knew she was leading the distraught woman a bit, but she was hoping to jog her memory.

Janet's blue eyes were wide, her voice breathy with effort. "There was a regatta, and…I…I stopped to watch. I headed toward the water…"

When Janet seemed about to lose her train of thought, Rebecca prompted, "Did you see something there? Hear something? Can you remember anything that you saw?"

"That's just it! I can't make sense of what I *can* remember. There are so many colors!"

"What colors, Janet?" Rebecca asked quickly, writing the word on her pad and circling it. *What the fuck?*

"I don't know!"

"Do you remember a man? Did you see a man, or a woman and a man?"

"No."

"Did you hear a woman scream?"

"No." She looked at Catherine, her face pale. "I'm sorry…I can't remember. I'm trying…"

"I know you are. It's all right," Catherine comforted her. "Close your eyes for a minute, and tell me anything you see—any image—any picture in your mind at all."

"Just the number."

Rebecca sat up straight in her chair, her face tense. "What number?"

"Ninety-seven."

"Ninety-seven what? Were there letters with the number?"

"I can't remember…please, I just can't remember."

"That's all right, Janet," Catherine intervened, sending Rebecca a warning glance. "You've been wonderful. We'll talk again when you're a little stronger."

Rebecca forced down a protest. She *knew* Janet had seen something important. She could feel it. She also knew it would be futile to try to prolong the interview. Clearly Catherine felt the young woman had had enough.

The detective pocketed her notebook and stood up, angry and frustrated. She looked at the battered, terrorized woman in the bed, so pale and fragile under the thin, impersonal sheets—an innocent victim of fate and circumstance. Janet Ryan and the others were her charges now, and she intended to bring them justice.

CHAPTER NINE

Catherine stood with Rebecca in the hallway outside Janet's room. She couldn't miss the hard stillness of the detective's face. "Not much help?"

Sighing, Rebecca passed a hand across her face, consciously trying to shake the anger from her mind. "Not much." Letting her feelings rule was not going to help her get the job done. "There's something there, though. I'm sure of it."

"I'm almost positive Janet walked up on the rape," Catherine said as they began to walk. "That would explain both her extreme reaction and the symptoms she's displaying now."

"Can you press her on the number...and try to find out more about the colors?"

"Sorry, not right now," Catherine replied, still thinking about Janet's obvious fragility. "She's blocking because she's not psychologically prepared to cope with what she witnessed."

Rebecca suppressed her impatience. She had no doubt Catherine was right, but she *needed* this woman to remember. This powerlessness was eating her up inside. "Will you let me know when I can talk to her again? I really need her, Catherine."

"I know, Rebecca. Of course."

The detective stopped in front of the elevator, at a loss for words. She didn't want to say goodbye, and she wasn't sure she should do anything else. The bell rang, announcing that the elevator had arrived. Catherine was so close to her she couldn't seem to think. Then Catherine's hand was on her arm, her fingers softly caressing, her green eyes holding Rebecca's with a tenderness she could drown in.

"About last night..." Catherine began. "I didn't mean to rush—"

"I want to see you again," Rebecca interrupted. "Not here, and not about the case."

Catherine realized she had been holding her breath. She let it out with a soft sigh as the elevator doors slid open. It took all her willpower to step back and let go of Rebecca's arm. Touching her was such an unexpected pleasure. "Yes. Yes, I'd like that, too. Very much."

Rebecca stepped in, then held the door back with one hand to keep it from closing between them. Several people in the rear stared. "Tonight? I'll come by..."

"Yes...dinner..."

The elevator bell chimed with annoying regularity while the door bounced against Rebecca's palm. She grinned at Catherine, who was smiling faintly, her eyes searching Rebecca's face—memorizing every detail.

"I'll call when I'm through," Rebecca said as the doors closed.

"Just come," Catherine called, hoping her voice carried through the metal. "Any time."

Rebecca drove back to the station with her thoughts divided between Janet's scanty recollections and the exchange with Catherine at the elevator. Catherine elicited a physical response so intense it was actually painful. She was hard and throbbing, again. It was all she could do to keep her mind on the traffic. *A visit with Flanagan ought to cool me off.*

She walked through the first floor of the station house, moving deftly around a small clump of people trying to get the attention of the duty sergeant behind the tall counter just inside the door. The hallway itself was nearly blocked by the feet and legs of people waiting for visiting hours or for someone to hear their complaints and who had stretched out on the benches lining the wall. Avoiding the obstacles, she pushed through the steel fire doors at the end of the hall and started down the stairs to the basement. Dee Flanagan, the senior criminalist, her crime unit lab, and by way of a series of underground tunnels, the morgue could all be found on that lower level.

Stopping first at Dee's small, windowless office, Rebecca noted the usual clutter of journals, model reproductions, and containers of yogurt in various stages of consumption piled on the oversized metal desk in the middle of the room, but no Dee. She was probably in the lab.

At forty, with twenty years of experience and a degree in forensic analysis, Dee didn't have to do bench work. She didn't have to get her hands dirty or her feet wet in the field. And she didn't have to work nights. But she did—routinely—because she was a perfectionist and something of a control freak.

Rebecca loved it when Dee handled her cases. She found the Crime Scene Investigation chief bent over a series of plaster footprints lined up on a bench in the wet room—a long, narrow, brightly lit space where the crime scene techs processed the gross evidence from a crime scene. Bags of trash, clumps of dirt, torn clothing, abandoned cigarette butts, gum wrappers, and discarded condoms all sat in labeled boxes and clear plastic evidence bags. Representative samples of the debris would undergo more definitive examination under the microscopes, in the spectrographs, and via the gas chromatographs in the adjoining high-tech lab.

"Those mine?" Rebecca asked, pointing to the shoe casts. She put her hands in her pockets to curry good favor as she walked up to the small, trim, tomboyish woman with short dark hair and a perpetual curl to the end of her surprisingly full mouth. Flanagan didn't like anyone touching anything in her lab.

"They'd better not be yours, Frye," the smaller woman snapped, barely affording the detective a glance. "If you haven't learned by now not to contaminate a scene, you should be on traffic."

"You turn up anything?" Rebecca persisted, ignoring the jibe. Traffic was one step up from the property room in terms of inglorious assignments.

Flanagan turned and leaned her hips against the counter, shaking her head. "Not much yet. Lots of shoe prints, but without a suspect, they won't help us. Bike tire treads...ditto. Same with the semen analysis. This one matches the other two, by the way. I *can* tell you it's the same guy, but without his cooperation, I can't match it to anyone." She looked as irritated and frustrated as Rebecca felt.

"What about the trace evidence from the newest victims, Myers and Ryan?"

Dee Flanagan raised an eyebrow, studying the tall blond detective.

She'd never known Frye to jump to conclusions. "You're certain the other woman—Ryan—was part of this?"

Rebecca nodded. "She was there. I think she tangled with him. She saw something, at the very least."

"Darla Myers had his semen on her but not much else." The scientist consulted her notes. "There were a few nylon fibers on her skin that didn't come from her own clothes. Could have come from him."

"Can you match them to anything?"

Flanagan shrugged. "Generic sports clothing, most likely. No help there. Maybe Maggie will have better luck with the chemical analysis of the material, but I doubt it. I'll tell you one thing, though," she added.

Rebecca's pulse speeded up. "What?"

"Darla Myers didn't put up a fight, if that's what you were theorizing. No scrapes on her hands, no broken nails, no tissue or fiber *under* her nails, and no evidence that she even tried to block any of the punches to her face. She was beaten after she was unconscious, as near as I can tell."

"It fits," Rebecca said grimly, feeling the rage again and quickly stifling it. "When will you have the rest of it for me?"

"When it's done," Flanagan said curtly.

"Call me. Any time," Rebecca replied as she turned to leave.

Flanagan just grunted, her attention already focused again on the shoe casts she had spread out for sizing.

Rebecca was almost out the door, finally done for the day, when her pager went off. For a moment she debated not answering it. She was on her way to Catherine's, and she hadn't thought of much else for the last hour while she brought her case notes up to date. The memory of Catherine's face, her voice, the touch of her hand kept drawing her attention away from the task of organizing and filing reports. She wanted to see her more than she had wanted to do anything for a long time.

Before she could take the final step through the doorway, her pager vibrated again. *Damn.* She turned around and took the front stairs two at a time back up to the third floor. Leaning over the counter at the intake desk, she announced, "Frye here. What's up?"

The frazzled dispatcher, sweating profusely in her blue uniform, looked up from the computer console. "Jeff Cruz is not responding to his calls. The captain wants to see you, pronto."

Swearing under her breath, Rebecca hurried to the glass enclosed office at the end of the hall and rapped at the door marked "Captain John Henry" in peeling black letters. The black man behind the desk was fiftyish, fit, and big. His iron gray hair was cut short, and his demeanor was blunt and authoritative. The white shirt he wore was stiff with starch, and his tie was tightly knotted, even in the ninety-degree heat.

"Where's your partner?" he barked without preamble as Rebecca entered his office.

"I don't know," Rebecca said, surprised by the question and suddenly a little worried. Jeff didn't go AWOL. "I was in court this morning and doing some follow-up on the rape cases after that. He said that he had a meet with Jimmy Hogan about some intel. Jimmy thinks Zamora's crew might have a piece of the kiddie porn business in the Tenderloin, but we've never been able to link any of them to it."

"Yeah, yeah, I read the file. Where was the meet?"

"I don't know. Jimmy and Jeff set it up."

"And you didn't ask?"

Rebecca shook her head. "It sounded pretty routine, Captain."

Captain Henry didn't comment. Cruz and Frye were his best team, and he gave them a lot of slack to run their own cases. It wasn't unusual for them to be involved with other divisions, particularly Narcotics, on cooperative investigations. They weren't careless. If Cruz was in trouble, he had walked into something he hadn't expected. "It doesn't seem routine any longer."

"Agreed. I don't like it either, Captain. Something's off. We need to find him—fast."

"We've got an all points out on him and his car. We'll get a fix on him soon."

"What about Hogan?" Rebecca asked, her stomach roiling. "Can we reach him without endangering his cover?"

"That's harder. He's been under deep for months. Even his contacts in Narco don't know how to reach him. He calls them on his own schedule." The captain fanned his hands out over his desk, his eyes troubled. "I can tell you that no one's heard from him, but that doesn't necessarily mean anything. We have to assume that they're both out there loose somewhere."

Rebecca turned abruptly and headed toward the door. She had to find Jeff, and she knew him better than anyone. It could take all night for a cruiser to spot his car. She wasn't going to leave him out there alone.

"Frye!" Henry barked, his commanding voice stopping her in her tracks. "I want you here coordinating the search until we have something definite."

"Let Rogers do it," she said, whirling to face him, her jaw set stubbornly. "He's *my* partner. I can find him."

"I want *you* coordinating, Frye." He stared back at her. His expression changed slightly, and he lowered his voice. "We've got two missing cops already. I don't want you out there alone."

"But Jeff—"

"That's an order, Sergeant."

She gritted her teeth and nodded. "Yes, sir."

Catherine glanced at the clock. It was close to eight p.m. It wasn't late by cop standards, or by doctor standards either. She knew from experience how often an unexpected phone call or a last-minute meeting could disrupt even the most important plans. She had a feeling that she was on the verge of being stood up and knew better than to take it personally. But she couldn't help the sharp, stark pang of disappointment.

Chapter Ten

When Rebecca entered the squad room, the noise level suddenly dropped. Feet shuffled, someone cleared his throat, a few people looked away. Everyone knew what she was feeling—her anger, her helplessness, her fear—and no one quite knew what to say. So they handled it the way they always did, by doing the job, by carrying on. Someone put a lukewarm cup of coffee in her hand and mumbled a halfhearted, "Don't worry. He's probably off with the old lady getting his pipes cleaned."

She nodded back, sat at her desk, and began making calls. A half hour later she had ascertained that no one had seen or heard from Jeff Cruz after he left the squad room at 1:30 p.m. She tried his pager and cell phone and contemplated calling his house. But she knew he wasn't there, and so did everyone else. He wouldn't have gone home for the night without checking in with her first. Yeah, maybe now and then a cop disappeared for an hour in the middle of a slow day, and nobody commented on it. But not at end of shift. Everyone checked back in, cleared the day's work, touched base with their partner, and *then* checked out.

Finally she just sat, fists clenched in her lap, and watched the clock. The men from the day shift stayed, even though many of them had been on duty for close to eighteen hours by that time. Gina Simmons, a young rookie, came in silently, piled boxes of pizza on the littered coffee counter, and left without saying a word. But she scored points, and someone, someday, would remember and give her a break. Rebecca shook her head when someone offered her a slice. Everyone stood around in groups eating and spilling bits of oil and cheese on the floor.

The call finally came in at 10:30. A cruiser had spotted Jeff's department sedan on a deserted pier at the waterfront, tucked under an overhanging abutment, where it hadn't been seen before from the road. Rebecca was on her feet and halfway to the door when a hand on her arm restrained her.

"I'll ride with you, Sarge."

Rebecca turned toward the stocky man beside her, shrugging off the hand impatiently, and when she saw to whom the hand belonged, she had to struggle to control her temper. She had never liked William Watts. He was a cynical, sarcastic cop, who didn't seem to give a damn about his job. She couldn't figure out why he was a cop, and she didn't want to deal with him now.

"Not tonight, Watts," she said.

He was trying to step in front of her as he jerked his head toward the closed frosted glass door at the far end of the room. His face impassive, he said flatly, "Captain's orders."

"I don't have time for this bullshit." She turned on her heel and headed toward the stairs. Watts hurried after her.

Rebecca gunned her Corvette out of the station house lot and slapped the flashing red light onto her dash. When the traffic ahead didn't yield fast enough, she veered around it into the oncoming lanes. She and Watts didn't speak, but when he reached into the inside pocket of his rumpled, out-of-style sports coat and pulled out an equally battered pack of cigarettes, she gave him a look that made him wince. He slipped the pack back into his pocket and stared out the window.

They were the first detectives to reach the scene. Half a dozen cruisers were pulled off the four-lane highway at odd angles, and men with dogs were moving along the waterfront. Flashlight beams sent fleeting beacons of pale light skittering across the river's surface.

Rebecca parked and climbed out at the entrance to a huge, deserted, blacktopped parking lot. She stood in the semidarkness and surveyed the area, her nerves settling as her cop instincts kicked in. *Do the job. Just do the job.*

The halogen lights spaced along the highway behind her penetrated the darkness for a fair distance into the lot, enough to make out Jeff's car parked under the overpass fifty yards away. The river on the far side looked nearly black. To her right, a huge crane loomed like a lonely sentinel over the abandoned site of someone's waterfront dream. To her left, facing the water, stood a cluster of darkened buildings—the maritime museum, an attached souvenir shop, and a curbside food stand.

She headed deliberately toward the buildings with Watts close behind. She neither spoke to him nor acknowledged his presence.

"Why not the crane?" he asked, out of breath from the pace Rebecca had set.

"Too obvious during the day. There wouldn't have been enough people around for cover. And Jeff and Jimmy would have wanted to keep their meeting private, just in case someone was tailing Jimmy," she answered, still not looking at him.

"Yeah, but the way I see it—"

She turned so fast he collided with her, his bulky form bouncing back a step off her surprisingly hard body. "Look, Watts," she seethed. "I don't give a rat's ass *what* you think. I *know* my partner. So just keep out of my way, or better yet, get lost."

Watts held both hands up in the air in front of him. "Okay, Frye, okay. You're the sergeant. I'll just tag along like a good little boy."

Wordlessly, she walked away. If Jeff had met his contact in the late afternoon, there wouldn't have been much activity anywhere except at the museum. They wouldn't have needed much time together. He hadn't left voluntarily; he would have taken his car. Something went wrong, and it happened right here. She tried not to think about what might have happened, focusing on her search.

She walked around the maritime museum, a square concrete structure with a jutting upper level that was probably supposed to resemble a ship. It didn't. She was looking for an alleyway, or a loading dock—some secluded area. She reasoned that someone had surprised the two cops in the middle of their rendezvous, and she doubted that anyone would have tried to move two uncooperative men very far in daylight. So whatever went down, they would have needed an isolated location nearby. But for what purpose? It was unlikely that anyone would hold two cops hostage or try to extort information from them. She didn't want to think about the most likely reason—that someone was sending them a message to stay clear of Zamora and his organization.

There was nowhere to hide two men anywhere around the museum. She shined her flashlight on the beer and burger stand, closed and shuttered for the night. There was a large green commercial dumpster behind it. Rebecca approached it slowly, sweeping the ground around it with her light. Holding her 9mm automatic in the other hand, she illuminated bits of refuse, a soggy cardboard box, a dented milk crate— nothing unusual. She looked at the dumpster, a knot of tension burning in her gut, slipped her weapon into her shoulder holster, and pushed the top up. Taking a deep breath, she played her light over its contents. It was half full of crushed boxes, rotting vegetables, and broken bottles. That was all.

"Uh, Sarge…" Watts said from the spot where he had been standing in the shadows.

"What?"

"There's a shipping platform just north of the marina, about a hundred yards from here. It's below ground level. They used to use it to tie up the tugs. Can't really see it from the pier unless you know it's there."

"Show me."

He led her along the edge of the pier; the water, ten feet below them, rolled against the huge wooden pilings and concrete walls with a surprising degree of force. An occasional spray of water, redolent with diesel fuel and river life, misted their faces as they walked. Almost exactly where Watts had predicted, there was a narrow set of stairs barricaded by a length of chain. The stairs would be easy to miss unless you were looking for them. The chains were rusted from years of disuse and exposure. Rebecca could make out moss-covered stone steps and some kind of platform anchored against the pier, floating unevenly on the water. Carefully, she stepped over the chain and started down the steps.

When she reached the bottom, she stepped gingerly onto the slippery, water-soaked, ten-by-twenty-foot dock and stood for a long time, playing her flashlight back and forth over the scene. She took a few deep breaths, wondering why everything had gotten so quiet. Her heart pounded in her ears, and she heard the breath moving in and out of her chest. She focused, taking in the tableau before her.

They were lying side by side—no apparent sign of a struggle. Hogan and Cruz had each been shot once in the back of the head. There were dark stains on the dock in irregular patterns spreading out from under both men. Rebecca noticed that Jeff's tie was neatly knotted under the button-down collar of his light blue oxford shirt. His gun was still in its holster. She wanted to reach down and close his eyes, but protocol dictated that she couldn't touch him. She put her hands in her pockets and looked away, her eyes burning but dry.

Standing at the edge of the dock, she could see across the water to their sister city. The shoreline sparkled in the moonlight. The river churned two feet below her, and the cold wind off the water whipped her light jacket around her. She didn't notice the cold or that she was shivering. It was so quiet.

"Sarge?" Watts called from above. "Frye? You find anything?"

"Yes," she answered hollowly.

"You want an ambulance?"

"No."

Chapter Eleven

Rebecca finally left Shelley Cruz at three in the morning. There hadn't been any way to make it easy. There never was. She had held her, rocked her silently, her own tears unshed. The last time she had seen Shelley had been at a barbecue in the Cruz's backyard, one Saturday after she had finally succumbed to Jeff's relentless pestering to visit. She remembered Jeff in a police academy T-shirt and jeans, movie star handsome, smiling at Shelley with a look that said he considered himself the luckiest guy in the world. His young blond wife had returned the gaze with equal intensity. Now he was dead. The fairy tale was shattered, and Shelley Cruz's life would never be the same.

Rebecca still felt cold. She was glad for that. She couldn't afford to let the pain surface. If she did, it would break her. She was a cop, and people died on the street every day—needlessly, senselessly. This time it was her partner, her best friend. She'd handle it like she knew Jeff would have if it had been her—like a cop. But first she needed to obliterate the image of him lying so still, and so damn alone, out on that dark, cold dock. Just for a little while. Then she'd be ready to carry on.

She drove to a run-down bar on the fringe of the Tenderloin, an eight-block section of the city where the bars were open all night, solace was for sale on the streets and tendered in dark alleys, and nobody cared about your name. No one wanted to, and even if they did, the rule of the streets dictated that your identity and your particular brand of need would be forgotten in the morning. The bar was nearly deserted, as she expected it to be. No one who had anywhere to go, or anyone to go to, was still about. Like her, the few people at the bar, leaning protectively over their drinks while staring into the glass searching for answers, sought no company. She didn't bother to check the shadowed corners for anyone who looked like trouble the way she normally would in a place like this. She didn't care. In fact, a little trouble would be welcome. She'd have an excuse to strike out, to vent her rage, and release the terrible ache in her chest that had nowhere to go but inward.

The bartender looked up disinterestedly from the girlie magazine lying on the long counter in front of him. Nothing surprised him anymore, not even the appearance of a good-looking woman in a dive like this. Besides, this one didn't look like she wanted anything but a drink, fast. "What'll you have?"

"Scotch, double—straight up."

He poured it neatly, slid it in front of her, and moved away.

Rebecca stared at the glass for a long moment, then reached for it with a steady hand.

Catherine woke instantly at the first buzz of the doorbell. Her ability to move from deep sleep to instant attentiveness was ingrained from years of medical training. She sat up, glancing at the digital clock beside her bed. It read 4:53 a.m. She reached for the robe that lay across the foot of the bed, swung her long legs to the floor, and pulled it on. She had been naked under the covers. Hastily, she tied the belt as she hurried through the living room, snapping on a table lamp in passing.

As she fumbled with the deadbolt on her front door, she asked, "Who is it?"

"Rebecca Frye."

Catherine hesitated, surprised. She had assumed when Rebecca neither showed up for dinner nor phoned that she had been detained at work. At least that's what she had hoped. There was always the chance, of course, that Rebecca had simply forgotten about their…date. Or she had changed her mind and wasn't interested in pursuing anything personal between them after all. Whatever brought the detective to the door at this hour must be serious, and Catherine felt a quick surge of anxiety.

"Just a second." She slid the chain off and hurriedly pulled the door open. Rebecca was slouched against the doorjamb. She looked terrible. She was in the same clothes that Catherine remembered her wearing at the hospital nearly eighteen hours before, and the previously impeccable charcoal linen suit was now grimy and wrinkled. That handsome face, starkly illuminated by the security light above the door, was white and drawn, and there was a frightening vacancy in her normally vibrant blue eyes. Her short, thick blond hair was disheveled, as if she had run her hands through it countless times.

Catherine grasped her arm and pulled her inside, closing the door soundly behind them. "What is it?" she asked, leading Rebecca to the sofa. "Are you hurt?"

"No," Rebecca answered hoarsely, sinking heavily into the plush cushions, her head dropping back wearily. She took a deep shuddering breath, turning her face slightly toward the woman who sat close beside her. "My partner, Jeff Cruz, was murdered tonight. Executed. Him and another cop," she said flatly, her pain-filled eyes not registering the psychiatrist's shock. She didn't feel Catherine move closer, nor the protective arm she slipped around her shoulders.

"God, Rebecca! I'm so sorry."

"He was twenty-nine years old. He'd only been married a year. He was a good cop." She thought of the five years that she and Jeff had been partners. She saw him every day, spent more hours with him than any other human being; they talked about things they wouldn't tell their wives or lovers; they shared horrors and faced dangers that no one else could understand. There was no way to describe the hole his loss left in her soul.

"He must have been very important to you," Catherine said gently, her hand resting softly on Rebecca's rigid back. *Tell me.*

Rebecca shrugged, staring at the floor, her face wooden with exhaustion. "We're cops. He looked after my skin, and I looked after his." Her voice broke on the next words. "Until today."

So much pain. Catherine remained still, resisting the urge to gather Rebecca in her arms and comfort her. That's what she wanted to do, had an almost overwhelming *need* to do. But that was not what Rebecca needed. Not yet. *Talk to me; let me listen.*

"Tell me about him?" For a long moment, she thought Rebecca would withdraw. Holding her breath, she waited.

Finally, haltingly, Rebecca began to speak. She spoke softly, as if she were talking to herself.

"I wasn't hot to have a rookie partner at first, especially a young hotshot like him. I figured he'd be too cocky to train and too arrogant to admit he had anything to learn. I was wrong. He wanted to be a good detective, and he'd listen to whoever could teach him something. He listened to me. He came along fast. In just a few months, we were really a team."

"Were you friends, too?" Catherine asked quietly. *Keep talking. Let me do this for you.*

Rebecca clasped her hands between her knees, stared at them, thinking about friendship. Friendship between cops was a funny thing. It was something mostly unspoken, but it was the one thing you really needed—someone to count on.

"He took a chance for me a few years ago. My life was a mess. *I* was a mess. My lover had left me. She said I was never there for her. And that even when I *was* around, it wasn't enough. She was tired of being a cop's wife; she needed more." Rebecca laughed bitterly. "She was right, though. I wasn't taking very good care of her. After Jill left, I drifted in and out of affairs; none of them worked out. I was drinking. Pretty soon, I was drinking during the day—on duty—and Jeff knew it. I was a hazard—to him, to myself, to everyone."

She stopped then and looked at Catherine, expecting to find rejection or disgust. That was certainly the way she felt about herself. Instead she found kind acceptance in Catherine's eyes and the soft smile that welcomed her each time they met.

"What happened?" Catherine prompted softly.

"He came to me one night after a shift. He said he knew that I was drinking on the job, that he didn't want to turn me in, but that he couldn't afford to have a lush for a partner. I was pissed. I told him to turn me in if that's what he wanted. I didn't care anymore."

Rebecca laughed softly at the memory. "Jeff is a bit shorter than me, and slim for a guy. But he grabbed me by the lapels and slammed me into the wall. His face was in my face, and he was yelling. He said, 'Listen, you stupid fuckup. You're my partner, and I *care*. So your old lady ditched you. Big deal! You think that hasn't happened to a hundred other cops? You think you're special 'cause you're a dyke? Well, you're not. You're just a cop, just like the rest of us. So you either get it together fast, or I'm through with you.' He shook me around a little. He was pretty hot. I just stared at him. He'd never let on before that he knew about Jill and me. I was trying to think of something to say when he stomped away."

Catherine smiled with tender sadness at the image, thinking what a good man Jeff Cruz must have been. Then she realized Rebecca was shaking, her face a study in loss. *This must be killing her.* She pressed a little closer, her arm tightening around Rebecca's waist. "What did you do?"

"I drove to an AA meeting that night. That was four years ago. We never talked about it again."

"He trusted you, Rebecca. And you didn't let him down." She felt some of the tension in Rebecca's tight muscles dissipate, but she knew the pain remained. "Where have you been all night?"

"After I told Jeff's wife about…about him, I went to a bar."

"Did you drink?" Catherine asked evenly.

Rebecca laughed harshly. "I sat there with it in my hand for a long time."

"What stopped you?"

Rebecca met Catherine's gaze, her defenses shattered by the memories she hadn't wanted to relive. "I thought about you. I don't know why…I…I just thought…if I told…if I came…Ah, Jesus, I don't know why I came. I'm sorry…I…"

Catherine stroked Rebecca's cheek lightly with her fingertips, pushing the hair back from her forehead. She hadn't meant to touch her, but listening to her, watching her struggle not to give in to her agony, was breaking her heart. Rebecca wasn't her patient, and she wasn't a psychiatrist at the moment. She was a woman wanting desperately to comfort the woman she cared for. She leaned slowly forward, whispering, "You were right to come. I'm so glad you did."

At the touch of Catherine's hand on her face, the fiber of Rebecca's resistance snapped like a straw in the wind. The unconditional tenderness pierced her armor like the pain could not, eclipsing her consciousness until there was no reality except the hazy green of Catherine's eyes, the heady aroma of her scent. She needed the respite of this woman's embrace more than she needed air to breathe.

"Catherine," she gasped and found Catherine's lips, bruising them unintentionally with the force of her kiss. She devoured Catherine's mouth, sucking her, drinking her in—desperate for her. Already past thought, she pushed her back against the couch, fumbling with the tie of her robe, wanting to feel her skin. She groaned in surprise when Catherine yanked her shirt from her trousers and slid her hands up her back, the sensation of warm hands on her skin making her impossibly aroused.

Her blood was molten, searing her veins—everything moving so fast—all so good, too good to stop. Moaning, drowning in the feel of Catherine's tongue thrusting insistently against hers, she struggled to contain her need. But it was far too late—once unleashed, she could not call it back. Desperately, she pulled away from the kiss and lowered her mouth to Catherine's breast, catching the nipple between her lips.

"Oh, God," Catherine cried, holding Rebecca's face to her, forcing her nipple harder into Rebecca's seeking mouth. She closed her eyes, arched her back with the sharp pleasure of it. "Rebecca…"

Rebecca couldn't hear the plea. She was burning, the very breath in her lungs evaporating from the heat. When she felt Catherine's arms tighten around her, pulling her close, she lost it. Flinging one thigh over Catherine's, she pressed her down on the sofa and slid on top of her. "I can't…I can't…I'm sorry," Rebecca choked brokenly, aching with the fierce rush of blood through her pelvis, consumed by the agonizing pressure of Catherine's leg between hers, her clitoris ready to burst. Eyes closed, she thrust frantically, unconsciously, driven by instinct and need.

"Yes…yes," Catherine urged, driving her hips upward, forcing Rebecca to the edge.

"Ooh…," Rebecca moaned, hips pumping erratically in a frenzy of release. Head flung back, arms rigid, she cried out with each wrenching spasm. Finally she collapsed, shaking, into Catherine's arms, groaning faintly with the lingering pulsations, gasping for breath.

"Rebecca, Rebecca," Catherine murmured, gently running her fingers through the damp blond hair as she cradled Rebecca's cheek to her breast.

Rebecca closed her eyes and let herself drift in the solace of Catherine's body. Surrendering to the salvation of that strong, sure embrace, she savored a peace she had long forgotten.

CHAPTER TWELVE

Rebecca sat up with a jolt. The sun streaming through the bay windows into her eyes had awakened her. As consciousness returned, memory did also, and pain rode the coattails of remembrance. The finality of Jeff's death twisted through her, an unrelenting ache she would carry with her for a long time. She drew a shaky breath, trying to ease the fist of agony in her chest and looked around the room. *Jesus, God...Catherine's living room.*

The sight of her jacket neatly folded over the arm of a nearby easy chair brought back vivid images of the night before—Catherine listening to her; Catherine consoling her; Catherine comforting her. *And then you just about jumped on her. You must have been out of your mind, Frye! God, what must she think? Of course, you didn't give her much choice, after all. Christ, you came all over her like a kid on his first date. And she probably just felt sorry for you.*

Her face burned with a conflicting mixture of dismay and renewed desire. She remembered her loss of control with embarrassment, uncertain whether she had the courage to face this compassionate woman after what had happened. Even as she struggled with the thought, she yearned to touch her again. The *want* was so powerful it left her shaking. *I need to get out of here. I don't know what the hell is wrong with me.*

She pushed herself reluctantly to a standing position and started to straighten her disheveled clothing. As she tucked her shirttail into her trousers, she discovered her shoes and belt beside the sofa. *God, where is my gun?* She looked about frantically, relaxing slightly when she saw the shoulder holster hanging on the knob of the closet door. She couldn't believe she hadn't noticed Catherine removing that. It was part of her.

"Everything all right?" a soft voice inquired.

Rebecca turned around to find Catherine in the kitchen doorway, watching her, a faint smile on her lips. She looked more beautiful than Rebecca remembered. Her wavy hair, highlighted in bright sunlight, shone with rich reddish tones streaked throughout the darker auburn. Here and there a faint silvering of early gray only served to accentuate the elegant planes of her face. She wore a pale green silk dressing gown, and the look of desire in her deeper green eyes sent a bolt of arousal directly between Rebecca's legs. Her head began buzzing, and she was instantly wet.

"Catherine, I..." she began tentatively, searching for words through a faint fog of uncertainty and desire. She ran a hand through her hair. "I should apologi—"

"Shh, don't even think of it," Catherine commanded, her smile deepening as she crossed the space between them.

"It's not how it looks," Rebecca tried again, watching her draw near, suddenly powerless to move. Captivated by the intensity of that sensuous gaze, she forgot what had been so important to explain. "I don't usually do that."

"No, I don't imagine you do."

"Listen...if you want me to go..."

Wordlessly, Catherine reached out and curled the fingers of one hand in Rebecca's hair, pulling her head forward into a kiss. It was a deep, sure, demanding kiss that left them both breathless.

When she released the stunned woman, Catherine teased, "Does that answer any questions for you?"

Rebecca took a long, shuddering breath. "I'm sorry about last night...I mean...the way I...the way it..." *I didn't mean to come like that. I couldn't stop it. I was crazy for you.*

"Don't be sorry. You were beautiful, and believe me, I have never enjoyed anything more. Being wanted that much is very exciting." She paused, ran a hand lightly over Rebecca's chest. "Don't you know how much I've been wanting *you*?"

Rebecca shivered as Catherine's fingers brushed over her breast. With a groan, she pulled the astonishing woman into her arms. She kissed her mouth, the soft skin of her eyelids, the smooth slope of her neck. She felt Catherine's pulse quicken under her lips, and her own heart thudded loudly as she found that inviting mouth again. She jerked in surprise when Catherine's hands slipped under her shirt, cupping her breasts, teasing her swiftly hardening nipples.

"Easy," she gasped. "I'm locked and loaded."

Catherine laughed throatily and ignored her plea. She stroked the firm planes of Rebecca's abdomen, moving lower with each caress. "Be strong, Detective," she murmured.

Rebecca hissed in a breath as Catherine tugged at her fly. *One touch and I'll lose it. Again.* "You're dangerous," she growled, pushing Catherine's fingers away. "And I never got to finish what I started last night."

Reaching under the hem of the dressing gown, she ran her hand up the smooth, bare flesh of Catherine's thigh, the silk gathering around her forearm in soft folds. She slipped her fingers smoothly between Catherine's legs, into the waiting wetness, finding her clitoris, distended and slick with arousal. She stroked her, sliding the sensitive bundle between her fingers, tugging gently.

"Oh my God...Rebecca..." Catherine cried, clinging to her, her forehead pressed to Rebecca's chest, her legs shaking. "That's so good. So good."

Just as Rebecca felt Catherine grow rigid, a sharp cry of surprised pleasure escaping her lips, the beeper in the pocket of the folded jacket went off. She stiffened and paused at the sound.

"Don't...stopdon'tstop...ohGoddon'tstop..."

"No," Rebecca breathed against her ear, circling her harder, following the motion of Catherine's questing hips. "I won't. Don't worry."

Catherine jerked several times, moaning with each surge of release, and then grew still in the circle of Rebecca's arms. Finally, she leaned back, her face flushed, her green eyes still cloudy with passion. "Tell me that wasn't your beeper."

"I could, but I won't lie to you. I have to answer," Rebecca said huskily, her hands moving to Catherine's hips, still caressing her. Her own legs were trembling so badly she wasn't sure she could stay standing. She had been on the verge of coming herself—would in a second still—if Catherine touched her. "I'm sorry."

"God, it's not your fault," Catherine murmured, pressing her forehead hard against Rebecca's shoulder, trying desperately to steady herself. Shaking still, she stepped back reluctantly. "Go. Answer it. I'll get us some coffee."

When Catherine returned with two steaming mugs, Rebecca was standing by the tall window next to the front door with her back to the room, looking out onto the street. Catherine hesitated, reminding herself of the toll the last twenty-four hours must have taken on this woman and knowing that it wasn't the time for them to get involved. But, God, she wanted her. It made no sense, but it wasn't her mind that was doing the talking. It wasn't exactly her body either; it was an even more dangerous combination of the two. Need and desire, both physical and emotional, were conspiring to make her lose all sense of good judgment. Still, too many demands on someone in Rebecca's state right now could destroy her. She wanted her, but most of all she wanted her to heal. Then, she hoped, there would be time.

"What is it?" she asked, handing Rebecca one of the mugs.

"Internal Affairs." Rebecca's face was a careful blank. "They need to interview me, and they need me to go over our cases with them. See if we can turn up anything on Jeff's killing."

"Today?" Catherine wondered what kind of people would put Rebecca through something like that less than twelve hours after her partner's death.

Rebecca laughed grimly. "Try two hours ago." She set her mug down on the window ledge and turned to Catherine. "I wish I could stay. Being with you is…good." She stopped. She wasn't certain how it had happened, her being here like this with this woman who made her feel so much, and who made her long for even more. She hadn't been looking for it—hadn't even known she'd wanted it—but she recognized what she was feeling for Catherine Rawlings, and it scared her.

"You can always come back, Rebecca. I'll be here, and I *want* you to come back. Whenever you can, whenever you want."

Rebecca nodded. "I will." She strapped on her holster and pulled on her jacket. At the door, she turned to face Catherine one last time. "Thank you for last night…all of it."

Catherine held the door open, watching the detective walk quickly down the steps and up the street. *Come back soon, Rebecca. Come back safely.*

❖

An hour later, freshly showered, in a crisp white shirt and navy suit, Rebecca walked into the squad room, her eyes hard and her expression indecipherable. Men looked at her and nodded as she passed, no one saying anything. The general atmosphere in the room was subdued, without the usual banter and complaining. She walked directly to her desk and stared impassively at the man seated at the adjoining one.

"What the hell are you doing in Cruz's chair?" Her voice was granite. "And what the *hell* are you doing with those files?"

William Watts looked at the expression on her face and then glanced around the squad room for support. No one offered any. "Just getting acquainted with the caseload. The captain told me to tell you that you and me are going to be partnered up."

She stared down at him coldly, then turned on her heel and stalked away. By the time she reached Captain Henry's door, she was boiling. She pushed the door open without knocking and crossed the room toward his desk in two furious strides.

"What do you mean telling Watts we were going to work together?" she demanded, not even registering the amazed look on Henry's face. "I don't want another partner, and if I did, it sure as hell wouldn't be him. He's a lazy sleaze, and I won't ride with him."

The captain rose in one fluid motion, his arms braced on the desk as he leaned toward her until their faces were nearly touching. "Frye, if I tell you to work with Bozo the Clown, you do it. And you smile about it, too." He bit off each word, his face a thundercloud of anger. "Now you turn your ass around and get the hell out of my office!"

She met his angry gaze evenly, her fists clenched at her sides, trying unsuccessfully to lower her voice. "Listen, Captain—"

"No, *you* listen. You just lost your partner. It's tough…I appreciate that. But you've still got a dozen open files, including the River Drive thing. You can't do it alone, and Watts is available. If he's an asshole, learn to live with it. I don't care how you do it, just do it!"

"What's he got? Friends in high places?" she asked, her blue eyes dark with scorn, mindless of rank or protocol. All she could see was Watts sitting in Jeff's chair, at Jeff's desk—where Jeff should be right now, telling her about his night with Shelley. She was shaking, but she didn't know that.

Henry's neck muscles tightened, and a flush rose to darken his features. His voice was deadly cold as he spoke. "I'm going to pretend I didn't hear that, Sergeant. Just this once. Because you're a good cop. But don't think I won't bust your ass out of here if you step over the line." He watched her carefully, wondering if she was even listening. "IAD wants to see you. Take care of that, and then get back to work."

She didn't reply, there was nothing she could do.

He watched her turn and walk away, wondering if he was making a mistake leaving her on the streets. She was one of his best. He thought she would crack if he put her behind a desk, so he had argued against it when the chief of detectives suggested it for her own safety, just in case the hit on Cruz had something to do with a case the two of them were working. Seeing her now, skittering on the edge of control, he hoped he was right.

Catherine knocked and then entered Janet Ryan's room. Barbara Elliot was sitting close to the bed, her fingers entwined with Janet's.

"Hello, Dr. Rawlings." Barbara's voice was tired, but her smile was genuine.

"Hello, Barbara." Catherine returned the smile as she approached the side of the bed. "Hi, Janet. How are you feeling?"

Janet looked better. The bruises still disfigured her normally attractive face, but the swelling had begun to subside. Both eyes were open now. Their expression was bright.

"I'm much better, thanks. I've been up walking a little, and I'm not taking the pain medication." She glanced at her lover fondly. "When can I go home?"

Catherine grinned. "I can see you're feeling better. The neurologists want to keep you a few more days, just for routine observation. I know it's hard being here, but let's be safe, okay?"

"All right, if you think it's best." Her disappointment was clear.

"I do," Catherine replied firmly. Then, her voice softening, she asked, "How are the flashbacks?"

Janet grimaced. "I'm still getting them, especially at night. Just bits and pieces...of my brother and me when I was small." She took a deep, quavering breath. "I never realized it had gone on for so long."

Catherine nodded sympathetically. "They may get worse as you recover from this attack, Janet. You may remember other things. We'll talk more about what to expect, but for now, I may want to try you on a mild sedative, nothing too strong. Let's think about going home in a few days, all right?"

Janet looked at Barbara questioningly.

"I really want Janet at home, Dr. Rawlings. Everyone is nice to us here, but it's so impersonal. I don't want her to come home until you think she's ready, though. Whatever you decide is fine."

Catherine spoke with them a few more moments, promising to look in on Janet later in the day, and then left to complete her inpatient rounds. When she stepped out into the hall, a neatly dressed young man moved hurriedly to intercept her.

"Dr. Rawlings? Is it true that Janet Ryan witnessed the rape on River Drive earlier this week? Has she been able to describe the assailant?"

Catherine stepped back a pace, nonplussed. "Who are you?"

"Mark Tyler. *Daily News*. What about it, Doctor? *Did* she witness the rape?"

"Mr. Tyler, you have no business being here." Catherine was furious. "If you want information, I suggest you speak to the police. I have nothing to say to you. And if I find you here again, I'll have security remove you!"

"Oh, come now, Doctor, surely you want this maniac caught," he persisted, blocking her path with his body.

She maneuvered around him. "Indeed, I do, Mr. Tyler, which is why I have nothing to say to you."

At last she was able to escape, wondering as she ducked into the stairwell how he had found out about Janet. The police had warned them to keep the circumstances of her admission quiet, and she thought they had succeeded. She should have known there were no secrets in a hospital. The police presence alone, no matter how understated, was enough to start rumors. Her first impulse was to call Rebecca, but then she thought it could probably wait until they spoke again about Janet. After all, she hadn't told him anything.

Chapter Thirteen

Watts saw Rebecca heading for the stairs in one hell of a hurry. He'd been hanging around outside the IAD offices, waiting for her to finish with the interview. He hurried after her.

"Where you going?" he demanded just as she reached the door.

She spun around, aware that he was right behind her. He took a step back, surprised.

"Look, Watts, I'm going out. Okay? Now go back to your paperwork."

When she began to turn, he grabbed her arm and stepped between her and the fire door. "Out where?"

Rebecca stared at the beefy hand on her arm and slowly raised her eyes to his. Her eyes were flat and so cold that his blood curdled. He hastily let his hand drop, but he stood firmly in her path.

"Watts…" she said menacingly, struggling to keep her temper under control. She had a fierce headache, and she was in no mood for conversation.

"Look, Sarge, I'm not any happier about this than you are, but that's the way it is. So it's a bitch. There's nothing we can do about it." He waited for some reaction, but Rebecca stared past him at some small spot on the opposite wall, her jaw clenching spasmodically. Watts shook a cigarette out of a crumpled pack, lit it, and leaned against the door, apparently content to stay there all afternoon. Another muscle in Rebecca's face twitched.

"I'm going to check in with Homicide, fill them in on some background on Zamora. Maybe I can help," she said reluctantly.

Watts blew a perfect smoke ring, watching it float and break apart, considering her words. "The Homicide dicks can handle the case, Sarge. They're not going to screw up when it's one of our own. Why not let them do their jobs. We've got plenty on our plates right here."

"I didn't ask for your opinion," Rebecca said heatedly, shouldering him aside and pushing the door open.

"Oh, fuck it," Watts muttered as he listened to her footsteps echo in the stairwell.

Rebecca slammed out through the door into the parking lot. Watts was right, and she knew it. Still, she had to see for herself that everything possible was being done to find Jeff's killer. *I have to do something.*

She slid into her car and started making calls. She finally tracked down the whereabouts of the investigating officers and drove to the waterfront. The crime scene crew was still there, too. She could see Dee Flanagan standing on the edge of the pier, just above the floating dock where Rebecca had found the bodies. Several other techs were scouring the parking lot, walking the grid, collecting evidence.

"I'm sorry, Frye," Dee said gruffly when Rebecca walked up beside her. Like Rebecca, like most cops, her way of coping with almost anything that angered or hurt her was to concentrate on the job.

"Yeah. Thanks," Rebecca said, her tone just as raw but her eyes revealing none of her pain. "Anything?"

Flanagan, dressed in faded but pressed jeans and a dark blue T-shirt with "CSI" stenciled in yellow on the breast above a police logo, grunted. "Plenty. This place sees hundreds of people every day—tourists, locals, homeless, kids looking for a place to make out, junkies looking for a place to score. Lots and lots of trace evidence. Ask me if I have anything that looks hot."

"Anything?" Rebecca repeated.

"Dick is what I got," Dee said with a grimace. "No shell casings. We're cutting out a section of the dock now that looks like it's got a slug in it. Let's hope it isn't too deformed to give us an image on the rifling marks...*if* we ever find a weapon to match it to."

Rebecca looked away, knowing that the bullet must have exited the skull of one of the victims and embedded in the wood. She hoped it hadn't been Jeff. "What *can* you tell me?"

Dee ignored the angry tone because she could see that Rebecca was suffering. "The ME has the bodies now, and I don't have a full report yet. But I do know that they were both shot at close range. No indication they resisted. It was probably over in a matter of minutes."

"Any sign of a weapon?" Rebecca asked dispiritedly.

"Not yet," Flanagan replied. "I've got techs searching drain pipes and dumpsters for a mile on both sides of the highway."

"Divers?"

Flanagan pointed to a twin-engine vessel bobbing on the river, "Police" in blue block letters on the bow. "They're in the water now looking for the gun. But I doubt a professional would have tossed it around here. And this guy was definitely a professional."

"Yeah," Rebecca agreed. "Will you call me?"

Dee Flanagan studied her. "You look like shit, Frye." Rebecca stared at her, and Dee nodded. "Yeah, I'll call you."

Rebecca climbed down to join the two Homicide detectives in charge of the case, who were standing beside the chalk outlines on the small loading dock where she had found Jeff and Jimmy Hogan. She stared at the spot, envisioning Jeff's body contained within the impersonal white lines. At length, she turned to the man and woman who were regarding her uncomfortably.

"I don't suppose you found a witness?" Rebecca asked, breaking the silence.

"Oh sure, and Santa Claus, too," the heavy-set, forty-something, disgruntled man replied. "We've had uniforms sweeping the area since dawn, rousting every vagrant in a six-block radius. Apparently, no one saw or heard anything last night. We're starting on the vendors and museum workers now, hoping somebody noticed something yesterday afternoon."

The small, dark-haired woman in an impeccably tailored, expensive looking suit extended her hand. "I'm Trish Marks. Sorry about your partner."

Rebecca shook her hand. "Thanks."

Marks nodded, then continued briskly, "We assume Cruz met Hogan sometime around four, based on the preliminary time of death. This place is still pretty busy then. Nobody would notice two men in a crowd."

"Perfect spot for a hit," Rebecca said flatly. "Anyone could have approached them, flashed some firepower, and walked them down to that dock without attracting attention. It's isolated down there, but if there were a crowd of civilians up here, Jeff and Hogan wouldn't have started a shoot-out. Often the easiest crimes to pull off are those carried out in broad daylight. Obviously, this time it worked."

Again, Marks nodded. "Most of the people who were here yesterday are probably miles away now—tourists. If we find a witness, it will be pure luck, but we're going to put it on the air. Set up a hotline number. Offer a reward for information leading to an arrest—the usual routine. We might get something that way."

"What about the people Hogan's been associating with? He must have gotten on to something a lot heavier than we expected. He made somebody nervous."

"We haven't had a chance to go through all his reports. He was pretty sketchy with his sources," the younger detective said. "There are probably a dozen possibles."

Rebecca raised an eyebrow, clearly irritated that they hadn't gotten to Hogan's notes yet. Her reaction did not go unnoticed.

"Listen, Frye," the man, who had yet to introduce himself, said pointedly, "we've been out here since two fucking a.m. We'll get to the reports. We'll roust anybody we have to, even without due cause. We'll find out who's behind this, okay? But cut us some slack here."

Rebecca's shoulders sagged slightly. She was tired. She knew these two and everybody else had been busting their balls all night trying to get a jump on the case before the slim trail went cold. But this was her partner, and she wanted more.

"Right," she said, straightening her back and heading toward the narrow stairs that led up to the pier.

"We'll keep you informed, Frye," Trish Marks called out. "And we'll get the bastard."

CHAPTER FOURTEEN

At 5:45 p.m., Rebecca found herself parked in a tow-away zone in front of the University Hospital, wondering why she had come. She had driven to the medical center directly from the pier, never even considering her destination. Now that she was here, she couldn't decide whether to go in or leave. She wasn't thinking very clearly. On some level she knew she had come because Catherine Rawlings represented the only sane haven in an agonizingly bleak landscape—a calm sanctuary she sorely needed.

Despite her despair, however, she resisted, distrusting the longing for comfort. If she relented, if she let down her guard and surrendered to her yearning for the solace of Catherine's embrace, what would she do if she were wrong? What would she do if Catherine found her lacking, as all the others had? Surely, it was much better never to acknowledge the need than to let it loose and be devoured by it.

God, what's wrong with me? I'm a cop—this is all part of the job. I can't fall apart just because things are a little rough. I've got to get myself together. She was reaching for the ignition key when a soft hand on her shoulder interrupted the action. Looking up, she realized Catherine was standing beside the car, studying her quizzically. Hesitantly, she smiled and said, "Hi."

"Hello. I saw your car as I was coming back from the outpatient clinic. What are you doing here?"

"I don't know," Rebecca answered dully. *I am so tired. I remember how warm your hands were on my skin.*

Catherine took a close look. Rebecca's eyes were red-rimmed and darkly shadowed; her hands trembled where they rested against the wheel. The combination of emotional shock and exhaustion was clearly catching up to her. This was not the razor-sharp, controlled detective who had charged into her office the night of Janet Ryan's assault. This was a woman on the verge of collapse.

The doctor pulled the driver's door open. "Move over, I'm driving."

To her own amazement and too numb to protest, Rebecca complied. As they drove, she stared at Catherine's hand resting protectively on her thigh, thinking how delicate Catherine's long fingers were. The hand felt good, there on her leg, like an anchor holding her in place. "My apartment..."

"I know where I'm going," Catherine replied with confidence, rubbing her palm in light circles on Rebecca's leg. She kept her eyes on the traffic, hearing the utter weariness in the detective's dull tone and wanting desperately to comfort her. Comfort, she imagined, was not something Detective Frye accepted easily.

Rebecca was surprised when Catherine pulled up in front of her own brownstone. She allowed herself to be led up the wide stone stairs and waited silently while Catherine opened the door. The living room in daylight was bathed in shades of muted grays and soft maroons as the late-afternoon sun streamed through sheer drapes and glinted off the walls. It was a beautiful place, warm and soothing and so very graceful. Just like Catherine.

"Take off your blazer," Catherine said gently as she slipped out of the light silk jacket she wore and tossed it aside along with her briefcase. She turned to Rebecca, who was still standing just inside the door, a faintly confused look on her face. "Here, let me get that."

Catherine tugged Rebecca's jacket off her shoulders and down her arms. Folding it neatly, she laid it over the back of a chair. She fumbled slightly with the shoulder harness but managed to slip it off the detective's body. Reaching down, she pulled the pager from her belt and placed it with the holstered gun on the chair. She kissed Rebecca lightly on the lips as she took her hand. "You're off duty now, Detective Frye," she whispered as she led the exhausted woman into her bedroom.

"You don't have to do this," Rebecca protested faintly as Catherine unbuttoned and removed her shirt.

"I know. But I want to," Catherine replied, pulling the belt free from the taller woman's trousers. As Rebecca watched, she neatly deposited the trousers on the chair and then undressed, too. Holding out her hand in invitation, she whispered, "Come to bed."

The sheets were cool against Rebecca's skin. When Catherine lay down next to her, she pressed her face against the fullness of her breasts, sighing. "You feel good," she murmured, moving just enough to nuzzle a nipple with her lips. "I think I'm waking up," she mumbled a moment later, running her hand slowly over Catherine's hip.

Catherine laughed softly and wrapped her arms around the drowsy woman. "There's plenty of time for that. You're going to get some rest now. Doctor's orders."

"Not good...with orders." Rebecca sighed and closed her eyes.

Catherine stroked the tight muscles beneath her fingers, feeling them gradually relax as Rebecca's breathing shifted to the steady cadence of sleep. Still caressing her, she, too, closed her eyes, now content, indeed more satisfied than she could ever have imagined, just having Rebecca safe in her arms.

It was dark when Rebecca opened her eyes, disoriented for an instant in the still, dark room. Quickly focusing, she became aware of Catherine asleep alongside her, softly encircling her with an arm flung possessively across her breasts. Rebecca lay motionless, savoring the new sensation of Catherine's skin against hers, turning carefully to see her face, not wanting to awaken her. She absorbed the image of Catherine in repose, memorizing each detail, surprised at how natural it felt to lie beside her.

Then she began a slow, careful exploration of Catherine's body, following the contour of her breasts and belly and hips with her fingers. Catherine pressed closer, murmuring softly in half-sleep. Rebecca gasped sharply in surprise as Catherine slipped one leg between hers and rolled over onto her with a throaty laugh.

"Hello, Rebecca," Catherine whispered, bracing herself above the length of Rebecca's firm body as she teasingly rocked against her. She was rewarded by Rebecca's deep groan of pleasure. "How do you feel?"

"Just fine," Rebecca whispered in reply, reaching for her.

A cry caught in Catherine's throat as Rebecca's hands found her breasts. She continued her rhythmic motion, thrusting steadily as they rode one another's thighs until they were both wet and moaning.

Suddenly she shifted to straddle Rebecca's body, entwining her fingers in the damp curls at the base of her abdomen. Tugging gently, she exposed Rebecca's erect clitoris, rubbing lightly with her thumb, drawing a groan from Rebecca as the skin tightened around the shaft. Rebecca reached between Catherine's legs, seeking to complete the circle.

"Ahh…" Catherine sighed as Rebecca slid into her. "That will make me come."

"Good," Rebecca gasped, arching under Catherine's continued caresses, the pressure about to peak. "I'm almost there."

"I…can…tell," Catherine managed, her eyes losing focus as she struggled to prolong the pleasure. "Don't…hurry."

"Then stop touching…me…there," Rebecca pleaded desperately, her hips lifting into Catherine's hand.

They were both moaning, answering stroke for stroke and thrust for thrust in perfect synchrony. Catherine worked to hold back the surge of heat for another minute, wanting to sustain their union, wanting to come with her if she could, but the spasms were building. They filled each other, stoking the fires of passion, trembling on the edge of consummation, until at last Rebecca groaned, "N-no more…God…" and began to orgasm.

Catherine gloried in the sight of Rebecca coming until her own climax crashed through her. Then she convulsed, whimpering with the unexpected force of it, eyes shut tight, head thrown back, until finally she collapsed into Rebecca's waiting arms.

When Rebecca stirred again, it was after midnight. She attempted to extricate herself from Catherine's embrace without disturbing her.

"I'm awake," Catherine said softly in the darkness, stroking the length of Rebecca's long form. She wanted to keep her close but let her move slowly away until she was but a shadow. "Do you have any idea how beautiful you are?"

"I know how beautiful I feel with you," was the quiet, intense reply. Rebecca sat up, brushing her fingers over Catherine's cheek.

"Are you leaving?" Catherine asked, knowing instinctively that after such intimacy, the very solitary detective would withdraw. She struggled with the disappointment, the professional in her understanding, but the all too human side wondering when, if ever, Rebecca would trust what they had shared. *Trust me,* is what she really meant.

"It's late. There are things I should have done earlier," Rebecca replied evasively. She was as content in Catherine's arms as she had ever been, but as her strength returned, so did the pull of the streets. How could she explain her restless need to immerse herself in the pulsing otherworld of the night? It was her domain, her reality, the reminder of who and what she was.

"Where are you going?" Catherine asked, sitting up now, too, saddened at the distance between them but determined to hide the feeling. Her body still throbbed with the aftermath of their lovemaking, and she wanted only to hold Rebecca until the morning. She would not have that tonight, perhaps not any night. It was a possibility she was not yet ready to face. Rebecca moved her too deeply, aroused desires too powerful, to think about that now. Her heart, her soul, had been marked by the searing intensity of Rebecca's presence and, for the moment, her presence would have to be enough.

"I'm going to cruise through the Tenderloin. I've got contacts there. I'll talk to people, listen to the rumors going around," Rebecca said, swinging her legs over the side of the bed. Instantly, she was aware of the absence of Catherine's touch. Her skin registered the loss. She was suddenly cold, although the night was warm.

"What are you looking for, Rebecca?" Catherine asked quietly, knowing that the answer she sought went deeper than the next few hours.

Rebecca pulled on her pants, looked around for her shirt, and answered absently, "News about Jeff…word about the rapist. You never know what's out there."

Catherine tried to absorb the realities of Rebecca's life, wondering if she would ever truly be able to understand them. Who but another cop could appreciate the soul-numbing inhumanity that was an everyday occurrence in the world inhabited by this restless woman? She was willing to try, and she was determined not to allow Rebecca to shut her out.

Catherine started to rise. "Let me get you some coffee."

"No. I don't want you to get up." Rebecca pushed her gently

down, then leaned to kiss her. "I want you to stay here, where we were together, so I can think of you like this until I see you again."

Wrapping her arms around Rebecca's neck, Catherine returned her kiss. "All right," she replied huskily. *You can't possibly imagine how tender you are or you'd never let it show.*

Because Rebecca had asked, Catherine remained in the dark, the bed growing cold, and listened to the detective move about in the other room. She didn't sleep again until long after the outer door clicked shut.

CHAPTER FIFTEEN

Rebecca cruised slowly north on Thirteenth to Arch, the heart of the Tenderloin, with the top down on the Vette and jazz playing softly on the radio. Nightclubs, bars, adult bookstores, and seedy hotels were crowded together, all of them lit by garish neon signs, their doors standing open to offer glimpses of the entertainment inside. The sidewalks were crowded even at three a.m. with prostitutes, johns, pushers, pimps, junkies, and panhandlers—all the flotsam that society had cast out or forgotten. The prostitutes in their crotch-high, faux-leather skirts and tight, skimpy tops leaned against buildings or strolled languidly through the litter-strewn streets. Many Rebecca recognized by sight, more than a few by name. Arresting them was not her goal— they were no more criminals than the hungry who stole for food.

When citizens of the adjoining newly gentrified blocks complained that the undesirable activity was encroaching on their neighborhoods, the cops would round up some of the girls to placate city hall, knowing full well that the prostitutes would be back on the streets and plying their trade within hours. All the participants in the charade knew it was a futile gesture. Rebecca chose not to hassle the women but rather to keep an eye out for new faces, especially the very young. She always hoped to get to a few before the streets became the only way of life. Occasionally, she succeeded. Nevertheless, she was still a cop, and when she needed information, she used the resources at her disposal to get it.

She pulled over in front of a bar that sported a flashing yellow sign reading, "Girls! Live Nude Girls!" She wondered absently if anyone besides her found that sign absurd. It wasn't the bar she was interested in, but the thin blond stationed in front of it. The woman was about five foot five, heavily made up, with an expanse of leg showing that left little to the imagination. Her hair was bleached, in a punk cut, and she kept one eye on the cars cruising by as she talked with several other women. She might have been twenty, or twelve. When she saw Rebecca climb out of her car, her face twisted into a frown.

"Hiya, Sandy," Rebecca said softly as she approached. The others in the group drifted quickly away.

"Jesus, Frye," the girl hissed, looking quickly over her shoulder. "What are you trying to do to me? I'll be poison to every john on the street tonight after this."

"So you can get a good night's sleep, then," Rebecca said, turning so her back was to the building, keeping a watchful eye on the slowly moving traffic and passersby. She was alone, and it was no secret she was a cop. "I need to talk to you."

"Is that all?" Sandy said with contempt. She'd had too much experience with cops who wanted more than just information to trust any of them.

Rebecca met her angry gaze evenly. "That's all, right now."

"I don't have much choice, do I?"

"No, you don't."

"Can we talk inside? You're killing my business out here."

Rebecca nodded and followed the girl into the dark bar, taking a table well away from the small platform where a woman did a tired bump and grind for the few patrons. Sandy signaled for a drink. Rebecca put a twenty on the table.

"So, what do you need, *Detective*?" Sandy asked in a bored voice. "I'm fresh out of discount blow jobs. Or are you going to pretend you're not into that sort of thing?" She took a healthy swallow of her drink, scanning the bar for anyone she knew. It wasn't good PR to be seen with a cop.

Rebecca ignored the taunt. "Two cops were killed the day before yesterday. What do you hear about it?"

Sandy rolled the shot glass in her hands and regarded Rebecca coolly. She didn't actually dislike the good-looking cop; in fact, Frye was one of the few cops who didn't harass the working girls. She'd even let Sandy out of the police van one night after a raid rather than bring her downtown for the empty exercise of booking. Still, Sandy didn't want the detective to get the idea she was her private snitch or anything. And it didn't help her reputation any to appear too chummy with the cops. There was something different about the tall, blond detective tonight, though. She seemed almost human, like she had feelings, like she was hurting. *You're losing it, girl. Cops with feelings?*

"There's nothing going down that I've heard," Sandy said finally, which was pretty much true. They'd all heard about the shooting, of course. Usually when something like that happened, it brought the whole police force down on them, like they were the source of all the city's problems. Probably this cop was just the first of many.

"What about the chicken trade? Any new faces in town?"

Sandy snorted in disgust. She hated the child procurers and pornographers as much as she hated the pushers. Like most of her friends, she stayed clear of them. "Since that big bust six months ago, it's been quiet. I heard there might be a new house open somewhere in a very ritzy location, but it isn't down here."

"Who's running it?" Rebecca asked nonchalantly, hiding her surprise at the information. She had been instrumental in cleaning out half a dozen establishments supplying children for all types of amusement in the citywide crackdown to which Sandy referred. If they were up and running again, there had to be big money behind it. *Could that have been what Hogan was on to?* It would take an organization as big as the Zamora crime family to start up the kiddie industry again. It took money, muscle, and overseas connections, because much of the advertising and clientele was established through Internet sites in foreign countries. She hadn't heard that the feds were looking into anything local, and she should have if anything serious was going on.

"No one knows, and that's the truth. There're more than a few people who'd like to find out."

"Yeah," Rebecca muttered in disgust. "Where there are kids, there's money." She looked at the young woman across from her, already cynical and hardened. There was nothing Rebecca could do to change her future, but maybe she could make a difference with a few of the really young ones. She pushed back her chair, leaving another twenty with the change on the table. "Thanks, Sandy. Keep your ears open. I'll be back."

"Hey, Frye," Sandy called, pocketing the money quickly. "Who were the cops who got killed?"

"Just cops."

CHAPTER SIXTEEN

Rebecca was still in the car when the sun came up, so she stopped at an all-night diner for breakfast before a quick detour to her apartment to shower and change clothes. The traffic was light, and her thoughts wandered, returning unbidden to memories of the previous night.

Just recalling the sound of Catherine's voice made her skin burn. The *images* of Catherine threatened to unhinge her—images of passion; images of splendor and surrender and desire; images that promised to hold her captive for eternity. Being with Catherine had been physically exciting, more fulfilling than she had ever dreamed, and easily the most frightening thing she had ever experienced.

She was relieved when the station house appeared, and she pulled into the lot on squealing tires. Work was just what she needed to put Catherine Rawlings into perspective. It was too early for the day shift to arrive, and she walked unnoticed through the quiet halls. When she pushed open the door to Vice, she was astonished to see Watts at Jeff's desk, *his* desk now, with a half-eaten pizza in front of him. She wasn't certain, but she thought he was wearing the same suit as he'd had on the day before. He was the only one in the room.

He glanced her way, grunting a greeting as he reached for another slice of the now congealed pizza. "I was just going to call you, Sarge," he said around a mouthful of crust slathered with thick tomato sauce and cheese.

"What could be so important at five thirty in the morning?" Rebecca commented, not really caring what Watts had to say. She couldn't stand to see him sitting in Jeff's chair. She noticed a stack of folders beside the desk. Her and Jeff's open case files. *Could Watts actually be working?*

"Thought you might like to read the morning paper," he said, tossing the early-bird edition onto her desk. He went back to eating, munching the cold crust, his face expressionless as he watched her pick up the paper and glance at it without much interest. Then he saw her eyes darken, and he braced himself.

"What the *hell* is this," she exploded, staring up from the headlines that proclaimed, "River Drive Rape Witness Found!" She regarded him in wordless astonishment, and he shook his head grimly.

"Read it. It's very interesting," he flatly intoned.

She began to read aloud, her voice tight and angry. "Sources reveal that a witness to the brutal rape of a college student on the River Drive last week may have been found."

What followed was a sensationalized review of the previous two assaults, but it was the last paragraph that caused Rebecca to clench her fists in frustration. "Dr. Catherine Rawlings, a noted psychiatrist at the University Hospital declined comment, but unnamed sources confirm she is the primary physician of a patient who witnessed the most recent attack. The patient's name has not yet been released, nor has a description of the assailant been made public." The article finished with an indictment of the police for failing to keep the public informed.

"Jesus Christ," Rebecca cursed, tossing the paper aside. "I can't *believe* the asshole put Catherine's name in the paper! He might as well have put Janet Ryan's in, too. We'll need to tighten security down there right away. Catherine didn't want us to put a guard on Ryan, but we'll have to now. God damn it."

"I already called the patrol commander. He said he'd post someone down there in an hour or so, as soon as the day shift signs in."

Rebecca regarded Watts with surprise, but she was too disturbed by the article to appreciate his quick thinking. "*This* kind of media coverage we do not need. It engenders public hysteria and distrust. If that isn't bad enough, it jeopardizes the whole damn investigation. If the perp thinks we may have a lead on him, he could change his pattern or stop temporarily, and then we're screwed. He could move to another city altogether, and we'll never get him." What she didn't add was what really worried her most—the perpetrator might try to silence Janet Ryan, now that he knew where she was.

"Looks like somebody talked," Watts remarked with disgust. "Probably the shrink."

"It wasn't her," Rebecca stated flatly, knowing that Catherine would never endanger Janet Ryan. What she couldn't understand was why Catherine hadn't told her about the reporter.

"She knows almost as much as we do," Watts continued unperturbed, fingering the reports in front of him. "She's been present every time you've talked to the Ryan kid—"

"I told you, Watts. It *wasn't* her. Now let it drop," Rebecca barked. She was feeling the effects of the long night, and the nagging headache was back. "Why don't you find out where that leak came from?"

"Yeah?" he said belligerently. "And just how do you suggest I do that?"

"Get that little twerp from the *Daily* and shake it out of him," she said, heading for the door.

"Hey! Where you going?" he called after her.

"The morgue."

He didn't ask her anything else.

"You don't want to be down here, Frye," Dee Flanagan said sharply when she looked up from her microscope to see the detective striding through the lab. Hogan's and Cruz's bodies were still down the hall in the autopsy room, and that wasn't the kind of memory a friend should have. "Besides, we aren't open yet. It's not even seven o'clock."

"You're always open," Rebecca said, ignoring the frown on Flanagan's tanned face. "Did you look at the slug you dug out of the dock?"

"Maggie has it now. I told you I'd call. You're just gonna piss off Homicide by poking around in their case."

"Yeah, yeah," Rebecca muttered as she threaded her way down the narrow aisle constricted further by equipment stands, boxes of supplies, and makeshift work areas. She went through the far door into the brightly lit room beyond and looked for Maggie Collins, a slender, blue-eyed redhead. Maggie was fifteen years younger than Dee Flanagan and her head technician, as well as her lover.

When she saw Rebecca, Maggie asked quietly, with just a hint of Ireland still in her voice, "Dee know you're here?"

"Yep."

"Hmm," Maggie mused, setting aside a labeled tube of something that looked like it had been scraped off the inside of a dumpster. "Slipping a bit, is she?"

"Nah," Rebecca assured her. "I was moving fast, and she didn't have a chance to tackle me."

Maggie smiled, a smile that melted hearts. "Ah, that's all right then. You'll be wantin' the report on the gun that killed Jeff?"

"Do you have something?" Rebecca asked hopefully.

"Not as much as you'd like, but something," Maggie responded, directing Rebecca's attention to a large computer monitor. She slid a disk in and deftly worked the cursor through a series of images until she had a gray object that barely resembled its previously cylindrical shape centered on the screen. "That would be it—9mm standard automatic. Best guess is a Mauser."

"Hell," Rebecca exclaimed when she saw the condition of the bullet. "You'll never get bore marks off that thing."

"Don't you be pullin' such a long face, Sergeant," Maggie muttered, her Irish thickening as she frowned in concentration, highlighting several areas of the distorted fragment and bringing up the magnification. "This section here shows enough of the land and groove pattern that I can make a match if you bring me a firearm to test it against, or even another bullet from the same weapon."

"You're beautiful."

"She is," Dee said as she walked up behind them, "but you should leave this alone, Frye."

Rebecca fixed the Crime Scene chief with a steady stare, and said in a low, dangerous voice, "He was my *partner*."

"All the more reason to let Homicide handle it."

For a moment the two women faced each other in stony silence, and then Rebecca said, "I can't."

Flanagan continued as if she hadn't heard. "We've pretty much finished up with all the exemplars from the River Drive rape site. There's nothing there that will help until you have a suspect and can search his place for physical evidence. I can tell you this with certainty, though—Janet Ryan was involved in a physical altercation with your perp. The skin under one of her nails matches the DNA from the semen on all the rape victims. I got the preliminary analysis back just now. You have your witness."

"Yeah," Rebecca snapped, tired and frustrated and knowing that

Dee was right to tell her to back away from the homicide. "If she ever remembers anything."

"Why don't you do us all a favor and concentrate on *that* case. Trish Marks is a good homicide cop, and even Charlie Horton isn't going to screw around when it's a cop who has been taken out. Give them some room to work."

"Thanks for the info on Ryan," Rebecca said, walking away without bothering to pretend she could leave Jeff's death alone. No one would have believed her anyway.

CHAPTER SEVENTEEN

Catherine finished her second cup of coffee and glanced up at the cafeteria clock. It was 7:15 a.m. Residents and students were beginning to gather in tired clumps to discuss the night's events and the day's demands over breakfast. She was one of the few staff present. The surgeons had already come and gone on their way to the operating room, and it would be relatively quiet for the next hour until the outpatient clinics opened at 8:30. She had come early for one specific reason—to intercept Hazel Holcomb before the chief of psychiatry's busy schedule made her inaccessible for the day.

Catherine saw the familiar figure moving through the coffee line at precisely 7:30, carrying a coffee and danish as she had each morning for the fifteen years that Catherine had known her. She was nearing sixty, but her age showed only in the gray of her hair and a slight thickening of her body. Her brisk step and quick piercing gaze were as youthful as ever.

Hazel's face registered faint surprise when she saw Catherine beckoning to her from across the room. As she settled into the chair across from her younger colleague, she said, "I don't suppose this is just a pleasant coincidence, is it?"

Catherine flushed in embarrassment. Hazel had been her supervisor when she was a resident, and they had since become friends. She always meant to call her just to chat or perhaps have dinner, but work always seemed to take precedence, and there never seemed to be time for it. Perhaps more than anyone else she knew, Catherine valued her opinion. Hazel had the ability to provide insight without judgment and the wisdom to hold her counsel until the patient—or friend—was ready to accept it.

"No, it isn't," Catherine admitted. "I have a professional matter I want to discuss with you. Do you mind me interrupting your breakfast time?" She knew that this was probably one of the few private moments Hazel would have all day.

"Your company is always a pleasure, Catherine. Tell me about your problem." While Catherine relayed the details of Janet Ryan's involvement with the recent assaults and her subsequent amnesia, Hazel absently nibbled at her breakfast, absorbing the tale.

"And what about all of this troubles you?" Hazel finally asked astutely. "It sounds as if your patient is recovering faster than you had hoped."

"I'm not sure how hard I should be trying to reverse her amnesia," Catherine said. "Obviously, it's vital to know exactly what she witnessed. It's critical to the police investigation. On the other hand, I have to think of Janet's psyche first. She is a sexual abuse victim herself. Her brother repeatedly raped her throughout her childhood. I'm certain that the shock of witnessing the assault this week triggered many old terrors for her."

"Enough to account for the amnesia?" Hazel asked, while dunking the corner of her cheese danish into the steamy black coffee.

Catherine shrugged. "The beating she took by itself may account for the amnesia, but she's having more frequent and more detailed flashbacks from her early childhood—previously unremembered episodes of abuse. That is a result of witnessing the rape, I'm sure."

"She must be very fragile right now," Hazel commented sympathetically.

"She is, of course. She's been working with me both individually and in group for some time and has made a lot of progress. But this whole event has brought up a great deal for her to handle all at once."

Hazel pushed her chair back slightly and sat quietly regarding her friend and colleague. Catherine had been the brightest resident she had ever trained and was now the most accomplished psychiatrist on her staff. Hopefully, Catherine would assume her own position as head of psychiatry when she retired. She knew Catherine to be both an empathetic therapist and an accomplished theoretician. She also knew that when Catherine sought her advice, it was often simply to confirm what she already believed.

"What do you think would happen to Janet if she were to recall the details of this recent trauma before she was emotionally prepared for it?" Hazel asked at last.

Catherine thought carefully before replying. "I can't be sure, and that's what's bothering me so much. There's a good chance she would handle it well. She has a supportive partner, and she's made great progress with resolving much of her confusion as to her own responsibility—or *lack* of it—for the abuse in her childhood." She hesitated, thinking aloud. "But there is still a possibility that she might see her inability to prevent this rape as a reflection of what she considers to be her failure to protect herself from her brother. That kind of guilt, even though unfounded, could be damaging."

"That's your answer, then, isn't it," Hazel said calmly. "She'll remember when it's safe for her to remember. Until then she needs to be supported and reassured that her inability to remember is natural and healthy."

"Of course. You're so right." Catherine felt a wave of relief as she often did when Hazel grasped the essence of some professional dilemma and reduced it to its simplest form. "I'm afraid I momentarily lost sight of exactly what my issues are. My responsibility is to her welfare first. I guess I've allowed myself to think too much about what will happen if the rapist isn't apprehended quickly. I owe it to Janet to be cautious."

Hazel recognized the look of self-accusation that crossed Catherine's fine features, clouding them for an instant with self-doubt. *Ever the perfectionist.* "Don't be so hard on yourself, Catherine," she said softly. "This is not a simple matter. There *are* many important issues here. Are the police pressuring you to force Janet along?"

"Oh, no," Catherine replied quickly. "Rebecca has been wonderful with Janet."

Hazel picked up immediately on the change in Catherine's tone, but she didn't comment on it. Catherine, however, flushed slightly and hastened to explain.

"Rebecca Frye is the detective in charge of the rape investigation. She's very good with Janet. She's frustrated, of course, because she doesn't have much to go on. But she's allowed me to handle Janet my own way."

"Sounds unusual for the police," Hazel noted dryly. "It hasn't been my experience that the police are particularly sensitive about how they elicit information."

"Rebecca *is* unusual. It's more than just a job to her. Oh, she's a police officer, down to her last cell, but she's also sensitive and kind. She *cares*. This investigation is stalled, and it's wearing on her." As she spoke, she thought about the exhausted woman who had sought comfort in her arms just a few hours before, and she warmed to the memory. She remembered too how eagerly—desperately—she'd given herself to Rebecca, and she flushed again.

Hazel knew Catherine too well not to notice. "How serious is this…with this police woman?" she asked pointedly.

"Oh, Hazel. I wish I could answer that." Catherine met Hazel's gaze evenly, but her eyes betrayed her uncertainty. She sighed deeply and shook her head. "I hardly know her, really. We only met a little over a week ago, but my feelings for her are so strong. It's completely unlike me." She spread her hands in a rare gesture of helplessness. "There's a connection I can't explain. I suppose I should be able to, but I can't. I'm afraid I'm quite taken with her already."

Hazel wasn't all that surprised. She was probably the person who knew Catherine best, and she had watched her hold herself apart from potential relationships—unsatisfied by casual encounters, not given to sexual liaisons; searching, seeking; unconsciously waiting for some deeper connection—and being continually disappointed. She knew it had been some years since Catherine had even seriously dated anyone, and she suspected that Catherine's detachment had grown out of her disillusionment with love. For all of Catherine's training and knowledge of life, she remained, at her core, a true romantic. And she remained a woman, Hazel feared, who might never find the soul partner she so desired.

"Well," Hazel said, "I think I can understand your dilemma better now." She raised a hand to halt Catherine's quick reply. "Oh, I do not for an instant doubt your professional judgment or your ability to protect your patient. But one's head is hardly clear when one is falling in love."

Catherine blushed fully and looked down at her hands. "Do you think I'm foolish?" she asked softly.

Hazel reached across the table, touching Catherine's hand gently. She had never seen her so uncertain. "Not a bit," she replied. "It's normal and healthy…and about time."

"It may turn into a disaster," Catherine went on, voicing her fear for the first time. "She sees the worst of people every day, and she's distrustful and emotionally remote because of it. But she's also burying her tenderness, her caring, and her fear just to maintain her balance. She's afraid of being hurt. She wouldn't say that; I doubt that she even realizes it. I'm not sure she's even *capable* of knowing her feelings for me...or for anything."

"She's not alone in that, Catherine," Hazel said sadly, "but I can see that she's touched you in a way that no one has in years, and I doubt that she could have done that if she were truly emotionally bereft. Trust to time...and try to take care of yourself."

Catherine smiled her gratitude and straightened her shoulders. Pushing back from the table she said, "I've got to make rounds."

"I'll walk with you," Hazel replied as she picked up her tray.

They accompanied each other in friendly silence, strengthened as always by their encounter.

CHAPTER EIGHTEEN

After running a quick check with the patrol officers who had been running down leads on cars parked illegally along the Drive the day Darla Myers and Janet Ryan were attacked—and coming up empty—Rebecca pulled into the hospital parking lot. It was just before eleven a.m. She took the now familiar route to the psychiatry wing with a surge of excitement spiraling through her belly. Even though she was bone tired and still reeling from the shock of Jeff's death, the memory of awakening beside Catherine, of making love to her, made her entire body feel charged. She was aware of the quickening of her heartbeat and a low pulse of desire just from the anticipation of seeing her again.

Get a grip, Frye. Catherine still held the pivotal piece in the puzzle of her case—access and insight to Janet Ryan—and she couldn't afford to let her personal feelings get in the way of her professional obligations. Time was running out. Too many people depended on her to do her job right, and she was going to have to push for the information she needed. The next victims were even now going about their lives under the assumption that they were safe, never thinking that around the next corner some madman waited to destroy their future. It was her responsibility to see that that never happened.

She stepped off the elevator into the hushed hall of the inpatient ward, the image of Darla Myers and the other victims as vivid as they had been the first time she looked at their battered bodies. A woman in a blue smock was bent over a stack of metal folding charts behind the white counter of the nurses' station, busily cross-checking medication cards. She looked up and smiled when she heard Rebecca approach.

"I'm sorry," she said. "Visiting hours aren't until one o'clock."

Rebecca pulled the slim black leather folder from her pocket and displayed her identification. "I'm looking for Dr. Rawlings. Is she around?"

"I think so," the friendly African American woman replied as she checked her watch. "She should be finished with the residents in a few minutes. There's a conference room just down the hall. Do you want to wait for her there?"

Rebecca nodded. "That's fine. I'll find it," she added, motioning the nurse to stay seated. "Would you tell her I'm here, please?"

There was little of interest in the conference room, and as she always did in the midst of a troubling case, Rebecca let her mind wander back over the investigation, hoping to turn up some detail that might give her a fresh lead. Jill had always complained that even when Rebecca was with her, she wasn't really *with* her, because mentally she was still working. Rebecca couldn't disagree.

Hands in her pockets, she paced around the perimeter of the room, sorting facts and cataloguing data. There was something that kept nagging at her about these assaults—something she had seen or heard that might be significant—but she couldn't quite bring it into focus. She knew from experience that the swirling impressions would eventually consolidate into a coherent image and, hopefully, bring the greater picture into sudden relief. The tantalizing clue was often the key to a puzzle whose separate pieces then quickly fell into place. *Then*, she hoped, she would be able to close the gap between herself and the man she sought.

Unfortunately, the process couldn't be rushed. Eventually, her unconscious mind would work that tiny fragment free and allow it to float to the surface. It was the waiting for that moment to occur that drove her crazy because, in cases like this, time was a luxury she didn't have.

The door opened and Catherine walked in. All thoughts of the case disappeared. She had forgotten, although she couldn't imagine how that was humanly possible, how beautiful Catherine was. Twelve hours ago, they had been in one another's arms, and as she remembered Catherine's hands on her, her skin suddenly burned.

"Catherine," Rebecca said, and, to her own ears, it sounded like a benediction. Searching for a more professional tone, she cleared her throat and tried again. "Sorry to arrive unannounced."

"You shouldn't be. I'm glad to see you." Catherine brushed her fingers over the top of Rebecca's hand as she moved past her to a seat at the small conference table. "You don't look like a woman who's been up half the night."

The warmth in her smile and the intimacy in her voice reached deeper than the brief caress. Rebecca felt it in her bones. She flushed despite her resolve to remain detached, and she had to look away. If she didn't, she was in danger of drowning in the depths of Catherine's eyes. *I can't go there right now. I can't think about how much I needed you, and how damn right it felt.*

"It isn't about last night," Rebecca finally said, her tone stiffer than she had intended.

Catherine studied her intently, replying quietly. "An official visit, then?"

"Tell me about the reporter you spoke with."

"The reporter?" Catherine asked blankly. She wasn't used to being interrogated, and the abrupt change in subject caught her unawares. It didn't help her concentration any that the moment she had seen who was waiting for her, she hadn't been able to think of anything except awakening in the night with Rebecca caressing her.

"Have you seen the morning papers?"

"No, I've been on rounds until just now. Why, what is it?" She stared at Rebecca, aware of the tension in the detective's slim frame as she continued to pace. Her body was practically humming with it. "Rebecca?"

"There's an article in today's *Daily* announcing the fact that we have a witness to the rape." Rebecca was unable to hide the anger in her voice.

"They have Janet's name?" Catherine cried, horrified.

"No, not yet," Rebecca assured her grimly, "but they have yours."

"Oh, thank God," Catherine said, relieved to hear that her patient's identity had not been revealed. "Oh, of course! There was a reporter here yesterday asking questions—" She stopped and looked at Rebecca, her eyes filling with concern. "You think I told him?"

"Did you?"

"No, of course not." She tried to ignore the quick flash of pain at the veiled accusation, reminding herself that even though they had been intimate, it had been very much a physical connection. Rebecca did not know her. "But he seemed to know that the police were involved with Janet's case. I assure you, Rebecca, I told him nothing."

"I'm sorry," Rebecca said with a sigh, finally sitting down next to the psychiatrist. "I didn't think it was you, but I had to check." Before she realized what she was doing, she grasped Catherine's hand and held it, circling her thumb slowly over the soft skin. She let it go reluctantly, leaning back in her chair because she had an overwhelming urge to touch her again. To keep touching her. "Can you think of anyone who might have talked to him?"

"A dozen people." Catherine's face revealed her frustration. "A hospital is the least private place in the world. Everyone is eager for a story, and every bit of human drama is grist for the gossip mill. It could have been anyone."

"I was afraid of that," Rebecca said angrily. "There's not much we can do about it now, but it makes it even more important that we find out what Janet saw. Can you help me with this?"

Catherine was quiet for a long moment, sorting through her thoughts, trying not to be swayed by the sight of Rebecca's drawn and tired face. She wanted so much to be able to offer some relief—not just to the detective but also to the woman. But she had a deeper obligation, one even greater than her growing affection for Rebecca.

"I'll do all I can. I'm seeing Janet for a therapy session later today. If I learn anything at all that I can reveal, I'll tell you immediately. I know that if she remembers any details she will want you to know."

"I may need to have Janet interviewed by the police psychiatrist," Rebecca said quietly. She saw Catherine's body tense and realized that she had offended her. She didn't want that—professionally or personally. "He may be able to recognize something you don't. It's routine."

"Of course," Catherine responded formally. "I'm not a forensic psychiatrist."

"Damn it." Rebecca shook her head impatiently. "I'm not suggesting you're not competent, Catherine, but he is trained in criminal investigation."

"May I be present at the interview?"

Thinking quickly, Rebecca replied, "I don't see why not. It might make it easier for Janet."

"I don't like it, Rebecca, but I can see why you might have to do this."

"Thank you," the detective said softly, realizing in that moment how much she had not wanted Catherine to be angry with her. It was hard enough keeping a clear head and her priorities straight around this remarkable woman without that. "I'd be pissed as hell if someone started interfering with how I ran one of my investigations."

"Yes, well, we have that in common."

Startled, Rebecca searched Catherine's face, looking for the anger she had heard in her tone. She couldn't find it, and wondered if that was due to supreme control or just a very balanced temper. "So...how pissed *are* you?"

"I'll survive," Catherine said dryly.

"Good. Then there's something else I need from you," Rebecca continued.

"There's more?" Catherine couldn't suppress a chuckle. The woman was certainly relentless.

"I need some insight here. Something about this case feels off. It's not like the usual sexual assault, if there is such a thing. What do you know about serial rapists? This doesn't seem to fit with what I'm used to seeing."

The doctor nodded, happy to be on safer ground. It was difficult being at odds with Rebecca over the issue of Janet Ryan, and getting more difficult every minute to concentrate. *God, ever since I walked into the room, I've wanted to grab her by the lapels, pull her close, and kiss her. This is so very much not the time.*

Focusing on the detective's question, she answered, "Most rapes occur between acquaintances; case in point is the all too prevalent date rape. Next are those common to particular settings—groups, or gang rapes, in bars or at parties. And, of course, the repeat rape of young children by adult sexual abusers, generally family members. The type of patterned, serial rape you're dealing with is actually quite unusual. In broad psychiatric terms, it's a sociopathic activity, a crime perpetrated out of some deep-rooted psychopathology."

"Such as?"

"Oh, any number of things—low self-esteem, attributed, often incorrectly, to powerful female figures such as a domineering mother or a failed relationship with a woman; anger at feelings of impotence or lack of control, especially his frustration at not being able to direct events around him. The rapist often feels like a victim of social or personal injustice and translates that into anger against women. The rape is rarely purely sexually motivated, but, of course, sex is equated with power, especially in our culture. So, the rape represents an attempt to control events, to gain superiority over the perceived persecutor."

"Are you saying that these rapes are the result of a disease?" Rebecca asked suspiciously. *Wouldn't a defense attorney just love that.*

"No," Catherine responded firmly. "Make no mistake about that. These assaults are a crime, regardless of what psychopathology may underlie the motivation."

"What can I expect in terms of the pattern of these attacks?" Rebecca asked, making notes as she listened.

"It's hard to say. There isn't anything particularly ritualized about them. As far as I'm aware, the only similarities are the site and the fact that all of the victims have been joggers."

"They've all been young and fit, but you're right, there hasn't been any physical similarity beyond that fact." Rebecca took a deep breath. She had never shared information with civilians, but then Catherine defied preconceived definitions. "There is something else, though. All of the victims were sodomized. And also, there was no vaginal penetration."

Catherine raised an eyebrow as she considered this new information. "Well, I could theorize, of course, but I doubt that it would help you much."

"Go ahead. You never know what may help."

"It could be that the rapist is potent only that way. Fear of vaginal intercourse, of losing one's penis, is not that uncommon with sexually maladjusted men. There is also the possibility that he is acting out a fantasy in which the victim's femaleness is a detractor."

Rebecca stopped writing and looked up. "You mean a homosexual fantasy?"

"Possibly."

"Terrific," Rebecca said with disgust. "That would definitely help public opinion of gays."

"No, no. It's not likely that he *is* gay. It would be much more likely that he is suppressing homosexual ideation, ideation that would be perfectly normal were it not for the fact that homophobia is so ingrained in our society. If he *is* sexually inadequate with women, such ideation would be even more unwelcome. As I said, I'm only theorizing."

Rebecca snapped her notebook shut and rubbed her face in frustration. "I can't do anything but wait for his next move, and that means waiting for him to attack another woman."

"What about staking out the area?"

"We try," Rebecca said derisively, "but it's pretty difficult with only a few people to cover twenty miles of riverfront."

"I wish I could help you more."

"You can. You can help me find out what Janet Ryan saw that night."

Catherine remained silent, torn between conflicting emotions. There was nothing she could say to change the circumstances and nothing to add to what she had already said. At length, she stood up, not wanting to leave but knowing she had to.

"I want to see you again, Rebecca," she said at last. "Not here, and not about police business. I want to be somewhere where we can just be together. And I want to be able to touch you."

Rebecca rose quickly and, in one motion, pulled her close and kissed her firmly on the mouth. Her hands traveled the length of Catherine's back, caressing each curve with trembling hands. When she stepped back, her heart was racing.

"And I've been wanting to do that since you walked into the room," Rebecca said, her voice low and thick. She touched Catherine's cheek softly, and then she was gone.

Watching the door close behind the detective's retreating back, Catherine took a deep breath and tried to get her bearings. It was the middle of the day, and sexual arousal tended to interfere with her concentration. It didn't escape her notice that Rebecca had deftly avoided mentioning when they might see one another again. She almost wished that Rebecca's hands on her hadn't felt so good. Almost.

CHAPTER NINETEEN

Rebecca's beeper sounded as she rode the hospital elevator to the ground floor. She was grateful for the interruption, because she had been replaying the way Catherine had felt in her arms. Good. So good. *Too good.* Her nerve endings were jangling from just one kiss. Threading her way through the logjam of wheelchairs, elderly patients shuffling behind steel-framed walkers, and clumps of disoriented visitors, she reached a public phone and called the station.

"Frye here," she announced when the switchboard operator answered. She edged her way out of the path of a speeding adolescent who raced between slower visitors and waited impatiently for her call to be put through.

"This is Watts," the heavy male voice intoned in a bored voice.

"What do you want, Watts?" Rebecca snapped, unable to hide her dislike. She had managed not to think about him for almost half a day.

"I got a courtesy call from one of the Homicide guys, a just-letting-you-know kinda thing."

"Yeah, sure," Rebecca said dismissively, watching through the large windows fronting the lobby as a line of ambulances rolled around the corner. "That usually means they're trying to pawn a case off on us. What is it?"

"They rolled on a dead body call late last night. A desk clerk down on Filbert found a very cold hooker in one of the upstairs rooms that rents by the hour."

Rebecca waited for more and was rewarded with the faint background buzz of the phone line. "Watts," she said in exasperation, "we don't have time to track down some faceless john who got too rough with a hooker. Tell Homicide we don't want it."

"Yeah," Watts said. "You're probably right. The whore was just a kid...thirteen, they said."

"Fuck!" Rebecca expelled a ragged breath. "I was hoping we had quieted down that action."

"Funny thing about it. The ME called in a preliminary report— seems the kid was beaten to death first, then sodomized. The semen analysis showed up blood type A."

"Jesus," Rebecca exclaimed. "Same as with all of ours. Why didn't you just say it might be our perp? Give me the address. I'll meet you there."

She knew the place. The Viceroy Hotel. It had once been a respectable hotel, housing long-term tenants and the occasional tourist. With the decline of the surrounding neighborhood and the gravitation of junkies, prostitutes, and drug dealers into the area, anyone who could afford to had moved out. Now the hotel was a stopover for hookers and their clients, junkies waiting for their next fix, and the lonely wino who had scrounged the price of a thin mattress for the night.

Rebecca made the cross-town trip easily, despite the rush of late lunch hour traffic. Watts was waiting in front of the four-story building, looking apathetic and bored. His crumpled suit, too tight across his bulging middle, had once been expensive but now reflected the neglect and disinterest that was evident in the man himself. She knew that he had once been considered a sharp detective, but apparently, something had changed. He looked every inch the burnt-out veteran, just putting in time until his pension came up. Even if she didn't resent him for taking Jeff's place, she wouldn't want to be saddled with him; he was clearly a loser.

She joined him wordlessly, and they pushed through the hotel's double entry doors into a dank, dimly lit foyer. The high-ceilinged room, once elegant with its ornate moldings and stately tiled floors, was now shabby and tawdry. Threadbare chairs sat haphazardly on scattered, worn rugs of indeterminate color. Piles of old magazines lay strewn randomly over the surface of a few scarred end tables.

Beyond the sitting area was the reception counter where the desk clerk, a thin, graying man of obscure age, leaned on his elbow, watching them impassively. The room was empty except for an old woman who reclined on a sofa against one wall, snoring softly. The clerk clearly read them as cops and continued to stare at them without speaking as they approached.

Watts flipped his badge open and leaned against the cigarette-scarred counter. "You Bailey?" he asked without preamble.

"That's right," the man said. His breath smelled of liquor, and he looked as if his face hadn't seen a razor in days. His soiled shirt and shiny trousers were in no better shape.

"You find the body?" Watts continued, making no effort to introduce Rebecca. She was irritated but saw no benefit in making a show out of it. She let Watts carry the ball.

"Yeah, I found it."

Watts nodded slightly. "Says in the report that you called it in at 3:42 a.m."

"Probably. Didn't look at no clock."

"How come you're on the desk now? Where's the day shift?"

The man looked at Watts blankly. "I work the day shift."

Watts paused for a moment, a befuddled frown on his face. "That so? Then how come you were here in the middle of the night? You work the night shift, too? Pretty dedicated fellow."

The desk clerk's face registered dismay, and he looked quickly around the room. Rebecca had the sense that he was looking for an exit, and she stepped slightly to the left, blocking the hinged section of counter that led out from the narrow space between the mailboxes and the registration desk. She slowly moved her hand to unbutton her jacket, allowing her access to her automatic. She wasn't sure what Watts had in mind, but he was certainly after something. It would have helped if he had briefed her first, but they were in it now.

Watts studied the clerk, his face still creased with confusion. "You got other work here, maybe?"

"Like what?" he asked uneasily. He seemed to be developing a twitch in the corner of one eye.

"Like maybe you run a few of the girls yourself?"

At Watts's suggestion, the man gave a frightened snort and backed away from the counter. "Uh-uh. No way, no way at all. I never pimped...I swear. I just..." he stammered into silence.

"You just *what*?" Watts asked.

"Nothing."

Watts turned to Rebecca and raised a questioning eyebrow. "What do you think, Detective Sergeant Frye? Isn't soliciting clients for prostitutes a felony in this state? Maybe we should take Mr. Bailey here for a ride downtown."

Following his lead, Rebecca nodded agreement. "You're right, Detective Watts. Mr. Bailey does seem in clear violation of the law."

Bailey squeaked in protest, words tumbling out of his mouth in a rush. "Wait a minute! I didn't solicit for nobody. The girl was up there a long time, and I just went to see. There she was—spread out on the bed, naked except for those shorts around her ankles. She was cold already…I could tell that from the door. So's I called the cops…that's what a citizen is supposed to do, ain't it?" He glanced from one to the other, hoping for a sign of approval.

They returned his gaze impassively. Then Rebecca stepped a little closer to the counter and said softly, "Why were you watching her, Mr. Bailey?"

He looked uncomfortable and shifted from one foot to the other. He seemed to come to some decision, speaking slowly. "They pay me a little to keep an eye on the girls. You know, to see how many tricks they turn, see if they're holding back on what they give their pimps. I don't do nothing but keep an eye on traffic, so to speak."

"Who pays you, Mr. Bailey?" Rebecca asked, keeping her body between Bailey and Watts. They were playing good cop/bad cop all right. She only wished that Watts had given her some notice.

"You can't arrest me for watching hookers. That ain't no crime!"

Watts moved closer to Rebecca. "It is if you're an accomplice to the act—which you are, Bailey."

Bailey blanched but remained silent.

"Who went up there with her, Mr. Bailey?" Rebecca asked suddenly.

"Didn't see him," he answered quickly. Too quickly.

Rebecca turned to Watts. "Maybe Mr. Bailey would remember if we took him downtown. What do you say, Watts?"

Watts appeared to be thinking, his brow knit in consternation. "Yeah…you might be right, Sarge. But then we'd have to fill out all those reports and probably run Bailey through the computer. You know how long those computer checks take." He sighed as if the idea didn't appeal to him much. "And then if we find paper on him, we have to look at every place he's been and every little thing he's been doing here. It will take forever."

Bailey watched them, scarcely taking a breath. Finally, their silence drove him to speak. "Look. I don't pay much attention to the johns…they're in and out of here all the time. Dozens of 'em. This girl Patty…she was popular, you know? Young stuff like that attracts a lot of action. She'd be up and down those stairs ten times a night."

Rebecca suppressed a shudder, pushing from her mind the image of a young girl laboring under the bodies of countless men. She kept her gaze noncommittally on Bailey's pale face.

"The last guy—I just glanced up when they went by—he was white. Young, I remember that. Made me wonder for a second why such a young dude would have to pay for it." He shrugged. "Who knows? Maybe he was a virgin."

"You never saw him before?" Rebecca asked, hoping to encourage Bailey to continue his musings.

"Nah. I probably would have remembered if he was a regular."

"Is there anything that struck you as unusual about the guy?" Watts asked.

Bailey appeared to be considering the question, but his face remained blank. Chances were he had become too inured to the decadence around him to notice specifics.

"Don't think so," he said slowly. Suddenly, his face brightened, as if he had had a revelation. "I do remember he had a bag with him…one of them gym bags." He chuckled absently to himself. "Maybe he kept those shorts in there."

"What shorts?" Rebecca prompted, looking at Watts. Watts shook his head slightly, signaling he had no idea what Bailey was talking about.

"You know," Bailey said, "those little shorts she had on, like I said before. She wasn't wearing them when she went upstairs."

Rebecca felt a surge of excitement. "What was she wearing when she came in?"

"One of those little leather skirts and a—what do they call 'em—tank top?"

"Were her clothes in the room when you found her?" Watts asked.

Bailey shook his head. "Didn't see 'em, but I didn't look too close."

"You didn't lift anything for a little souvenir?" Watts probed.

"Uh-uh. No way. Didn't touch a thing. I looked, I saw her…that was it."

Rebecca knew they could check that out in the report filed by the uniform who responded to the call. She thought they had enough from Bailey for now, and she explained to him that they would need him to meet with the police artist to sketch a composite of the man who had accompanied Patty Harris on her last trick. Despite his protest that he didn't really see the guy, he agreed to meet them at the station later that day. He seemed more willing to cooperate now that they had conveniently forgotten about his role in the prostitution business.

Rebecca and Watts went upstairs to view the crime scene, but they didn't expect to find much. CSI had already been there, and the charcoal residue of fingerprint powder lay like a pall over everything. An iron bedstead tilted on uneven legs in the center of a dingy room that had once been white. The mattress was thin and stained. There were no rugs on the worn wood floor and only a curtain remnant to block the view of a deserted building across the alley. A single bulb hung from a central ceiling fixture, its globe long broken. It was an empty, abandoned place, much like the people who used it for their hasty couplings. The oppressiveness of the room permeated their consciousness quickly, and they left after a rapid survey, neither of them speaking.

Once outside, Rebecca turned to Watts as he stood back against the building out of the wind, attempting to light a cigarette. His match kept blowing out. "That was a nice piece of work with Bailey, Watts," she said. His questioning had been sharp, and they had worked well together.

His cigarette finally caught, and he took a deep drag. He didn't acknowledge her remark as he started toward the car. "Guess we'll have to start questioning all the hookers down here," he commented, pulling open the door to his battered green Dodge sedan. "See if there's a john around who likes girls in gym shorts."

Rebecca nodded, her thoughts in tune with his. "It might be a coincidence, but it's the only lead we've got. It wouldn't be the first time a perp hit on the prostitutes when he couldn't score elsewhere. It's certainly better than cooling our heels, waiting for him to strike again."

"Yeah. Beats doing callbacks on parking ticket violations, too. We're not gonna catch this guy that easy."

"I've got some contacts here. Let me chase this a while," she proposed. "You can check with the Homicide guy who took the call and review the uniform's first on-scene report. Maybe they talked to someone who saw something."

Watts shrugged. "Suits me. I'm going to grab some lunch first."

He didn't invite her along, and Rebecca didn't suggest they go together. She agreed to meet him at the station later to see what Bailey and the police artist had come up with. Maybe, finally, they had a break.

CHAPTER TWENTY

It was after eight p.m. and Catherine was exhausted. She had spent the afternoon at her office seeing private patients—five fifty-minute sessions with a scant ten minutes between to jot notes and clear her head before the next one arrived. Each patient expected her undivided attention and appropriately so. She loved her work, but there were times when it took all of her effort to stay connected and focused during a session.

Her workdays seemed to be getting longer despite her frequent resolutions to reduce her evening office hours. Since her teaching responsibilities at the medical school now included directing the psychiatric resident training program, as well as supervising the outpatient clinic *and* the inpatient service on a rotating basis with other staff psychiatrists, she had less time for private patients. Even as her personal time steadily disappeared, she constantly found herself making one more exception and adding yet another patient to her already crowded schedule. On days like today, though, she was glad to see the last patient leave.

As she pushed the stack of patient files into her brief case, the phone rang. She had told Joyce to leave a half an hour ago, so she was alone in the office. She stared at it as it rang again and decided to ignore it. The switchboard would pick it up in a few more rings, and if it was anything urgent, they would page her. Then it occurred to her that it might be Rebecca, and she snatched up the receiver.

"Hello," she said, a hopeful anticipation in her voice.

"Dr. Rawlings?" a soft male voice inquired.

"Yes?" Catherine was disappointed and worked to hide it in her response.

"Is she feeling better now?" the voice continued.

Catherine frowned, annoyed and confused. "I'm sorry. Who is this?"

"I understand that she will be going home soon."

"I don't know to whom you're referring," Catherine said carefully. Something in the caller's oddly uninflected tone made her wary. "What did you say your name was? Are you a patient?"

"Of course you know her, Dr. Rawlings," he said, a harsh note creeping into his voice. "The girl who saw me in the park. The one who watched me fucking that other one."

Catherine took a slow deep breath, pulling her briefcase closer and scrambling inside with one hand for her cell phone. Maybe she could call Rebecca while he was still on the line.

"I'm glad you called," Catherine said, working to keep her voice steady despite the sudden racing of her heart. "I was hoping that we could talk. What shall I call you?"

"Don't try to be clever." There was a soft chuckle through the line. "You understand I can't tell you that. They're looking for me, you know. But they're too stupid to find me."

"Who do you mean?"

"The police. They have no imagination." Another soft laugh, dismissive, arrogant. "Do *you*, Dr. Rawlings?"

"I think so," she answered. She'd found her cell phone, and she held it, forgotten, in her hand. His voice was mesmerizing, the tone of voice she'd heard from hypnotized subjects—distant, disembodied. Fascinating in a viscerally disturbing way. "What is it you want me to know?"

"Can you imagine lying on the ground, your face in the grass, with my big hard cock up your ass?"

He might have been asking her if she would like to take a stroll in the park. His tone was casual, almost relaxed.

"Is that what you're imagining right now?" she asked him in the same conversational tone, trying not to push too hard. Meanwhile, her mind worked frantically, searching for the right words to engage him, draw him out, make him reveal himself, while allowing him to believe that *he* was in control. "Is that what happens with the women?"

"I won't tell you *that*, Doctor," he responded, an edge of anger in his voice for the first time. "Did you really think I'd tell you what I do to them? You insult me if you think I'd be that easy. But you'll see, won't you? Believe me—the next time…you'll see."

"What are you going to do?" Catherine questioned, allowing a bit of her eagerness to show. She wanted him to keep talking, because eventually he would slip. He'd mention his plans or give her a clue to who he was. "I'd like to hear—"

The click of the line being disconnected was the only response.

"Damn," she muttered in frustration as she sagged back in her chair. "Damn, damn, damn."

For a moment she wasn't certain what to do. The call had shaken her, disoriented her. The professional part of her mind was intrigued by the interaction, but, personally, she was repulsed by the soft, cool voice that had reached out to her like an unwanted caress. She almost felt his hands on her and couldn't help but imagine what his victims had experienced. Trembling suddenly, emotionally raw, she realized that there was only one voice she wanted to hear.

"Hey, Frye," the night sergeant shouted across the squad room. "There's a call for you."

Rebecca frowned and gestured no with her hand. She and Watts were expecting Bailey to finish with the police artist any second, and she was eager to get a look at her suspect's face.

The desk sergeant shrugged. "The lady says it's an emergency."

Annoyed, Rebecca considered telling him to take a message, and then thought that it might be one of her contacts. She'd spent several hours late in the afternoon talking to prostitutes and street hustlers, hoping for a lead. No one knew anything, but it was too early in the day for many of the working girls to be around. Maybe this was one of them now. "Put it through over here, Riley." She grabbed up the handset. "Frye."

"It's Catherine, Rebecca. I'm sorry, I wouldn't have called, but—"

"It's okay," Rebecca interrupted immediately, detecting a difference in Catherine's usually calm voice. "What is it?"

"I just got a call from a man…your suspect…Janet's attacker…At least, I think it was him," Catherine replied, her voice curiously flat.

The stress was taking its toll, and she felt somewhat detached from everything at the moment.

Rebecca caught her breath and was on her feet in an instant, grabbing for her jacket with her free hand. She shrugged it on, the phone clamped under her chin. "Where are you?"

Watts glanced up at her from the opposite desk, his expression curious.

"At my office."

"I want you to lock your office door and turn down the lights, then move away from the window and wait for me. Do *not* open the door for anyone. Anyone. Even if they say they are a police officer. Do you understand?"

"Yes, I've already locked the door."

"Good. I'll be there in ten minutes."

"I'm fine, Rebecca," Catherine said, some of her usual control evident in her tone. "Really."

"I know that. Just do as I say."

"Of course I will."

Rebecca slammed the receiver into the phone cradle and cursed viciously under her breath; she was so furious she couldn't quite see clearly. *This sick bastard has gone too far. He just made it personal.* She turned toward the door and almost ran into Watts.

"Where're you going?" Watts was standing nonchalantly between her and the exit.

Rebecca stared at him, blinked once to clear the angry haze from her mind, and forced herself to think. She should tell him about a possible contact from the suspect, but all she wanted was to see Catherine, to be sure she was all right. *I don't want to have to be a cop for just a couple of minutes.* She remained wordless, and he watched her, no expression on his face. Taking a deep breath, she made a decision and replied, "We may have a phone contact from our boy. He may have just called Dr. Catherine Rawlings. I'm going there now."

Watts raised both eyebrows and whistled softly. "Things are heating up, aren't they? Guess I'd better tag along."

"Let's go, then," she said resolutely. She couldn't prevent him from accompanying her, as much as she wanted to go alone. *Damn the job.*

She made it from the station house to the university in less than eight minutes. Watts looked a bit green when he climbed from the front seat of the Vette. When she knocked on the office door, calling to Catherine, she unconsciously held her breath until she heard the lock being turned. The door swung open and Catherine stepped forward, looking pale but composed. She stopped short when she saw Watts behind Rebecca.

"Thank you for coming, Detective," she said quietly.

"Dr. Rawlings," Rebecca said just as quietly, wanting desperately to enfold her in her arms, if only for just a second. Aching to touch her, she instead followed the doctor through the waiting room into her private office, Watts trailing behind.

She took one of the chairs in front of Catherine's desk, and Watts sat beside her in the second one. "This is Detective Watts," Rebecca said, pulling her notebook from inside her jacket. "Can you tell us what happened?"

Catherine relayed in detail the brief conversation. Her memory was excellent, honed from years of retaining an entire hour's session with a patient. Rebecca and Watts each took notes, interrupting now and then to be certain they got the conversation verbatim.

Rebecca stiffened when Catherine clinically stated the caller's sexual intimations. Despite all her encounters with brutality and perversions, she'd rarely experienced such swift fury, and her focus wavered. When Catherine finished, Rebecca was momentarily wordless, struggling to set her personal reactions aside. She started slightly as Watts asked a question; she had forgotten he was there.

"Did you recognize the voice, Doctor?"

Catherine shook her head, a look of faint surprise on her face. "No," she said, "of course not."

"Never can tell." Watts gave a noncommittal shrug. "Could be someone you know...or maybe someone you treated?"

Catherine regarded the blank face of the man seated beside Rebecca contemplatively. She sensed a clever mind behind the facade of apparent disinterest. Her curiosity was piqued, and she wondered where his train of thought was leading. Without consciously realizing it, she resorted to professional objectivity and began to review the events dispassionately, as if they had happened to someone else. The familiarity of the process was just what she needed, and, immediately, she began to feel more comfortable and in control.

"I would recognize the voice if I'd heard it before, I'm sure of that. He was casual, and yet…so intimate." She didn't notice Rebecca flinch at her choice of words. Watts gave no sign of noticing it either.

"Why do you think that he called you?" Watts probed.

"He wanted to make contact…to boast a little. He wants someone with whom to share his experience," she mused aloud.

"What do you mean?" Rebecca asked, trying to keep her voice even. She didn't want her own reactions to interfere with Catherine's assessment of the events. She forced down the rage that threatened her detachment and struggled to view the psychiatrist as the critical component she had become in this case. Nevertheless, she was aware of a faint nausea that made it difficult for her to swallow. *God damn him to hell for involving Catherine in this.*

Watts glanced at Rebecca nonchalantly. He gave no outward sign that he had noticed the strain in her voice or the tense way she sat forward in the chair, looking like she might launch herself out of it at any second. "Go ahead, Doc."

"He's pleased with himself," Catherine said, shifting her attention toward Rebecca. Her gaze was remote as she sorted impressions and formulated opinions. "He's performed an important act, you see, and he's established himself, done something powerful—won a little victory. And he wants to be sure someone appreciates this."

"So why call you?" Watts asked.

Catherine shrugged. "I don't know—"

"Catherine," Rebecca interrupted urgently, "this is very important. Are you sure he isn't a current patient or someone you might have treated years ago?"

Catherine shook her head. "I don't treat many men. I'm certain I would know."

"How about pulling your files on all the men you've seen…say in the last five years?" Watts suggested. "Maybe we can find something there that jogs your memory."

Catherine straightened in her chair with a start. "Absolutely not, Detective. It's out of the question."

"Look, Doc," Watts pressed, his tone suddenly harsh. "This guy picks *you*—you of all the people in the city—to have a little chat with. He calls *you* to share a few *intimate* details of his latest fuck. Now, I gotta think that's not a coincidence. Like maybe he's got a little thing for you or something?"

"Back off, Watts," Rebecca ordered, fighting to control her temper. Watts's crude interrogation of Catherine incensed her, and, had Catherine not been present, she would have told him to shut his fat fucking mouth. As it was, it was all she could do to keep her hands off him. "If Dr. Rawlings says he's not a patient, then he's not a patient."

Watts settled back in his chair apparently unperturbed. "Yeah, if you say so."

"I'll review all my files, Detective," Catherine offered. "If there's anything there at all I think may be relevant, I'll look into it."

"Absolutely not!" Rebecca exploded. "You are not to pursue any contact with anyone you think may be involved with this case. For God's sake, Catherine, this man is a psycho; he's already killed two women, and a third may die."

"Oh, I don't know, Sarge," Watts mused softly. "Might not be a bad idea. Maybe the doc can come up with something for us. We ain't got shit now."

"Leave it alone, Watts," Rebecca said, cold fury in her voice.

She then looked at Catherine, her blue eyes dark and angry. There was something else there, too, a fear she couldn't quite hide. "Promise me, Catherine," she said urgently, not caring that Watts was sitting beside her.

"Yes, of course," she answered quickly, despairing at the anguish in Rebecca's eyes and hating the conflict her involvement had created for the detective. "I only meant that I'd look into previous records. I have no intention of physically pursuing this man." She was pleased to see the slight easing of Rebecca's stiff shoulders.

"We'll need to put a tap on your office and home phones," Rebecca said, her mind beginning to function again. "I'll order round-the-clock surveillance and put a man in your office, too."

Catherine sighed deeply, hating the words she was about to say. The last thing she wanted was to make Rebecca's already overwhelmingly difficult job any harder. "I can't let you do that, Rebecca."

"What?" Rebecca looked up from her notebook, astonishment flooding her face. She was immediately enraged, her patience completely frayed, while Watts looked almost amused. "Why the hell not?"

"I can't have my phone lines monitored. It's an invasion of my patients' privacy. And a man lurking about in my waiting room would be too unsettling for some of them. I just can't allow it," Catherine said as gently as possible.

"Catherine," Rebecca began, her tone dark with exasperation. *This* was too much. She couldn't deal with this professional bullshit any longer, not when it put Catherine at risk. Confidentiality was one thing, but this was carrying it too damn far. Not only did she need to protect Catherine, but also she had to have access to this guy if he called again. Before she could continue, Watts interrupted.

"How 'bout this, Doc. We put a tape recorder on your phone, and if our boy calls, you record it. And we'll have somebody watching your office from a car on the street. Would that work?"

Catherine considered carefully for a moment. "The tape recorder sounds fine, but I can't have someone watch my patients come and go."

"God damn it to hell!" Rebecca barked.

"Okay for now," Watts said, slapping his thigh briskly. He turned to Rebecca, his face carefully revealing nothing. "Talk to you outside for a moment, Sergeant?" He rose and strode deliberately to the office door, leaving Rebecca to follow angrily behind.

"What the fuck do you think you're doing, Watts?" she barked as soon as the door closed behind her. "It's not up to you how we run this case. I'm the primary, and I'll say how we handle this surveillance." Her face was two inches from his, and it took all of her control not to punch his already misshapen mug.

Watts reached unperturbedly into his jacket pocket and fumbled for a cigarette. He lit it, took a long drag, and exhaled slowly. "Looks to me like the shrink is one stubborn lady. If we're gonna get anything out of her, we've gotta go real slow and treat her gentle, like a virgin on her first date."

"Jesus Christ," Rebecca murmured. "You are the worst piece of crap I've come upon in years. If you think I'm going to leave her here like some piece of bait, you're stupider than you look."

She was having trouble thinking straight, but she couldn't seem to clear her head. She'd been up for nearly three days running with only a few hours of sleep. Jeff was dead, for God's sake, and now some piece of slime had slithered into her world and touched the woman she...she...she *what*, for Christ's sake? The woman she let hold her when her heart was breaking? The woman whose body she sought for comfort and a few hours' peace?

Oh God, what am I doing? How could I have let this happen now, in the middle of a case like this? She sagged slightly against the wall and stared numbly at Watts, who continued to puff contentedly on his cigarette.

"Sorry, Watts," she said at length. "You're right. We can't force her to do anything, and even a tape is better than nothing. Probably can't use it as evidence, though."

"Doesn't matter if we catch the guy. We won't need the tape…we'll have a DNA match from the semen. We just have to get our hands on him to make the case. Fuck the tapes then."

Rebecca stared at him wordlessly. He was right again.

"Let's see if Cath…if Dr. Rawlings has anything else to add," she said tiredly, feeling ineffectual and unaccountably defeated.

Watts stubbed out his cigarette on the expensive parquet floor in the hallway outside Catherine's office. "Why don't you do it? Not much more there, and I'm ready to call it a day." He strolled away, leaving Rebecca staring at his retreating back.

CHAPTER TWENTY-ONE

Catherine slumped tiredly behind her desk and, even from two rooms away, could hear the angry voices outside in the hall. The excitement of the last few hours had dissipated, leaving her drained. She knew Rebecca was angry, and she understood, or thought she did as much as anyone could, the frustration and powerlessness that she must feel right now. To have this man, whose identity had eluded the police so thoroughly, suddenly reveal his presence in such an arrogant and taunting manner was an insult too bitter to contemplate.

And, Catherine reminded herself, *now the man who has escaped her has made me an involuntary participant in all of this. She has got to feel torn between her professional obligation to maintain contact with* him *and her personal desire to shield me from him. What's making it even worse is that I can't cooperate with her investigation the way she wants. This on the heels of her partner's death. What were they thinking to let her keep working?*

But Catherine knew the answer to that question. This was what Rebecca did. This was who Rebecca was. She stared uneasily at her office door, wondering what future difficulties the return of the two detectives would bring. Clearly, Rebecca and her associate did not see eye to eye on the best way to proceed. Catherine imagined it must be very hard for Rebecca to deal with a new partner so soon after Jeff Cruz's death, especially since Rebecca had had no real opportunity to mourn him. *Of course, she'll never have time to deal with his death as long as she can drive her feelings into some hidden corner by working twenty hours a day. I suppose she's placing me in the same category—someone who creates feelings she'd rather avoid.*

Rubbing at the tension between her eyes, she sighed softly and leaned her head against the back of her tall leather chair. Sometimes it was hard being a psychiatrist; it was too hard facing what many others never really saw. Now and then she longed just to live from moment to moment like most of the world, not really knowing, or caring, *why* she did or felt something. She longed to abandon for just a few hours her awareness of the struggle it was merely to survive.

When Rebecca let herself back into Catherine's office, she found her asleep. They had kept the room lamps turned down deliberately in case anyone was watching from the street, and now, a pale sliver of moonlight fell across the slumbering woman's face. Only Catherine's soft, steady breathing broke the nearly dreamlike stillness in the room. Rebecca sank into the chair in front of the desk, remembering that the last time she had seen her like this they had been lying naked together.

For one brief moment, she forgot the case, and even Jeff's death, content just to look at Catherine. Her face was soft in sleep, with only a hint of fine lines at the corners of her full lips to suggest that she was not as young as she appeared at first glance. She looked very beautiful to Rebecca, who rose finally and walked around behind the desk. "Catherine," she murmured, shaking the dozing woman's shoulder gently.

A faint smile touched Catherine's lips as her eyes fluttered open. Her gaze widened with pleasure when she found Rebecca bending over her, an unexpectedly tender expression in her deep blue eyes. There was something else in Rebecca's face, though—a tightness around the fine mouth and a weariness in the shadowed gaze that she had never seen before, not even when Rebecca had come to her in the first hours after Jeff's death. Instinctively, she reached out to stroke the cheek now just a whisper away and spoke without thinking. "What is it, love?" she asked quietly.

Rebecca's heart lurched at the words. *He's found you now, and I can't stand the thought of him anywhere near you. He could hurt you, and I don't think I could bear it. The idea of this madman touching you, even talking to you, is driving me crazy, and I don't know how I'm going to leave you. I don't know how I'm going to work. Ah God, I don't know what I'm doing standing here wanting you so much I hurt all over.*

"Rebecca?" Catherine asked again, pushing herself upright, her fingers lingering on that troubled face.

Rebecca forced herself to keep quiet. Her demons were her own problem, and it was time she began acting like a cop instead of allowing Catherine to take care of her again and again. She turned her head slightly and kissed Catherine's palm. "I need to take you home," she whispered quietly.

Catherine drew her hand away, recognizing the barrier that Rebecca had subtly erected. Rebecca might touch her, but she would not share her pain. Despite her understanding, Catherine was hurt. She needed to know this woman, *all* of her, not just the parts the rest of the world was allowed to see. She already knew Rebecca's strengths—she could see them in her body, feel them in her touch, hear them in her words. But what of her fears and her needs? Would that part of Rebecca's life always be closed to her?

"I have my car here," Catherine answered, knowing, even as she struggled with disappointment, that this was not the time to search for answers, nor the time to expect Rebecca to lower her defenses. The investigation and her partner's death were taking too heavy a toll on the detective's physical and emotional reserves as it was.

"No." Rebecca shook her head. "I don't want you to drive home alone. Not tonight...not after this call. I don't think you're in any danger, but I'm not taking any chances. I'll take you home and pick you up in the morning. You can come back for your car then."

Catherine started to protest but then thought better of it. An argument now would not help either of them, and she suddenly realized she was exhausted. It was nearly ten o'clock, and, once again, she had missed a meal. "Burger break on the way?" she asked, rising stiffly from her chair.

Rebecca grinned at last. "I'll do better than that, my dear Dr. Rawlings. I'll treat you to pizza."

"You're on," Catherine replied, slipping an arm around Rebecca's slim waist.

The unexpected embrace caught Rebecca by surprise. She suddenly pulled Catherine close and held her fiercely. "I have to go out again," she whispered into fragrant hair. "Things are beginning to move in this case, and I've got to stay on top of it. I wish I could stay with you tonight, but I'll have one of the black-and-whites cruise by your place every half hour or so."

"I'll be fine." Catherine leaned back in Rebecca's arms, her clear green eyes meeting the deep blue ones now filled with worry. "I know that you're concerned, and I understand that you have work to do. But I'm concerned, too. You haven't slept enough in three days to account for one good night's sleep, and you won't be very effective if you can't think straight." *And you could be hurt, too.*

"I'm all right," Rebecca said softly, silencing her with a kiss.

It was a slow, deep kiss that spoke of all that had gone unspoken between them—of need and longing and dreams long forgotten. It kindled desire in them both, and when they broke away at last, they were gasping.

"I don't want to let you go," Catherine murmured, sliding her hands under Rebecca's jacket, up her back. "God, you feel good."

Rebecca leaned into her, fusing her taller, leaner frame to the gentle curves and planes of Catherine's body, kissing her again. Her hands traveled unbidden to Catherine's breasts, feeling the softness of silk and the hard peak of her nipples beneath her fingers. "I'm not going anywhere," Rebecca whispered against her ear. She moved her mouth lower, catching the skin of Catherine's neck with her teeth, making Catherine moan softly. "Not. Just. Yet."

Catherine pulled at Rebecca's shirt, loosening it from her trousers, searching for her skin. She traced the muscles of Rebecca's back, up and down her sides, and finally onto her abdomen, all the while feeling the blood rush from her head and pool in the center of her—hot and heavy and demanding.

Rebecca groaned, fired by the urgent play of Catherine's hands over her skin. With one hand, she raised the hem of Catherine's skirt, slipping up over hot smooth flesh, pressing against the restraints of her lingerie. "I want you so much," she said hoarsely, insistent now as she fumbled with the buttons of Catherine's blouse.

Legs trembling, Catherine moaned as Rebecca found her way inside her bra, fingers closing hard over her nipples. The swift sharp pressure streaked downward, drawing liquid heat shimmering from her core. "I should lock the door," she gasped, both hands pulling at the buckle on Rebecca's belt. She couldn't seem to control herself. She was going to explode if she couldn't get her hands on her soon.

"To hell with that—I've got a gun," Rebecca rasped. She raised her head and looked around, eyes wild and fierce. Wordlessly, she slipped her arm behind Catherine's knees and lifted her, carrying her the few feet to the couch. Laying her down, she pulled Catherine's clothing aside and knelt on the floor next to her. Fingers stroking soft skin, she pressed her face against the warm flesh of Catherine's thighs, breathing in her passion. With her lips, she sought the source, thirsting for the taste of her, desperate to absorb her into every cell, groaning as wet heat welcomed her. She slid both hands under Catherine's hips, guiding her against her mouth. She immersed herself, seeking and probing for Catherine's very soul.

"Oh yes, Rebecca," Catherine cried, her hands twisted in Rebecca's thick hair. "I want you there...right there..."

As Catherine grew hard under her tongue, Rebecca brought a hand between Catherine's thighs. She pushed inward as she sucked harder, working the rapidly quivering shaft between her lips.

"Rebecca..." Catherine breathed, her voice an urgent whisper. "Make me come...please...now..."

Even as she heard the words, Rebecca felt the muscles spasm around her fingers, and she knew it had begun. She increased the pressure with her tongue, gripping Catherine as her hips heaved upward. She continued to stroke the pulsing flesh with her lips and tongue long after Catherine's cries had ceased and her limbs quieted. Finally, Rebecca pulled herself up onto the sofa and stretched out beside Catherine, pulling the sated woman into her arms. Catherine's arms came around her, and she felt soft lips on her neck.

"You're wonderful," Catherine sighed contentedly. "I'm completely demolished."

Rebecca laughed quietly, tightening her hold. "I needed to touch you so much I couldn't stop myself." She pressed her lips to Catherine's cheek. "I had to be that close to you."

"I know," Catherine said softly. "And I'm right here."

For a time all too brief, reality vanished as they slipped into sleep.

Chapter Twenty-Two

A relentless pain in her left side pulled Rebecca from a restless slumber. She shifted carefully on the office couch and reached between her body and Catherine's to reposition her shoulder holster against her rib cage. Her watch showed that it was nearly three a.m. Her head ached and her body felt empty, drained. She realized she hadn't eaten since early the previous morning. That, combined with sleep deprivation, was sapping her strength, but she couldn't seem to stop. She had a rapist-serial killer and Jeff's murderer on the loose. She had four other open cases, none of which she had touched in days. She forced herself upright and swung her legs to the floor.

"What are you doing?" Catherine asked sleepily, curling her body against Rebecca's back and stroking her softly.

"There are things I need to do that can't wait," Rebecca said quickly, turning on the couch to face her. "I'll take you home now, if that's okay."

"No," Catherine said, sitting up beside her. "It's already very late. You don't need to take me home. I'm up now, and you should do what you need to do. I'll just work here until morning."

"How about I swing by and pick you up in a few hours? Can you sleep a while here?"

"You don't need to come back," Catherine said softly as Rebecca rose and began straightening her clothes. "But I'd like it if you did."

Rebecca stopped, her eyes meeting Catherine's. Then she leaned down and kissed her, and Catherine kissed her back. The kiss, possessive and demanding, lasted long enough to arouse her again, and she was uncomfortably aware of the fact that she was still swollen and throbbing. "I'd like it, too," she murmured against Catherine's mouth. "What time?"

Catherine thought about the next day's schedule while she worked to ignore the pulse of desire that tingled along her nerve endings. "I have to be at the hospital at nine o'clock for rounds, and I should shower and change before that. Can you be here at 6:30?"

"Yes. Lock the door when I leave and don't open it until you hear my voice. And *don't* answer the phone."

"But what if *he* calls again?"

"Then *he'll* have to wait. I don't want anyone to know you're here alone," Rebecca replied vehemently.

"Yes, I see. Of course." Catherine met her steely gaze, reading the worry and anger in her eyes. "I won't take any chances. Please don't worry about me tonight. I'll be fine here, and you'll be back soon."

Rebecca's face softened suddenly. "Thanks. I know it's hard being ordered around—"

Catherine stood and stopped her with a gentle hand to her lips. "Nonsense. In these matters, you're the expert and I trust you."

Rebecca reached for Catherine's hand and squeezed it, then continued to hold it as she turned away. "Come lock the door behind me." At the door, they exchanged one last, brief kiss, and then the detective slipped out into the hallway.

"Be careful," Catherine whispered as the door closed firmly. She stood motionless for some moments, listening to the footsteps echoing down the empty corridor. The room suddenly felt chilly, and she pulled her raincoat from the rack behind the door and threw it around her shoulders.

She was worried, and she knew she had good reason to be. Rebecca was in far more danger than she was at the moment. She was all too aware of how quickly reflexes and thought processes could be impaired by fatigue and stress. She fought the anxiety, knowing she could not influence Rebecca's behavior—that, in fact, Rebecca was behaving in the only way she could under the circumstances.

Once again, however, understanding was small comfort. She sighed deeply, pulled the coat tighter around her shoulders, and resigned herself to wait out the rest of the night on her own therapy couch.

Rebecca slowly turned the corner onto Locust Street, a seedy area populated with adult movie theatres, nondescript bars, and the grime-streaked facades of hotels indistinguishable from one another save for their neon signs blinking hopefully into the dark. Even at 4:00 a.m.— the darkest, loneliest part of the night—there were still a few people on the streets. The vagrants were all tucked away in their cubbyholes, in doorways or on subway grates, covered with bits of carpet or old clothes, their possessions gathered under their arms for safety. Here and there, a few prostitutes huddled in pairs or leaned singly against storefronts, hoping for one more trick before morning. And cars continued to cruise slowly by, the drivers' faces cast in shadow as they surveyed the possibility of a quick antidote to their isolation.

She circled the six-block area several times until she finally saw her, standing alone in the doorway of an adult bookstore, her long legs bare to mid-thigh despite the inevitable chill of the hour. Rebecca pulled the Vette to the curb and rolled the passenger window down. "Get in," she directed, just loud enough to be heard.

The girl's surprised look of hopeful anticipation quickly turned to dismay when she recognized the detective. "Aww, man! Can't you leave me alone? You're gonna ruin my business."

"Come on, don't make me get out," Rebecca said, pushing the curbside door open.

"Uh-uh. No way. You don't have nothing on me…"

"Do you want to talk to me in here, or should I just walk around the streets with you a while?"

"Oh Jesus, I don't need this," she swore as she quickly crossed the pavement and slid into the low-slung front seat, the scant skirt riding high along her shapely thighs.

"Put your seat belt on," Rebecca said as she pulled away from the curb.

Sandy snorted in disgust. "If you cared so much about my well-being, you'd stay the fuck away from me. People down here start thinking I'm a snitch, I could get hurt."

"What people?" Rebecca said nonchalantly, her eyes on the road. The girl was right about getting hurt, and it wasn't something that Rebecca intended to let happen. She protected her contacts. But it was more than that with this one. Every now and then, Rebecca thought she caught a glimpse of tenderness beneath Sandy's bravado, an uncommon humanity that the life had not yet destroyed. "What people?" she asked again.

"Just people. And, besides, I don't have any tips for you. Nobody knows nothing about no kiddie racket...or if they do, they aren't telling me."

Rebecca's head turned slightly and met the gaze of the young woman beside her. The eyes that looked back were the eyes of the street—bitter and far older than her years. "It's not about the chicken business."

Sandy looked surprised for an instant but quickly recovered with an expression of disinterest. "Well, what?"

"A hooker was found dead last night at the Old Vic. Young girl, about thirteen."

"So?" Sandy feigned indifference. "It isn't the first time. She OD'd or what?"

Rebecca shook her head. "Looks like the john did it." She looked directly at Sandy as she said, "I don't want it to happen again. I want this guy...and I need help."

Looking down at her hands, Sandy remained silent, unconsciously picking at a broken nail. "Sometimes ya can't tell, ya know? A guy looks like Mr. Straightsville, and the next thing you know, he wants you to tie him up or let him piss in your mouth. It happens. You try to be careful, but sometimes you just can't tell." Her voice was flat as she spoke, and she didn't raise her head.

"I know. That's why I'm telling you this. You need to be careful. And tell the other girls, too. I can't give you anything on him. I don't have anything."

Sandy raised her head defiantly. "And if you did, you wouldn't tell us anyhow, would you? Afraid we'd scare him off."

Rebecca shrugged. She wasn't here to make friends, and she knew that if she were perceived as too soft, she'd lose whatever power she had to pry information out of women who had every right to be suspicious of her. She was a cop, and even if she didn't use physical force or sexual intimidation to get what she needed, she was still a cop.

"Probably not," she said and wondered if it were true. She ignored the pointless question and continued, "Try to find out if any of the other girls have noticed a particularly strange guy lately—white, probably late twenties, most likely prefers ass fucking."

"Yeck," Sandy said. "Most girls stay away from that. But it depends on how much, you know. Some'll do anything for the right price."

"Yeah, well, ask around...see what you can turn up. You call me, okay? I want to hear something from you in twenty-four hours."

"And if I don't feel like it?" Sandy asked with a pout.

"You keep testing, don't you?" Rebecca countered, her tone flat. She sighed. "Then I guess I'll have to start visiting you every day—out in public—like you're my new sweetheart. *That* would not be good for business."

"Maybe we could work something else out," the girl said, her tone suddenly practiced and seductive. She turned on her seat and rested one hand on Rebecca's thigh. The muscles were as unyielding as stone, but, undeterred, she slipped her fingers further around the detective's thigh, tracing the inside trouser seam with her nails. "I could be your secret sweetheart, and you could get information from some other girl." *Balling you would be a lot nicer than most of my tricks, and it would be a lot less risky.*

Rebecca glanced down at the hand between her legs, saw a flash of bare thigh as Sandy leaned close. "Information. That's all I want from you. Anybody hassles you—for any reason—you call me. Now move your hand."

Sandy sighed and flounced back into her seat. "Had to ask."

"Right." Rebecca pulled the car to the curb. "Go home, Sandy. You're not gonna retire on what you'll make the rest of the night." As she pulled away, she watched the woman in her rearview mirror slowly wander off into the cheerless dawn.

CHAPTER TWENTY-THREE

Shortly before five a.m., Rebecca returned to her apartment. The first thing to greet her, besides the customary stale air of a space left too long undisturbed, was a pile of junk mail that had been pushed under her door, which she kicked aside. She went straight for the kitchen, emptied the grounds from the basket of her coffeemaker, and poured water into the appliance. She found half a pound of espresso in the freezer and measured out enough for four cups, but only poured in water for two. She needed the extra jolt of caffeine after the nearly sleepless night. Leaving the coffee brewing, she headed for the bathroom.

Her jacket and slacks would have to go to the cleaners. They looked like they'd been slept in. Come to think of it, they had been. She laid her gun on the toilet tank, threw her underwear at the overflowing hamper, and turned on the shower. She stood under the pulsing stream for a long time before she lifted her arms to lather some shampoo into her hair.

With her eyes closed against the frothing suds, her mind replayed random images—the dead girl in the hotel room; Jeff lying so quietly on his side, just a trickle of blood behind his ear; Janet Ryan, eyes pain-filled and terrified, enclosed by sterile white walls and cold white covers. And then she thought of Catherine—calm and determined when caring for a patient; soothingly gentle when Rebecca came to her exhausted in body and soul; vibrant in the throes of passion. Nightmares and deliverances, all tumbling through her restless, fevered mind. One thought, though, kept haunting her. *He knows Catherine's name.*

She twisted the knobs viciously and stepped from the shower, gasping at the chill in the room. The face looking back from the mirror above the sink was haggard and lined with fatigue, but the eyes were clear and hard with determination. Dark, furious eyes. He had made a mistake killing that hooker. He'd changed his pattern; he'd gotten eager; he'd gotten sloppy. The desk clerk had seen him, and if one person had seen him, there would be others. She had a tiny thread to grasp now, and she would follow it wherever it led until she could get a bigger piece and then another piece until all the pieces came together.

He had made an even bigger mistake calling Catherine Rawlings. Rebecca wanted him now—wanted him not just because he was terrorizing women on her turf—she wanted him because he had come into her world and touched someone who mattered to her. She wanted him now...no matter what it cost. "I'm coming for you," she whispered into the stillness of the room. "Oh, yes, you fucker, I'm coming."

Invigorated by her shower, she pulled on a clean navy summer-weight suit over a pressed white shirt and poured the coffee into a large plastic-topped travel mug. She maneuvered quickly through the empty streets just ahead of the morning rush hour traffic. The area around the medical center, as always, was alive with activity, and she was forced to circle several times before she found a parking space near Catherine's office. She hurried through the deserted hallways, anxious now to reach her. Her knock was answered immediately.

Catherine, looking rumpled and weary, greeted her with a smile. "You have no business looking so damn good when I know you haven't slept all night," she said, relieved to see that Rebecca, although obviously tired, seemed clear-eyed and fresh. She reached for Rebecca's hand and pulled her into the room. Impulsively, she slipped her arms around her waist and kissed her.

"Everything all right?"

"Yes. I'm just glad you're here," Catherine sighed, not adding that she was also relieved that the detective was safe.

Rebecca held her gently for a moment, savoring the closeness. After so long, she supposed that it should have felt strange to hold a woman, but holding Catherine was anything but strange. What *was* strange was how right it felt. Standing there with Catherine in her arms, she felt anchored, as if in this one place, the world made sense. In Catherine's embrace, she felt at home. "Are *you* all right?" she said at length, not loosening her hold, not wanting the moment to pass.

"I've had better nights," Catherine said, her head resting on Rebecca's shoulder, "but the morning looks pretty damn good right now."

Rebecca grinned at the woman's resiliency, hugged her briefly, and stepped back. "I'd better get you home."

"Yes, duty calls." Catherine sighed resolutely and moved away to gather her briefcase and papers.

Once she was back in the car, Rebecca's mind returned to the case. She was desperately trying to weave a tapestry from an assortment of disconnected threads. Somewhere there was a pattern, some detail she had overlooked or failed to recognize that would begin to make a whole of the scattered pieces. She knew that she'd need to sit down with the murder book, the voluminous file that contained every piece of evidence related to the case—every police form, witness statement, and ME's report—and reread it all again. Maybe something there would jog her memory.

Catherine recognized the distant look in Rebecca's eyes and left her alone with her thoughts. She was startled when Rebecca's voice broke the stillness.

"How is Janet Ryan doing?"

"Oh, physically she's making good progress. She would actually be ready for discharge if it weren't for her psychological state. I'm just fine-tuning her medication now, and then she should be ready to go home. Unfortunately, the assault has triggered flashbacks which are difficult for her to deal with under the best of circumstances."

"Flashbacks?" Rebecca queried.

"Traumatic events will often provoke memories of similar occurrences in an individual's past," Catherine answered, intentionally avoiding making direct reference to Janet's specific case.

"Similar occurrences," Rebecca echoed. "Like rape?"

"Sometimes," Catherine said.

Rebecca's jaw tightened, a sign Catherine was coming to recognize when Rebecca was angry or, more often, frustrated. She waited, knowing that Rebecca would continue when her feelings were once again manageable.

"No wonder Janet can't remember what she witnessed out there," Rebecca said, her voice carefully concealing the rage she felt at the brutality visited upon so many women by this maniac. Her fingers tightened on the wheel, the only sign of her anger. She reminded herself that she would somehow have to view this as just another case.

"Would she be able to look at a police sketch of a possible suspect?" Rebecca asked at length. "With you present, of course."

Catherine considered her answer carefully. "I'm not sure," she answered truthfully. "Janet feels a tremendous responsibility to remember what she saw. She wants to be helpful and feels like she's failing because she can't give you any details. Any added pressure—like trying to sort through a photo array—could actually make it more difficult for her to remember the event. I'd like to reserve judgment on that until I can speak with her again. Can you give me until tonight?"

"Do I have a choice?" Rebecca asked, her frustration now evident.

"Rebecca," Catherine responded cautiously, "your responsibilities and mine don't have to be at odds here. I know you need Janet's statement, and, please believe me, I want to see this man caught as much as you do. But I simply can't place her in psychological jeopardy to do that."

"Even if it means another woman is raped and murdered?"

"Even then," Catherine answered quietly.

Rebecca couldn't miss the pain in Catherine's voice and knew suddenly how agonizing that decision was for her. "I'm sorry," she said, reaching across the seat to grasp Catherine's hand. "I'm sorry. I know you're doing what you think is best."

"Don't be sorry. You have to use everything you can to put an end to this madness. And I have to take care of the people who put their trust in me."

And now those people include me. Rebecca held her hand until she pulled the car to the curb in front of the brownstone, then followed Catherine silently to the steps of her building, searching the streets for any sign of someone who seemed out of place. The sidewalks were crowded with people hurrying to work, but no one took particular notice of them.

"Let me have your key," she said at the top of the steps, her eyes scanning the heavy oak door for signs of tampering. She opened it and led the way inside, making a quick search of the rooms, checking the windows and patio as she went. Satisfied that everything was in order, she turned to face Catherine. "You can go ahead and change; I'll wait."

Catherine smiled at her, appreciating once again the presence of this intense, driven woman in her life, wishing she could somehow reach into that barricaded soul and comfort her. Instead, she contented herself with a soft kiss, rewarded by the instant melding of Rebecca's lean body against her own. In this way at least, Catherine knew she could reach her, and she accepted that; for now, that was all she could do.

❖

Rebecca arrived at the station just after nine a.m. and was surprised to find Watts already at his desk, nursing a hot cup of coffee and a danish. He looked up when Rebecca sat down across from him with her own caffeine infusion.

His eyes scanned her face, giving no indication that he noticed the dark circles under her eyes or the fatigue lines etched in her naturally chiseled features. Nor did he comment on the slight tremor in the long fingers that held the paper cup of coffee. "Everything okay with the shrink?"

"She's fine." Rebecca looked for some hidden meaning behind his words but could make out nothing in his usual blank stare. She turned to the pile of papers on her desk in an effort to avoid conversation.

He wasn't dissuaded. "I think it's about time we went over what we got and figure out where to go from here before this creep bangs another broad."

Rebecca stared at him, so astonished by his comment that she forgot that she had been considering the same thing not an hour before. She leaned forward on her elbows and said softly, "Watts, you are a crude bastard, and I don't give a good goddamn what you think. I'm in charge here, and we'll do things my way."

Watts simply shrugged. "Don't think the captain's as patient as I am. He wants a status report so he can meet with the media this morning."

"Shit, just what we need. More media people nosing around." She looked at Watts and had the feeling they finally agreed on something. "Did the artist get anything out of Bailey's description?"

Watts grimaced. "It's pretty general, but I'm having copies run off and distributed to all the precincts."

Rebecca was taken aback, as she had been several times lately, when she discovered that Watts was actually thinking about his work. She stood abruptly. "Come on, let's get out of here."

Watts raised an eyebrow. "What about the captain?"

"We can't give him a status report if we're not here. And then the media won't have anything to write about, so they won't be able to tip off our boy. Who knows what little tidbit might send him running for cover?"

Watts grunted noncommittally, but he rose to his feet to follow, grabbing a stack of photocopied sketches as he went. He handed the police sketch to Rebecca as they pulled away from the station. She glanced at it quickly and felt her hopes plummet when she saw how nonspecific the rendering was.

"Just what we need," she sighed. "Everyman."

"Yeah," Watts agreed. "Ain't life a bitch?"

Rebecca ignored him as she drove aimlessly, her mind sifting through possible courses of action, trying to come up with something they had failed to do. "Have the Homicide guys had any recent assaults or murders of prostitutes that might tie in with this case? Maybe that kid at the Viceroy Hotel wasn't his first."

Watts pulled out his tattered notebook and made an entry. "I don't know. We should check it out. I suppose we ought to start interviewing all the hookers, too, and find out if anybody knows anything."

"I'm working on that. Leave a bunch of those fliers in the back. For what it's worth, I'll hand them around."

"Yeah, and tell them about his bag of tricks."

"What did you say?" Rebecca asked quickly as she pulled into a drive through at a fast food restaurant. "You want another coffee?"

"Yeah, black," Watts answered absently. "You know, his gym bag or whatever the hell it was that Bailey saw him carry in. Maybe if they can't remember his face, they'll remember the bag."

"Or what he brings in the bag," Rebecca mused, passing him his coffee and balancing hers on the seat between her legs. "Watts, all three victims on River Drive have been joggers, all wearing running shorts. The dead prostitute was found with running shorts that she wasn't wearing when she went upstairs with him. Maybe he needs them to get turned on."

"Yeah, well, I've heard of weirder stuff, but so what? You want we should put out a bulletin that no broads wear shorts outside the house?"

Rebecca sighed, deciding for once to ignore his crass mannerism, since he had a point. "No, but at least I can get the word out on the streets. Maybe one of the girls will have run into some john with that particular kink."

Watts grunted. "We don't even know for sure it's the same guy. We won't have a DNA match from the dead hooker for a while. Could be we're chasing our tails for nothing."

"Right now we don't have anything else to chase," Rebecca replied dispiritedly.

CHAPTER TWENTY-FOUR

Rebecca and Watts split up when they returned to the station house to hit the Homicide unit. He went in search of some old friends to chase down the possibility that other prostitutes had been assaulted or killed in a manner similar to the young girl murdered two nights before in the hotel. Rebecca sought out Trish Marks and Horton for an update on Jeff's case. They were obviously hassled and didn't look real pleased to see her, but they took the time to fill her in.

"What we've picked up from Jimmy Hogan's notes, which were none too helpful, and street rumors is that he was getting in pretty tight with some middle-level men in Zamora's organization. It might be that he was hit not because they made him as a cop but just because of plain old gang politics. Maybe he was stepping on somebody's toes," Trish Marks informed her. She offered a box of donuts in Rebecca's direction as she spoke.

Rebecca shook her head. "What about Jeff, then? Why did they kill him?"

"Wrong place, wrong time," Horton answered bluntly, grabbing two sugarcoated donuts.

For a moment Rebecca was speechless, the anger in her chest so thick she couldn't take a deep breath. *An accident? Oops, sorry about that? Just a big, cosmic fuck-you?*

Trish Marks must have seen something in Rebecca's face because she added quickly, "Look, Frye, we're not quitting. Okay? We're gonna shake down every soldier and bagman in Zamora's outfit. If we have to, we'll start leaning on his clubs and cite him for every ordinance and license infraction we can find until his attorneys don't have time to do anything except file extensions. Somebody somewhere knows something."

"Yeah. Thanks." Rebecca nodded. "I know you'll do what you

can." All three of them knew that if it was a contract mob execution, the hit man would have been hired from out of town, he was long gone, and there was no way anyone would ever find him except by luck.

She walked out of the building wondering what she would tell Shelley Cruz. *I'm sorry, Shell. It was just one of those things. You're a widow because Jeff got unlucky.* Justice. Where was Jeff's justice? What the hell was the point of doing what she was doing? That was a train of thought that had once upon a time landed her in a bar. She looked at her watch. *Noon. Not too early for a drink.*

Her beeper went off, and she considered not answering it. She didn't want to hear that the captain was waiting for his status report. She didn't want to hear that there was another rape on River Drive. She didn't want to hear about another dead child in a lonely room in some run-dowm hotel in hell. Whatever it was that kept her from driving to the bar, that kept her getting up every day and strapping on her weapon, that kept her reaching out for Catherine in the dark instead of swallowing her pain—stubbornness, pride, responsibility, hope—whatever it was, made her stop and call in.

"Watts wanted us to run you down," the dispatcher said when Rebecca identified herself. "Said you'd want to know that some doctor received an interesting package this morning. That make any sense to you? I got the message—"

She slammed down the phone and was out the door before the dispatcher could finish his sentence. She went lights and sirens all the way across town to the hospital and left her car in the emergency zone outside the ambulance entrance. Storming through the sliding glass doors, she nearly collided with a woman pushing a baby stroller.

"Sorry," she muttered as she swerved, racing to the elevator. The ride up to the psychiatric floor seemed to take forever. As soon as the doors opened, she saw Watts down the hall, leaning against the counter at the nurses' station, conversing with a woman in white.

"Watts!" she shouted, running toward him. "Where's Catherine? Is she all right?"

He intercepted her with a surprisingly strong grip on her arm and tugged her away from the curious eyes of the people gathered around. "Whoa...hold on. Jesus. Yeah, she's fine."

"Where is she?" Rebecca demanded, shaking off his arm but managing to lower her voice. "What happened?"

"I took the call because I was in the squad room. When I heard what it was, I figured you'd want to know."

"What *what* was?" She thought she might throttle him in half a second.

"Your doctor friend is pretty smart," Watts said, patting his pockets looking for his cigarettes. He stopped when he remembered where he was. "Someone sent her a dozen roses. And since it ain't her birthday, she thought that was kinda strange. I guess she figured you didn't send them."

Rebecca stared at him, but his expression was completely innocent. "Damn it, Watts. You've got about ten seconds to tell me what's going on before I shoot you."

"I *am* telling you. I'm waiting for the lab boys to pick up the flowers now. The card reads, 'Thank you for last night. I'll see you soon.' Hand printed, but the printing is pretty generic."

"Jesus Christ." Rebecca turned away, her face grim. "That's it. I want to see Catherine. We need to put a guard on her."

"I don't think that's such a great idea," Watts stated flatly. "Might scare him away."

Rebecca's temper finally snapped. She stepped up chest to chest with him, her voice low but lethal. "Get this clear, Watts. We are *not* using Catherine Rawlings for bait. You understand me? If I even hear you *thinking* it, I'll make you very sorry."

Watts seemed unperturbed by her threats. "Hey, I know how you feel—"

"No, you *don't* know how I feel, and you never *will* know how I feel. So let's just drop it. Now."

She could never remember being so frightened. She had been shot at, maced, and ambushed by street punks, but she had never felt the panic that infused her now. All she knew was that Catherine was being drawn into a very dangerous game, and she felt powerless to stop it. She set her jaw and took a deep breath. It was time for her to act like a cop. It was time for her to take charge of the situation, and that was exactly what she intended to do.

Catherine, as it turned out, had different ideas.

❖

"Rebecca, you must understand. For any number of reasons, I can't let you assign me to protective custody. I have responsibilities at the hospital and patients to see in my office every day. There is no way I can make arrangements for someone else to take over for me."

They were in the small office the doctors used for chart work and phone calls, a cramped room cluttered with coffee cups, stacks of official memoranda that no one ever read, and dog-eared copies of the DSM-IV that categorized the most recent diagnoses of mental illnesses. Catherine sat at the single table, watching Rebecca carefully. The detective stood with her back to the room at the dust-streaked window that faced a parking lot. Her silence was ominous, but Catherine was used to silences. She waited.

"Is there some other reason?" Rebecca asked at length, finally turning to look at Catherine. Her voice was curiously flat.

It wasn't often that someone surprised Catherine. She was an expert at anticipating reactions and predicting behavior. Not only was she trained for it, but also it was simply her nature. She had been attuned to the nuances of inflection and expression since she was a small child. Some children were.

Rebecca's question had taken her aback because rarely had someone gleaned *her* motives and unspoken intentions. Only Hazel had ever been close enough to her to do that, and she had known Hazel a very long time.

"I may very well be able to establish a relationship with this man. If we have some idea of the state of his mind, we may be able to predict his actions. It could mean saving a life, Rebecca."

"He fascinates you, doesn't he?" Rebecca asked softly, leaning against the windowsill, her eyes so dark they were nearly black.

Catherine wasn't sure if it was anger or fear she saw in the depths of Rebecca's eyes. Whatever it was, lying would not mitigate it. "You must be a very good interrogator," she murmured.

She took a breath and gathered her thoughts. "Yes, he fascinates me. The human mind fascinates me. There is something terribly wrong with this man's mind, and I want to know what…and why, insofar as we can ever understand the whys of behavior." She stared intently at Rebecca, who was regarding her with a completely impassive expression, except for a flicker of fire in her eyes now. *Anger. Good…much better than fear.*

"You understand that you are putting yourself in danger even talking to him?" Rebecca asked, unable to keep the edge out of her voice. "This isn't a game, God damn it."

"I know that," Catherine said, "but I am only proposing that we leave some avenue open for him to contact me. If I suddenly disappear, he won't call again. Talking, listening—that's what I do best."

"Don't you think I know that?" Rebecca retorted. *I know you hear me, even the things I can't say.* She turned her back again, looking out the window at nothing as she struggled to clear her head. All of Catherine's arguments made sense, and at any other time, she would have accepted the logic of maintaining contact with a psychopath like this. Christ, even Watts had been urging her to see the benefit of Catherine communicating with him. But she couldn't accept it.

"I know you're right," she said softly, her voice hollow. "If I were a good cop, I should be overjoyed that we finally have a way to get to this guy…" Her voice trailed off.

"No. This isn't about what kind of cop you are." Catherine went to her, put her arms around her, and leaned her cheek against Rebecca's back. Rebecca's muscles were taut and unyielding under her hands, the tension humming through her slender frame. She didn't acknowledge Catherine at all. Neither did she move away.

Catherine sensed that the rejection was not of her, but of the weakness that Rebecca perceived in herself. And she knew that much of this struggle was *because* of her. Her presence in the detective's life disrupted the professional control, threatened the absolute emotional distance Rebecca needed to do the work she did, to be the cop she was. This conflict, between caring and caution, was a battle Rebecca would face again and again, and Catherine understood that the outcome of this battle would determine just how much the two of them could share. That meant a great deal to her.

"Rebecca, I know you're worried about me," Catherine said quietly, still holding her loosely, determined neither to ignore the problem nor to allow Rebecca to face it alone. "We're involved with each other. We've made love; we've shared something of ourselves. It would be hard for you to let anyone do this; it must be even harder now. I imagine I'm not someone you can be objective about." *And not someone you must push away to satisfy your sense of duty. I hope.*

"I never should have let this happen," Rebecca said starkly, her back still to Catherine. "It's compromising my thinking, and that could mean jeopardizing your safety. I can't believe I'm in the middle of a case and I'm involved with one of the main participants."

"Well, I'm just as surprised as you are," Catherine persisted. "But, believe me, I, for one, am not sorry that it happened." *But I'm just as scared as you are. I never thought I'd ever feel this way about anyone, and I certainly didn't expect to feel so much so soon.*

She did tighten her grip then, needing to feel Rebecca's solid strength in her arms, needing the reassurance of her presence. She kissed the skin on the back of Rebecca's neck bared by the collar of her shirt. She knew she was taking her own emotional risks by admitting to Rebecca, and to herself, just how important this woman had become to her. But one of them had to make the first move. She waited, her heart loud in her ears.

Rebecca turned to her then, tightening her arms around her, holding her fiercely. "Neither am I," she answered, her voice rough with emotion. *I'm afraid to even think about how much you mean to me. I just don't know what I'd do if anything happened to you.*

"Good," Catherine answered, her breath a soft sigh.

Rebecca kissed her gently, a quiet kiss of tender caring, and then she closed her eyes, leaning her cheek against Catherine's hair. Her tension began to subside in the soft embrace of Catherine's arms. This woman's touch restored her, brought clarity to her overworked and stressed mind. She was continually astonished, and still a little afraid, of the woman's effect upon her.

"I don't suppose I could persuade you to have a police officer accompany you around until this is over, could I?" Rebecca asked, her lips against Catherine's forehead. "We can't leave you unprotected, Catherine." *I can't. No matter what anyone says.*

"No."

"At least at night, when you're at home?"

"Only if it's you."

"It's not in my contract," Rebecca whispered, leaning back to gaze into her face, amazed by the effect just looking at her produced. She wanted to forget everything except the tenderness of those full lips and the welcoming heat of Catherine's passion. She wanted to fall into the depths of those green eyes, drown in them, just let go. Never had peace been so close.

"It could be," Catherine answered, her lips finding Rebecca's. The kiss took her by surprise, the hunger, her own and Rebecca's, rising quickly. In a moment, she was gasping. She pushed back, not quite breaking Rebecca's grip. "We have to stop," she managed.

"Why?" Rebecca asked, a grin pulling at the corner of her mouth. The light glinting in her eyes was a dangerous mixture of amusement and desire.

"Because it's the middle of the day, in the middle of the psych ward, and I have to work," Catherine said emphatically, her voice stronger now that she could breathe again. She lifted a hand to Rebecca's cheek. "You look exhausted, Detective."

"I'm okay," Rebecca assured her.

"I'm sure," Catherine acknowledged, her fingers lingering on Rebecca's face a moment longer. "I should go," she said reluctantly.

"I'll drive you home later," Rebecca said quickly. "I've got a few hours' downtime coming, and the lab won't have anything new today."

"You can wait, if you do it in one of the on-call rooms, with your eyes closed," Catherine countered.

Rebecca sighed, aware of fatigue for the first time. "You're the doctor."

CHAPTER TWENTY-FIVE

Rebecca slept during the afternoon in an empty on-call room that the residents used at night. It was after six p.m. when Catherine roused her and close to seven when they reached Catherine's home. While Catherine went to get changed, Rebecca attached a voice activated recording device to the telephone.

"I'll have to erase any patient related calls before I can turn the tape over to you," Catherine reminded her when she walked back into the room and observed Rebecca setting up the machine.

"Just be sure that you call me the second he contacts you. Promise me that," Rebecca requested, looking over her shoulder at her. For a second, seeing her standing there in loose cotton pants and a faded shirt with the cuffs turned back, the detective forgot what she was doing. Catherine was just so damn…beautiful.

"I will, don't worry," Catherine said softly, watching Rebecca's gaze travel down her body, the blue of her eyes darkening with each second. She flushed as heat spread over her skin.

Reluctantly, Rebecca turned away to finish with the recorder and then walked through the apartment, checking the doors and windows, finally calling the local precinct to arrange for extra patrols to pass through the neighborhood. After that, she had done all she could do. The next move was up to him. Catherine was waiting when she returned to the living room, a question in her eyes.

"I'm sorry. I have to go out for a while. There are people I need to talk to—people I can only find at night. Will you be all right?"

"Yes. Will you?" Catherine replied, walking over to her, but not reaching out and touching. She concentrated instead on silencing her fears—not fear for her own safety, but for this intensely honorable woman. Whenever she saw the gun strapped against Rebecca's chest, she was reminded of what could happen every time the detective went out into the streets. Rebecca's world, her reality, was so different than Catherine's, where the injuries were not of the body but of the heart and spirit. The violence was no greater, perhaps, but its consequences so much more immediate, and so often irreversible. There were no second chances where deadly force was the weapon. The fear was new for Catherine, and something she wasn't certain she could get used to. Knowing that it was the price she had to pay for allowing Rebecca into her life, into her heart—this kept her from reaching out to her.

They stood, separated by inches, a lifetime of defenses between them. Catherine spoke first. "Can I expect you back tonight?" She placed her hand gently on Rebecca's arm.

With something very close to relief on her face, Rebecca whispered, "Count on it."

Rebecca found Sandy without any difficulty and was surprised by the lack of the usual protest when she stopped the car beside her.

Instead of complaining, the young prostitute crossed the sidewalk quickly, pulled open the door, and slid into the passenger seat. "Let's get out of here, okay?" she urged.

Rebecca pulled into the line of traffic and looked at the girl questioningly. "Why so glad to see me?"

Sandy grimaced. "Things are getting really weird out here. All the pimps are uptight because the cops are pulling them in, asking questions about all kinds of shit—kiddie porn, drug rings, the rackets. It makes the guys mean, and they take it out on us."

Rebecca reacted quickly. "You all right? Is there somebody you need me to talk to?"

"Oh sure," Sandy said with a snort. "That's exactly what I need— you hassling the men on my behalf. That ought to shorten my life span."

Rebecca swerved to the curb and parked, turning in her seat to face the young woman. Sandy was dressed conservatively, for her. Hip-hugger jeans and a blouse tied in the front that exposed an expanse of smooth firm abdomen and navel ring. She was pretty without the makeup that made her eyes look dark and wary. "Just tell me straight out. Is someone giving you a hard time?"

"Nah," Sandy said with a shrug. "I don't exactly work for one of the guys. I'm in a group, you know?"

Rebecca knew. Often one of the more experienced women would befriend a few younger ones, teaching them the ropes, giving them advice, often providing them with a place to stay. They, in turn, gave her a part of their earnings with which she paid off the pimps to leave *her* girls alone. It was a loose form of a union, and it kept some of the naïve, fresh-off-the-farm ones off drugs and out of the hands of the pimps who literally and figuratively abused them.

"Okay," Rebecca said with a nod, pulling back into traffic. "Then what *does* have you so spooked if some pimp isn't threatening you?"

"The last few days the Vice cops have been pulling in the girls, too, asking everyone about kinky johns and rough trade. It's making us all nervous. What's going on?"

Rebecca smiled at the reversal in their positions. Suddenly, she had become the informant. "I don't know for sure. There may be a loose cannon around—some guy who likes girls in gym shorts and gets rough."

"How rough?"

"Rough like dead."

Sandy leaned her head back against the seat and sighed. "Shit, we don't need this. Got anything on him?"

"Look in the backseat. There's a sketch of someone who might be him."

Sandy looked at the police rendering and snorted. "Oh, *him*. I must see ten dudes a night who look like this."

"Yeah, that's what I was afraid of," Rebecca commented grimly. "Like I said before—he's white, late twenties or early thirties, probably well educated, and won't seem like a nut case. And, this is important, he may have a gym bag or something like it that he carries clothes in. He likes his women to dress for his pleasure. Skimpy running shorts seem to do it for him."

"That's it?"

"Afraid so."

"What do we do if he shows?"

"If you can, don't work alone; stay in pairs or a group. That way, if he approaches one of you, someone else can call me. Try to get the word out as quickly as you can to everyone in the area. The girl he killed two days ago is the only prostitute we know about. I don't want there to be another one."

Sandy looked at the woman beside her, surprised by the vehemence in her voice and the stony set to her features. "Yeah, well, thanks," was all she said. Too many years on the streets had taught her not to trust what looked like kindness, because there was always a price attached. But she would remember the look on the tall detective's face, a look that made her feel a little safer.

When Rebecca knocked on Catherine's door a little after midnight, Watts answered. He stepped out onto the small front landing before she could say anything, pulling the door closed behind him.

"She's all right," he said quickly, noting the alarm on Rebecca's face. "Our boy phoned again. She called it in, and I came over. Figured you'd rather have me here than someone she doesn't know. I was just about to page you, but I wanted to see what the story was first."

Rebecca took a deep breath and nodded, relief and anger warring with her emotions. "What did he say this time?"

Watts shrugged, his hand on the doorknob. "This dame…excuse me, this *doctor*…is one cool cookie. She insisted on clearing the tape of *unrelated* messages before she'd let me hear it. She should be ready for us now."

"Thanks, Watts," she said as she pushed by him and stepped inside.

Catherine was seated in front of a small desk at the far corner of the living room with the tape recorder by her right hand. She was staring out the window and seemed lost in thought.

"Catherine," Rebecca murmured softly.

She turned at the sound of her name, and a faint smile flickered across her elegant features. "I'm glad you're back."

"I'm sorry I wasn't here when he phoned," Rebecca began, drawing close but keeping her hands by her sides, fisted tightly. *God, I want to touch her.*

Catherine silenced her with a quick wave of her hand. "It doesn't matter. You're here now. Shall we go over this?"

Watts had shuffled in behind Rebecca and was sitting on the couch across the room, his notebook on his knee. Rebecca walked past the seated woman to the window and looked out into the night sky. She didn't want Catherine to see her face when she heard this. She didn't trust herself enough.

"Go ahead," Rebecca said gruffly. She tried to prepare herself, trying to forget that it was Catherine this psycho had chosen to call. She needed to focus; she needed to find some clue to his identity, and now she had his voice—his words—to help her. Still, her stomach clenched when she first heard Catherine's voice on the tape.

Catherine:	*Hello?*
Male Voice:	*I'm so glad I found you home, Dr. Rawlings.*
Catherine:	*I'm sorry. Who's calling, please?*
Male Voice:	*You know me, Doctor. Did you get my flowers this morning?*
Catherine:	*Yes. Why did you send them?*

Rebecca listened to his voice, smooth and soft and seductive. Unconsciously, she opened and closed her fists, her eyes narrowing as she tried to ignore his intimate tone. She was surprised at Catherine's calm responses and then realized she shouldn't be. As a doctor, she was an expert in the art of interrogation, too—not the aggressive interrogation that Rebecca was used to doing, but the gentle subtle questioning that caused hidden motivations and long-buried secrets to surface. They couldn't have picked a better contact person in this situation, and that was something she was not happy to consider.

"I'm sorry," Rebecca said sharply, angry at herself as her concentration wandered. "Could you play that back again?"

Catherine glanced at her, concerned by the brittle tone in her voice and anxious for her loss of focus. She knew that the detective must be struggling for detachment, but she could not help her find it. "Yes, just a minute," she said steadily, rewinding the tape.

Male Voice:	*You know me, Doctor. Did you get my flowers this morning?*
Catherine:	*Yes. Why did you send them?*
Male Voice:	*Because I wanted to show you how special you are to me.*

Catherine:	*Why is that? We haven't met, have we?*
Male Voice:	*I know that you can appreciate the things I've accomplished. I know you'll understand.*
Catherine:	*What will I understand? What have you done?*
Male Voice:	*You know...with the girls. When I fucked them. I was...good with them. They'd never had it so good before. I took a long time with them, too. Do you know how that feels, Dr. Rawlings... to be fucked for a long time? I could show you. I know that you would enjoy it.*
Catherine:	*Tell me about the girls. How did you pick them? Were they special, too?*
Male Voice:	*It's not hard. They're everywhere, waiting for me. They're waiting for me to show them how good it can be. Sometimes they don't know it, so I just wait for them to come to me.*
Catherine:	*Where do you wait?*
Male Voice:	*They think they know where...the police. But they don't know* anything. *The next time it will be very special. I am powerful...my cock is powerful. Maybe next time you'd like to feel it, Dr. Rawlings. Would you like to feel my power inside you...would you?*
Catherine:	*How will I recognize you?*
Male Voice:	*You'll know, Doctor. It won't be long.*

"Jesus Christ," Watts breathed as the tape clicked off. "What a fucking nutcase."

"Not exactly a clinical diagnosis, Detective, but fairly accurate," Catherine replied grimly. Rebecca had not spoken, and Catherine wanted desperately to go to her. She could see from across the room that Rebecca's spine was rigid and the hand that rested against the window frame was closed into a fist so tightly her fingers were white.

Drawing a slow, deep breath, the psychiatrist forced herself to think objectively. "He's delusional, but not fragmenting yet. He was still careful not to reveal too much to me, but the very fact that he contacted me at all suggests that he's lost any sense of vulnerability. He doesn't think anyone can detect him or stop him. His hold on reality is slipping, which means he will become less and less predictable."

"And more and more dangerous," Watts commented in disgust. "Damn, I hate the friggin' loonies."

At last, Rebecca turned, keeping her gaze on Watts. "Did we get a trace?"

"Nope." Watts shook his head. "Just under the wire. He's smart, this one."

"Yes." Her face a careful blank, but her voice vibrating with tension, Rebecca continued harshly, "Double the patrols through the neighborhood. I've got the prostitutes alerted if he goes after one of them. Put a man on the street across from Catherine's office and one on the psych floor in the hospital, too...preferably a woman at the nurses' station."

"Rebecca—" Catherine protested.

"*Do it*, Watts." She finally turned to Catherine, her eyes simmering with repressed anger and the revulsion she had felt as she listened to that quiet, disembodied voice on the tape. "He's changed his MO, Catherine—he's got a specific target now. You. This is where he'll come."

She could envision his hands on Catherine's skin, forcing her down, violating her. She would not give this madman any opportunity to harm her. Not Catherine. His words were violation enough. Nothing, not even Catherine's professional responsibilities, would change her mind. If Catherine hated her for it, that's the way it would have to be. "Sooner or later he'll come after you, Catherine." *And when he does, I'll kill the bastard.*

Watts heaved himself to his feet. "Right. I'll meet you at the hospital in the morning."

Catherine stared at Rebecca as Watts lumbered out. "Why the hospital?" she asked quietly.

"I'll need to see Janet Ryan in the morning," Rebecca said flatly. She still had not met Catherine's eyes. She was afraid if she did she would lose what little control she had left. She was shaking—with rage, with apprehension, with a sense of powerlessness that nearly drove her crazy—and she hoped that Catherine could not see it. It would not help either of them to acknowledge just how far they were from stopping this guy.

"I want to be there when you question her," Catherine said quietly.

"All right."

"Is there no other way?"

"No. It's not a random victim any longer, Catherine. It's *you* he wants now."

Catherine looked into Rebecca's determined face and knew the decision was made. She held out her hand. "Is there time for you to hold me?"

Rebecca was across the room in an instant, gathering her close. "All night."

CHAPTER TWENTY-SIX

Rebecca awakened with Catherine enfolded in her arms, the sky beyond the bedroom window just beginning to lighten with the dawn. Catherine's head rested on her shoulder—her flesh warm beneath Rebecca's hands, her breath a soft whisper against Rebecca's skin, her heartbeat a steady, soothing rhythm against Rebecca's chest. She moved her lips to the soft skin at the base of Catherine's throat and lightly explored the sleeping woman's body. With trembling fingers, she traced the curve of breasts, followed the arch of hip, and smoothed the slope of firm thigh, marveling at the wonder that was Catherine.

Catherine's back arched and she moaned softly. She brought one leg over Rebecca's hips, pressing even closer, whispering urgently, "Do you know what you're doing to me? I'm on fire."

Rebecca smiled as she shifted, fitting the length of her body over Catherine's. "I hadn't meant that—not just then—but I do now." She kissed her, the hunger sudden, aching to fill the places left long untended in her heart, and in her soul, with the touch of a woman. This woman.

She was rewarded with a soft groan from Catherine, and her body tightened with an urgency that left her breathless. Her head grew light, every nerve in her body ignited, and fire streaked downward into a single pounding point between her legs. "Ah, God..."

Slipping a hand between them, Rebecca then pressed low over Catherine's stomach, wanting to be inside her, but Catherine was quicker and found her first—stroking through her wetness, teasing her until she was fully distended, stiff and throbbing. Rebecca closed her eyes tightly, willing herself not to come, and caught one swollen nipple lightly between her teeth, groaning in satisfaction at Catherine's swift gasp of pleasure. She tried to concentrate on the heat and softness of scented skin and not the building pressure as Catherine rolled her clitoris rhythmically between her fingers.

"You're so hard," Catherine murmured, her voice husky and deep. "I love the way you feel."

"Go slow, go slow," Rebecca begged. Moaning now, barely able to think, she clutched Catherine's shoulders, her hips thrusting against Catherine's hand. *Not yet, not yet, not yet,* she chanted silently, gritting her teeth, each second a sweet agony.

"Oh, I don't think so," Catherine breathed, feeling a fluttering beneath her fingers as Rebecca's orgasm began.

"Uhh…" Rebecca exhaled, shuddering, as Catherine pressed harder along her length. She tried but couldn't hold back any longer. The spasms started beneath those relentless, knowing fingers and twisted inward, the force causing her to jerk in Catherine's arms. When she cried out her release, again and again, she didn't feel the tears that followed swiftly upon the joy.

Catherine gentled her with tender caresses, holding her securely as she trembled. "It's all right, Rebecca. There's nothing to be afraid of here."

Rebecca lay in her arms, her heart pounding with hope and terror, yearning desperately for that to be true.

Catherine stood silently as Rebecca prepared to leave, feeling the distance grow between them and wanting very badly to prevent it. The woman across the bedroom from her did not *seem* like the lover who had cried in her arms just hours ago; yet, Catherine reminded herself, she was. What they shared in private was precious to her, because it was a side of herself that Rebecca kept hidden from the world. Her secret side—the vulnerable, all too human side—disappeared when she buckled on her holster and clipped her detective's shield onto her jacket. But it was there, Catherine knew, inside her still. As formidable and aloof as Rebecca appeared now, gathering herself for battle, Catherine admired and respected the tough street cop with a will of iron and a core of steel. *My tender warrior with the fragile heart.*

"How are you feeling?" Catherine asked. They had had so little time to talk in the tumultuous days since they met, and so much had happened to both of them. She wished that for just a few hours they could stop time.

Rebecca looked up to find Catherine regarding her with a look both tender and passionate, and she blushed slightly, pleased by the appreciative look on Catherine's face and embarrassed by the scrutiny. Nevertheless, she liked being the focus of Catherine's attention. "I'm all right. Last night...it helped."

"I'm glad," Catherine said softly, gathering her things as well.

Rebecca cleared her throat. "I know it will be difficult for you to have me around all day, but I just can't take any chances. As you said, he's becoming unpredictable, and there's no way to anticipate his behavior. I'm sorry."

"Don't be concerned about intruding," Catherine replied, kissing Rebecca quickly as she reached for her briefcase. "I can think of much worse things than having you around all day. And I do know that you're doing what needs to be done. I appreciate it."

Janet Ryan was sitting in a chair by the window when Catherine and Rebecca entered. The bruises on her face were fading, but she still appeared fragile physically. She smiled a greeting at Catherine and looked hesitantly at Rebecca, who pulled up a worn armchair and sat beside her.

"Do you remember me, Janet? I'm Detective Sergeant Frye. I spoke with you before." When Janet nodded, Rebecca continued, "I have more questions to ask you. I want you to tell me again everything you did on the day of the assault. Everything you can remember, even if it doesn't seem at all important. Start with when you woke up."

"I overslept," Janet began uncertainly. "I usually run in the morning and then take the train to work...but I was late. I was rushed that morning, so I decided to drive. I remember working...nothing unusual happened. I took River Drive home. The sun was still out... there were boats on the river. It seemed so peaceful I decided to stop. I parked...and walked down toward the water." She stopped suddenly, a fine sheen of sweat glistening on her pale face.

Rebecca tried not to appear anxious. Janet was speaking in a low monotone, and her eyes were slightly unfocused. Her memory for the events surrounding the rape was clearly improving. Rebecca desperately needed for her to remember, but she was afraid to push too hard.

"You're doing wonderfully, Janet," Catherine said softly from where she stood just to the right of Janet Ryan's chair. "Tell us about walking down to the water."

"It was so quiet; I could barely hear the cars on the road. There was no one around and then...I heard something—a scream..." Once again, she stopped abruptly. This time she was visibly agitated. Her hands trembled and her breath came in quick gasps. Catherine reached out and lightly rested her hand on Janet's arm.

"You're all right, Janet. You are safe here with us. Can you tell me what is frightening you?"

"There was a man...he was doing something to the woman on the ground. He was...hurting her...but she wasn't moving. I ran toward him, screaming at him to stop!" Janet looked wildly about the room, her gaze finally fixing on Catherine's face. "Oh, Dr. Rawlings! I can't remember! I just can't remember any more."

"That's all right, Janet. You've done beautifully. Really. I'll speak with you again this afternoon. I think we'll be able to talk about you going home, all right?"

Janet nodded gratefully and softly murmured goodbye as Catherine and Rebecca left the room.

"That's as much as you're going to get for today. She *is* remembering, but it will take more time."

Rebecca ran a hand through her hair, clearly frustrated. "What about trying hypnosis or drugs?"

"It's possible that either method might help spark further recollections, but I'm concerned that forcing the issue will be harmful to her in the long run. Her memory will return when her mind is healed enough to deal with what she experienced."

"Is that doctor talk for no?" Rebecca asked, but there was no edge in her voice.

"You're learning, Detective," Catherine laughed. "Was it helpful for you at all?"

"She's consistent, but I need the details." Rebecca shrugged in exasperation. "I can't help feeling that there's something there, and I'm just not getting it. Three times this guy rapes and murders a woman in a fairly well populated area of the park, and no one sees him coming or going. He's like the invisible man."

The sound of Catherine's name over the loudspeaker interrupted them. Rebecca was reviewing her notes from her first interrogation of Janet Ryan when Catherine motioned urgently for her to pick up the extension line.

"I'm so glad I found you in, Dr. Rawlings."

Rebecca recoiled slightly when she recognized the same smooth voice from the tape of the previous night. She swore under her breath in utter frustration. She couldn't believe how easily this guy could get to Catherine, despite all her efforts to prevent it. All her training, all that she *was*, seemed inadequate to protect her own lover from invasion. She forced herself to remain silent and listen.

"Why are you calling?" Catherine asked, her eyes on Rebecca. "What do you need?"

"I must see you."

"All right," she answered quickly, ignoring the violent negative gestures from Rebecca. "Come here to the hospital. I'll see you this evening."

Soft laughter. "Oh, Dr. Rawlings...you know I can't do that. Besides, I want this meeting to be private and romantic. I want *you* to meet *me* tonight. I'll tell you where later."

Catherine looked quickly to Rebecca for direction. Rebecca shook her head *No!*

"I want to talk with you," Catherine responded, sounding totally sincere. "I have a feeling it would be very interesting. *You* are quite remarkable. I'm afraid that I can't meet you tonight, however. Won't you tell me your name so that I can reach you, too?"

"Good try, Doctor," he said, his voice suddenly harsh. "The next time I talk to you, you'll be ready to do whatever I ask."

"Wait—" Catherine exclaimed as he broke the connection. She settled the receiver slowly into the cradle and stared at Rebecca, who hurried to her side. "I didn't handle that very well, did I?"

Rebecca covered Catherine's hand with her own. "You were fine. You had to tell him no."

"Perhaps I should meet him," Catherine mused, her expression distant and distracted. "If he wants to talk to me so badly, I might be able to talk him into giving himself up. Very often this type of personality craves attention, even to the point of accepting incarceration if it means more media exposure."

"Are you crazy?" Rebecca's eyes flashed angrily and her fingers tightened on Catherine's arm. "There is no way I'm going to let this guy anywhere near you. Don't even think about it; it's not going to happen. I need to call this in, and then I need to get someone to run a check on the phone records to this floor. It's a long shot, but you never know."

Catherine nodded, her thoughts elsewhere. If only she could get him to get talk to her...

CHAPTER TWENTY-SEVEN

The call came at a little after two a.m. Rebecca roused herself from an uneasy sleep, checked her pager, and reached for the bedside phone, trying not to awaken Catherine as she pushed the familiar numbers.

"Sorry to bother you, Frye," the night dispatcher said, sounding truly apologetic. "I know you ain't on duty—"

"It's okay," Rebecca interrupted, wide awake now. She sensed Catherine stir beside her and reached to touch her in the dark.

"I got a girl on the line who says she has to speak to you and nobody else. I should be so popular."

"What does she want?" Rebecca asked, surprised. She had expected it to be Watts or one of the other Vice cops.

"Won't say. I had to threaten not to call you unless she gave me a name. Sandy. She said you'd know—"

"Patch her through," Rebecca instructed, sitting up in bed, every muscle tense.

"Frye?" a faint voice questioned.

"Yeah, it's me, Sandy. What is it?"

"Anne Marie is missing. She was supposed to meet Claire and Rosie at the diner at one, and she never showed."

Rebecca didn't bother with the routine questions; she knew Sandy would never have called if there hadn't been real cause for alarm. "When and where did someone last see her?"

"She was working the corner at Thirteenth and Comac, about eleven thirty."

"I'll meet you there in twenty minutes. In the meantime, try to find anyone who saw her with a john tonight. Ask around. See if anyone knows where she takes her clients. And Sandy…get the girls off the streets." As Rebecca rose from the bed, Catherine sat up.

"What is it?" she asked, pulling the sheet up around her bare breasts.

Rebecca had arrived at her door at midnight, apologizing about the lateness of hour, a look of such hunger in her eyes that Catherine was surprised they had made it to the bedroom. She was even more surprised by her own swift arousal and the near-frantic need she had felt to touch Rebecca's skin—to feel her heart beat, to take her, to *have* her—with no barriers between them. They couldn't have been asleep more than half an hour when the beeper went off.

"Probably nothing." Rebecca pulled her shoulder rig over a black turtleneck sweater and reached for her jacket.

For some reason, she couldn't put voice to the dread that began churning in her belly the minute she'd heard Sandy's voice. She'd had a bad feeling listening to Sandy's story, and over the years she had come to trust those premonitions. She *wanted* to tell Catherine; she knew Catherine was waiting for her to speak. But she couldn't talk about it, couldn't say the words out loud, because then she would have to face the feelings. Feelings were dangerous things in her line of work. They tripped you up just when you needed to think clearly. And one misstep could be deadly.

"Rebecca?"

"I'm sorry the call woke you," Rebecca replied, leaning down to kiss her swiftly. She had hidden her feelings from everyone for so long, she couldn't change that now. "I just have to check something out, but I probably won't be back tonight. I can have an officer come to stay with you."

"I'd rather not, if it isn't really necessary."

Rebecca considered the situation. It was unlikely that the perp would try to approach Catherine in her home, and there were uniforms keeping a close watch on the immediate neighborhood. "Just don't answer the door, all right?"

Catherine nodded, aware that Rebecca had avoided her questions. She sensed Rebecca struggling to bridge the distance between them, but knowing that she was trying did not make the silence any easier. She hoped she would have the strength and patience to wait until Rebecca trusted her. "Just be careful," was all she said. "Call me when you can?"

"I will," Rebecca whispered, kissing her again, grateful for

Catherine's calm acceptance. She turned to look back from the bedroom door, warmed by Catherine's tender, caring gaze. She would carry that look with her into the night, a shield as important as any weapon she might wear.

❖

"No one knows where she went," Sandy said anxiously when Rebecca found her, shivering in a doorway near one of the busiest corners in the flesh-trade district. "But she always tricks somewhere close by. I can send some of the others around to ask."

"No," Rebecca said emphatically. "I don't want them wandering around out here tonight. Do you have a cell phone?"

"Uh-uh," Sandy chattered, still shaking, and it wasn't from the unexpectedly cold night. She was scared, and the grim expression on the blond cop's face wasn't helping.

"Here." Rebecca pulled hers from inside her jacket pocket. "Let me make a call, then you take this and go inside the diner," she instructed, pointing to an all-night dive across the street that was a favorite hangout for the denizens of the street. She held up a finger signaling Sandy to wait while she dialed Watts's number. Surprisingly, he grasped the situation quickly and said he'd start checking hotels in the area as soon as he could get dressed and make it downtown.

She handed the phone to Sandy. "Start making calls. Page your friends; I know most of them have pagers. Find out what you can about Anne Marie, and tell them all to head home. Tell them a raid is coming down any minute."

"Is there?" Sandy asked, eyeing Rebecca suspiciously. She'd called Frye half expecting to get blown off, but she hadn't known what else to do. She still found it hard to believe the cop didn't want something from her, not that the idea of being with her was all that bad. She *was* hot.

"Just *do* it, Sandy," Rebecca said, impatient to get to work. She gave Sandy her pager number and walked her to the diner. "Wait for me, okay?"

"Yeah, yeah," Sandy said, feigning disinterest, but she was lonely—and scared—the minute the detective walked away.

Rebecca spent forty minutes checking establishments that rented rooms by the hour, favorite places for prostitutes to take johns to trick. Nobody admitted to remembering anyone that fit the description of the woman Sandy had given her. She was beginning to think that maybe this was a false alarm, and Sandy's friend had just gotten lucky and hooked up with an all night trick. Hopefully, she was tucked away in some nice hotel for the rest of the night, her only worry being how to satisfy some salesman from Omaha. Then her beeper went off, and when she called from a pay phone, Watts answered.

"You ought to come on over to Twelfth and Locust, Sarge."

"Right," Rebecca responded, her heart turning cold.

She found Watts on the landing outside a numberless door in a nondescript hotel two blocks from the diner where Sandy still waited. "What have you got?" she asked curtly.

"The night manager thought the last girl to use this room didn't come down," he explained. "He was too deep into a bottle of Thunderbird to remember who she went upstairs with or when the john might have left."

She watched his face while he talked, realizing by now that she couldn't hurry Watts when he was telling a story. She didn't need to hurry him, though. She already knew how this one ended. "Have you been inside?"

"Just for a minute," he replied, his voice unusually heavy. "To be sure. Looks like our boy again."

His characteristic nonchalance was absent, and if Rebecca didn't consider it impossible, she would have thought he was upset. "She's dead?"

"Yeah."

Rebecca pushed aside her swift surge of anger at the senseless waste and at her own inability to put an end to it. *Later.* Silently, she shoved the door open.

A glance confirmed Watts's impression that they were dealing with the same perpetrator. The victim, young and slender, was lying face down on the thin mattress, a pair of blue nylon shorts pulled down around her ankles. Her street clothes were neatly folded on the cane chair that stood forlornly against a bare, water-stained wall.

"Be sure to check if all her clothes are here after the crime scene team finishes," she said. Watts grunted and made a note in his ever-present tattered notebook. "Did you get anything at all from the guy downstairs?"

"No, and I don't think we will. He remembers handing her the key. He didn't see the john go in or out. Didn't hear anything either."

"We'll have to round up all the prostitutes for questioning. Chances are this guy has been around for a while and maybe started getting rougher as he's come unglued. I'll talk to her friends. One of them must have seen her with him."

"I'll get some uniforms on canvassing the hookers," Watts responded.

"Let me use your cell phone?" she asked.

He handed it over as they leaned against the wall outside the crime scene, and she punched in her own number. She tried not to think about the quick surge of hope in Sandy's voice when she asked the girl to meet them at the hotel.

"Just come on down, Sandy," Rebecca finished. "I'll explain when you get over here."

Watts raised an eyebrow and Rebecca merely shrugged. "I've got someone who can ID her."

The Homicide team and the CSI lab van pulled up as Rebecca and Watts were on their way out. Dee Flanagan stopped next to Rebecca in the hallway.

"You catching homicides now, Frye?"

"Stumbled on this one. Check what you get against a similar— four days ago at the Viceroy."

"He's getting greedy, isn't he?" Flanagan remarked caustically, hefting her heavy crime scene case in her right hand. She started up the stairs, adding over her shoulder, "Yeah, yeah. I'll call you."

Rebecca turned at the sound of her name and saw Sandy at the bottom of the stairwell, a uniformed officer blocking her ascent. "She's with me," Rebecca said to the slim, dark-haired female beat cop. "You can let her up."

The uniform turned in her direction, caught sight of the gold shield on her coat, and almost snapped to attention. "Yes, ma'am."

Sandy gave the cop a haughty look and slid by her on the narrow stairs, brushing her breasts against the officer's arm in passing. Startled, the cop took a step back. "Rookie," Sandy muttered disdainfully, and for a second, Rebecca smiled.

Then she looked into Sandy's eyes and saw her terror. She steeled herself for what she had to do, taking her elbow in a firm grip as she said, "I want you to come upstairs and see if you recognize this girl."

Sandy didn't protest or even question. She'd known the minute she'd turned the corner and seen the patrol cars and the cluster of uniforms around the entrance. Whatever it was, it wasn't good. But then there was always a chance it wasn't her. Maybe someone else's number had come up unlucky.

Rebecca stopped at the door and called to Flanagan, "Can I bring in someone for an ID?"

Flanagan glanced up from where she was kneeling by the bed, peering at the dead girl's body. From their angle she looked like she was praying.

"Yeah...carefully. You know the routine."

"Don't touch anything, and stay right next to me," Rebecca instructed as she led Sandy to the bed.

The young woman stared motionlessly at the figure for a long moment, then turned away. "That's Anne Marie," she said, no hint of emotion in her voice.

"Come on, let's get out of here," Rebecca murmured, still holding her by the arm.

Sandy began to tremble as they descended the stairs, and by the time they reached the bottom, she was sobbing. Rebecca automatically put her arms around the shaking girl, whose street-hardened façade had finally crumbled. To the detective's surprise, Sandy held on to her tightly, pressing her face to Rebecca's chest.

"I'm sorry, Sandy," the detective whispered, softly stroking her hair. "I'm sorry."

"Never thought I'd like getting this close to a cop," Sandy said after a minute, her voice wavering. She wiped her eyes with the back of her hand and straightened her shoulders. She looked into Rebecca's eyes, read the undisguised pain in them, and said softly, "Thanks."

Rebecca was aware of Watts watching them expressionlessly from the opposite side of the lobby, but she ignored his flat appraising observation. She motioned the young female officer over from where she still stood guarding the stairs and flicked a glance at her name tag. "Mitchell, I want you to take Ms. Dyer home."

"Yes, ma'am," Mitchell responded crisply, eyeing Sandy with just the slightest bit of uncertainty.

Sandy surprised Rebecca again by offering no complaint. She promised to call as many of Anne Marie's friends as she could reach and to page Rebecca if she learned anything.

Rebecca and Watts headed back to the station to begin the long process of writing up the first-on-scene report. After that, there was nothing to do but wait for the preliminary findings from Flanagan's crew. She drove silently, her jaw clenched so tightly it ached, struggling to suppress the pervasive sense of helplessness that surrounded the case. She didn't think she could stand to see one more woman brutalized by this shadow of a man who continued to elude them. She sighed, gripping the wheel tighter, fighting the depression that would only make her less effective. She also ignored the insistent urge for a drink.

Mercifully, Watts was silent.

CHAPTER TWENTY-EIGHT

They had barely begun their paperwork when Captain Henry strode through the squad room and gestured with a quick nod of his head for them to follow. Rebecca glanced at the plain clock on the wall.

"It must be something big to get the captain in here at five a.m.," she remarked to Watts as they stood.

"Or something bad," Watts replied morosely.

"We need a break on this case," Henry said without preamble. He waved them to chairs in front of his desk and loosened the collar of his immaculate white shirt a fraction. The snowy collar contrasted dramatically with his deep mahogany skin tones. Regardless of the time, or the level of tension in his office, Captain John Henry was always the picture of composure. "When the media makes the connection between these dead prostitutes and the River Drive rapes, they're going to have a field day with us. We have one—and *only* one—thing going for us at this point, and that's the psychiatrist he's contacted. We've got to use her, and soon."

Rebecca's throat constricted and her head pounded. This was the last thing she expected, although if she had been thinking clearly she should have anticipated it. Where Catherine was concerned, she seemed to be incapable of thinking like a cop.

"No, sir. You can't—" she began, only to be interrupted by Watts.

"Uh, what she means, Captain, is that the shrink's probably a long shot. You know, a red-herring kind of thing. The perp's not going to be stupid enough to come after someone we know about."

Henry looked at Rebecca strangely but directed his reply to Watts. "That's not what our experts tell me. They say that he's delusional, and that his distorted sense of vulnerability is his weak spot. He's arrogant enough to believe that he can snatch someone right out from under us and get away with it. We need to use that to our advantage."

"Well, it's not going to be her," Rebecca said harshly, finally finding her voice. "I'm sorry, sir, but I just can't allow it."

Watts gave a small sigh and gazed out the window, waiting for the axe to fall. All he heard was the captain's voice, oddly soft.

"Sergeant, you've had more to deal with lately than any one person should, and you've done a fine job. Now let me do mine."

"Not with Catherine, Captain. Please." She leaned forward in her chair, her hands gripping the arms so tightly the tendons stood out in stark relief beneath her skin. Her face was taut with the effort it took not to bolt to her feet and shout at him. If shouting didn't work, she was prepared to beg.

The big man regarded her with compassion, but his voice was stone. "It's not up to you, Sergeant. We'll let the doctor herself decide."

Rebecca was about to protest again when she saw his gaze divert to the squad room behind her. With a sense of dread, she turned to see Catherine enter in the company of one of the night patrolmen. Attired in a cream-colored silk suit, the psychiatrist looked fresh and alert despite the hour; her face, as always, was composed and elegant. Rebecca jumped to her feet, more vehement protests on her tongue, when Watts quickly stepped between her and her superior.

He whispered urgently, "Not now, Sarge, for Christ's sake. You're no use to the lady if the Cap pulls you off the case."

Rebecca slowly settled back into the chair, waiting in stunned silence, avoiding Catherine's gaze as Henry rose to greet her. She didn't trust herself quite yet as she struggled to clear her head. Watts was right...again. There was nothing she could do to change what was happening. Now more than ever, she needed to be sharp.

"I'm sorry to inconvenience you at such an early hour, Doctor," Captain Henry said politely, standing to shake her hand. "Phillips, bring another chair for Dr. Rawlings," he instructed the uniform.

"That's quite all right, Captain. If you hadn't contacted me, I would have called you myself." Catherine glanced quickly at Rebecca as she took the proffered chair, realizing that this was going to be even harder than she had expected.

Rebecca looked shell-shocked, and the sight of her dazed distress tore at Catherine. Even someone with Rebecca's incredible reserves had a breaking point. Catherine knew what she was about to do was going to add to the physical and emotional strain the detective had been under since Jeff Cruz's death, but she had no other choice. She would just have to convince Rebecca that she would be fine.

"We're hoping that this killer will contact you again soon, Doctor," Henry began.

"He already has. He called at three this morning."

"Bastard," Rebecca swore swiftly.

Catherine continued, staring fixedly at the man behind the desk. "He told me he had murdered a girl tonight, a prostitute. Is that true?"

The captain looked at Rebecca for confirmation.

"We're not sure yet," Rebecca responded, her face a mask of tension.

Catherine contemplated Rebecca's inscrutable expression, then said softly, "The truth, please, Rebecca."

"Yes," she replied between gritted teeth, her ice blue eyes hard as she finally looked at Catherine. She saw the flash of sorrow, quickly hidden, in the deep emerald gaze that held her own. Beneath the pain in Catherine's eyes was a tenderness that hurt.

"He said *I* killed her," Catherine continued, her usual composure slipping for an instant as her voice broke. She took a deep breath, and her face was calm again. Only her eyes, glittering emerald stones, betrayed her rage. "He said that he killed her because I wouldn't meet with him as he had asked."

"That's bullshit," Watts interjected abruptly. "Uh, pardon me, ma'am, but nobody killed that girl except the person who crushed her skull, and it sure wasn't you."

"He said that he would kill one woman for every day I delayed. In my professional opinion, I believe that is entirely possible."

"Catherine, you can't let him make you feel responsible," Rebecca protested desperately. "It's just a trick to trap you into seeing him. I won't let you get involved in this—he's deadly, for God's sake!"

Catherine saw Watts grimace and the captain's formidable countenance darken with anger. She suddenly realized that Rebecca was jeopardizing her entire career out of fear for her safety. She understood it; she, too, would do anything within her power to keep Rebecca from harm. But, just as Rebecca had responsibilities and obligations, she did also. At the moment, however, she needed to keep Rebecca from destroying her career with another ill-timed outburst.

"I'm afraid you have nothing to say about it, Detective. What I choose to do about this situation is none of your concern." She turned her back on Rebecca's stunned face and said to Henry, "What is it you have in mind, Captain?"

"When he calls again, I want you to agree to meet him. You'll never have to actually engage him; we just need to lure him out into the open so he can be apprehended. We'll attach a recording device to you, and we'll know where you are every second. You'll be quite safe."

"He's lying, Catherine," Rebecca said flatly. "A million things can go wrong when you're wearing a wire, and we won't be able to put a tail too close to you because it might scare him off. You'll be alone with him—with plenty of time for him to kill you before we could reach you." She met the astonished eyes of her superior officer without flinching. "Tell her, Captain. Tell her that you're asking her to risk her life."

Catherine turned slightly in the chair so that only Rebecca could see her face. She reached a slim-fingered hand and rested it protectively on Rebecca's clenched fist. "It's all right," she said quietly. "I know you're worried, but this is something *I* must do. Please, Rebecca, trust me."

Rebecca's fist slowly relaxed and her fingers entwined fleetingly with Catherine's. Their eyes met and silently spoke.

I need you.

And I need you.

Rebecca squeezed Catherine's hand briefly, then let go and straightened her shoulders, facing Henry squarely. Her voice was steady. "If she's going to do this, I want it to be my show. I'll call the shots all the way, and I want to be her backup."

Captain Henry contemplated the two women. They were not physically touching, but the connection was nearly palpable. One was a stranger he felt he knew; the other was a cop he was just beginning to understand.

He settled back in his chair and nodded. "You've got it, Sergeant. Don't screw it up."

CHAPTER TWENTY-NINE

They waited in tense silence. Catherine had called Hazel Holcomb and arranged for coverage at the hospital; her home and office phone numbers had been patched in to a line at the station. She, Rebecca, Watts, and several other detectives were crowded into a small room filled with stale smoke and littered with half-filled paper coffee containers, soda cans, and fast food wrappers. Catherine had no chance to speak with Rebecca privately, so she contented herself with watching the detective work.

Rebecca had shed her jacket and leaned against the desk, one slender hip balanced on the edge, her sleeves rolled up to reveal her tanned, muscled forearms. A phone was tucked between shoulder and chin as she scribbled notes while she talked. Her height and leanness were accentuated by the fine tailoring of her shirt and gabardine trousers, the only interruption in the elegant line of her body the slash of leather across her back that secured her weapon to her side. Catherine had never felt so far from her, or more captivated by her. Every ounce of Rebecca's exceptional skill was displayed in her sure, certain movements, underscored by the steely determination in her face and the absolute command in her voice. Here was the strength that defined her.

The detective had been on the phone for nearly an hour, demanding surveillance equipment, requesting particular officers for special assignment, setting the wheels in motion to create an enormous web designed to trap her prey. To the other cops in the room, she appeared focused and self-contained. They were used to her calm under pressure and took no notice of the tension betrayed in the brusque tenor of her voice and the clenched muscles of her jaw. Catherine, however, knew her in a way that they did not, and she appreciated the effort such command presence demanded. She was too sensitive to the nuances of behavior to miss the signs of agitation and stress that Rebecca thought she was hiding.

Catherine wanted desperately to touch her, talk to her, make some connection with her—anything to let her know how much she cared, and how much Rebecca meant to her. She was continually frustrated in her attempts to draw Rebecca aside by the arrival of yet another person who had to see the Sarge on some urgent matter or by the constant ringing of the phones with yet another decision for her to make. When Rebecca did glance her way, there was the barest flicker of warmth before her eyes became impenetrable again. Whatever she was feeling toward Catherine at the moment, she hid well.

The low level of conversation in the room halted abruptly when the red phone, the one that was receiving calls forwarded from Catherine's home, rang. Twice before it had rung; both were patient-related calls. This time even the ring seemed different. Catherine waited for Rebecca's signal, then they both picked up at once.

"Hello?" Catherine said.

Rebecca could detect no nervousness in her voice. Even though she expected it, her stomach still tightened at the next words.

"Hello, Dr. Rawlings," the smooth, well-modulated voice said. "Did they find the girl yet?"

"What girl?"

"The one I left them. The one I killed for you."

"Yes," Catherine replied at a nod from Rebecca.

"Are you ready to meet me now, or will I have to kill another one tonight?"

"Where?" Catherine answered quickly, no longer looking at Rebecca. She would have to let her instincts guide her now. It was she, after all, he had chosen to contact, and she had the expertise to deal with him. *Oh God, I hope.*

"I can't tell you that now, can I, not with someone listening. We must keep it a secret a little longer. Drive to the statue of St. Joan in the park. You'll find an envelope under three bricks on the left side. Read the instructions and do as they say. And remember, Dr. Rawlings, I'll be watching you the entire time…just as I watched the others."

"When?"

"Seven o'clock tonight."

"If I come—" The line went dead.

Catherine looked to Rebecca, the receiver still gripped in her hand. Her heart was pounding, and that surprised her. She thought that she had been ready to hear his voice again, but his intimate, seductive tone had unsettled her. That was a good thing to know, because she needed to be in control of herself when they finally met. Instinctively, she knew that they would, even though Captain Henry had assured her that it would never get that far—that the police would apprehend him before he ever actually got near her. She didn't really believe that and, she was quite sure, neither did Rebecca.

"Time?" Rebecca asked sharply, but she already knew the answer.

Someone confirmed that the conversation had been too short for a phone trace. She went to the attached tape recorder, pushed rewind, and played the tape for the others in the room. For some, it was their first exposure to the sound of his voice.

Watts finally spoke, breaking the tense silence. "It won't play, Sarge. There's no way we can stake out the meeting place, because we won't have enough advance notice of where it is. A wire won't help much if we're too far away to get to her in a hurry. He's got the upper hand, which means that we might lose. It's got a bad smell to it."

Rebecca studied the disheveled man whose very presence she had resented up until now, and she couldn't help wondering if he had spoken first so that she wouldn't have to. And he was right. If she had said the same thing, there always would have been some suspicion that she had not acted impartially—that her judgment had been clouded by her personal involvement in the case. Those who knew her well would never believe it, but, still, her reputation would be tainted. She owed him, and she wasn't sure she liked that prospect.

"You're right, Watts. Let's send someone out to pick up the note. Maybe there's something in it that will give us a handle on him."

"Wait!" Catherine cried, ignoring the flash of anger in Rebecca's eyes as she spun around to stare at her. "You can't do that. If I don't go…if I disappoint him…he's going to kill again. Believe me, he's serious about that. And there's every possibility that he won't harm me. It doesn't matter *why* he fixated on me. He did. He thinks of me as someone special—he wants to share his victories with me. I'm his *audience;* I validate him, and he needs that. There's a chance if I can talk to him that I might be able to convince him to surrender."

"Can you guarantee that he won't harm you, Dr. Rawlings?" Rebecca asked pointedly.

"No, I can't." Catherine spoke softly, but her voice was steady. She looked at Rebecca with a plea for understanding in her eyes, and with a tenderness that said she appreciated Rebecca's concern for her. "But I can guarantee he'll harm someone else if I'm not there to pick up his note at seven o'clock tonight. There must be a way."

"There is," Captain Henry said from the doorway, where he had been standing quietly. "It's almost five. We have time to fill the park with undercover people between now and seven o'clock. We'll put a two-way microphone on you and a tracer on your car so we know where you're going at all times. And we'll put one detail behind you on foot when you get out of your car. They'll be close enough to intercept him if he gets close to you."

"It's loose, Captain," Rebecca interjected, her voice steady. "She might go where we don't have any people, or the tail might lose her. It's still risky."

"If it looks bad, you can pull the plug, Frye," Henry said. He watched her carefully, wondering what he would do in her situation. He thought he knew, but like so many things, you never know what you were made of until you were tested. And Detective Sergeant Frye was being tested now.

"I want to do it," Catherine said, pleading with her eyes for Rebecca's support.

"We go," she said. "I want everyone in the command room in ten minutes for a briefing."

Henry nodded and left the room, satisfied that he had made the right call in putting Frye in charge. Every cop there knew Rebecca Frye had put her career on the line by openly challenging her superior officer. To everyone's stunned surprise, he had handed the reins to her. If things went wrong, she'd bear the brunt of the censure. If they went right, she was looking at lieutenant's bars.

"Well, you heard the Sarge," Watts said grumpily. "Come on, everybody. Let's go. You've got ten minutes to piss before things really start rolling."

He succeeded in emptying the room, and Catherine found herself alone with Rebecca for the first time in eighteen hours.

CHAPTER THIRTY

I don't suppose there's any way to change your mind?" Rebecca asked, her voice resigned.

"No."

"For God's sake, Catherine, *why?*" She ran her hand through her short blond hair, trying not to pull it out in frustration.

"Because he's got to be stopped, Rebecca! And this may be the only chance." Catherine's heart ached at the anguish in Rebecca's eyes. She did not want to be the cause of it, for any reason, ever. "I'm not a fool, Rebecca, and believe me, I have no desire to be a hero. But surely you must see that I am the best person to draw him out."

"What I *see*," Rebecca replied angrily, "is you as his next victim." She turned her back and leaned both arms down on the desktop, breathing rapidly, desperate to dispel the nightmare images of Catherine on the ground, bloodied and violated. Every woman she had ever found, broken and abused, flooded her memory. All of them had Catherine's face. "God," Rebecca said, her voice breaking. "I couldn't bear it."

Catherine went to her, wrapping her arms around her, pressing her cheek to Rebecca's back. Softly, she confessed, "I'm falling in love with you, Rebecca Frye. And I have absolutely no intention of leaving you."

Falling in love. Rebecca closed her eyes, shutting out everything except those words—precious words, terrifying words—stirring emotions at once joyous and fearsome. Faced with her desire for Catherine, she was forced to confront her own loneliness and need. It was far too late to pretend that she could walk away from this woman and far too late to return to her safe, well-defended world where she kept her feelings buried.

"Please don't leave," she whispered too quietly for Catherine to hear as she turned, slipping her arms around the other woman's waist, brushing a kiss over the soft skin of her neck. She caressed her gently, running her hands over her back and arms. When she kissed her lips, all she knew was the rightness of holding her. "Catherine, I—"

A sharp knock on the door interrupted.

"Yeah?" she answered gruffly, reluctantly lowering her hands and stepping back a pace. Her eyes were fever bright as she stared at Catherine.

"Captain wants us, Sarge," Watts announced, entering after a moment. "He wants to review the operation, get the doc wired, and start moving people into position."

Rebecca continued to look into Catherine's calm eyes. "Are you absolutely sure?"

"Yes."

The next hour passed in a flurry of activity. Suddenly, it was nearly time for Catherine to drive to the statue of Jeanne D'Arc, situated along the Drive in the center of the large park, and pick up her next instructions.

"Let's go over it again," Rebecca said to the escort team waiting with Catherine. "Watts and I will be behind Dr. Rawlings with the directional receiver." She looked at the short, wiry woman who was the department's technical supervisor. "You're sure the transmitter on her car is set to go?"

"I fixed it to the undercarriage of the doctor's Audi myself," the female officer replied. "It's working fine. I set the frequency in your vehicle on the same channel. Readout is perfect."

Rebecca nodded in satisfaction. "Okay. Once Dr. Rawlings reaches the final destination point, all teams will converge on that site but maintain a perimeter of a hundred yards until contact is confirmed. I'll be on foot at that point."

Watts gave her a quick look. They hadn't discussed that part, but he knew better than to question her now. You didn't contradict the quarterback in the middle of a play.

"If at any point the doctor's safety is at issue, we will move in, whether we have contact with the suspect or not. Are we all clear on that?" She looked at each team leader individually, assuring herself that everyone understood that protecting Catherine was their top priority.

Reasoning that the suspect couldn't possibly hope to leave the park undetected with Catherine in tow, she assumed that whatever he had planned, it was going to happen at the rendezvous point. If he did try to leave, there were officers posted at every parking area and all the crossroads that intersected with the main drive. The only time that Catherine would be at risk would be the window between the moment he made contact with her and the time it took for Rebecca to reach her. She estimated that interval to be thirty to sixty seconds. And if it were not his intention to kill Catherine immediately, she would have enough time to close the gap. She knew full well how slim the margin of safety was; she fervently hoped that Catherine did not.

"If at any time you want to call this off, for any reason," Rebecca said firmly, looking at Catherine directly for the first time, "all you have to do is say so, and we'll get you out immediately."

"I understand," Catherine replied steadily.

If she was worried, she did not appear so to the room full of police officers. She had paid little attention to the logistics and strategies they were planning. She had already been fashioning her own plan of action.

She wanted to be emotionally prepared to meet the man whom most people would consider hopelessly insane. Her training had taught her to reserve such judgment until she had firsthand experience. In this case, she had no idea what form that experience might take, and she knew that being caught off guard could mean her life. Nevertheless, there was a part of her that looked forward to the opportunity that few professionals in her position would ever have. Deep in thought, she had actually been startled when Rebecca addressed her.

"Are you ready, Dr. Rawlings?"

"I'm quite ready, Detective Frye."

Rebecca straightened up, her eyes focused and intent. "Then let's do it."

"Roger that," Watts seconded emphatically as he led the procession of officers out of the room.

"Is the wire comfortable?" Rebecca asked as they headed down the corridor to the rear exit. She put her hand lightly on Catherine's elbow as they walked, just for the comfort of touching her.

Catherine smiled. "I won't be sorry to take it off."

"You know I'll be right behind you all the time. If you sense anything at all—a stranger approaching who looks odd, a noise that seems out of place, *anything*—just whisper. I have a receiver. I'll hear you."

They had reached the car, and Catherine turned to Rebecca, sliding her fingers along her sleeve and touching the back of her hand. "I know that you'll be there. That's what makes me feel safe. Don't take any chances, Rebecca. I don't think he'll hurt me, at least not right away. He wants to talk to me; he needs to tell me what he's done. He doesn't want to kill me. And I don't want *you* to get hurt."

"I hope you're right," Rebecca said grimly. *But I'm not giving him the chance to change his mind. As soon as he shows, it's over.*

Watts was already sitting in the car that would follow Catherine. Rebecca motioned that she would be right there. Now that she was faced with actually letting Catherine go, she wasn't sure she could do it. She stepped close to her, blocked from Watts's sight by Catherine's open car door, and encircled her waist with one arm.

"Catherine," she said urgently, aware that there was no more time. Suddenly, it was very important that she tell her. "I love you. Jesus…be careful."

Catherine heard the fear in her lover's voice and softly disengaged herself from Rebecca's embrace. "I promise. I'll see you soon."

Quickly, she slid into the car and started the engine. She was afraid that if she looked at Rebecca again, her own resolve would weaken. She needed all her strength to do what she knew must be done.

Watts pulled the unmarked police car up beside Rebecca and pushed the passenger door open. He handed her a vest across the front seat. "Get in, Sarge. It's time to nail this prick."

Rebecca tossed the vest onto the seat beside her as she slid in, mentally holding Catherine's image with the clarity of a photograph. She felt her fear turn to anger, and her anger focused into a raging fire. This was one woman he would not touch. She took a deep breath, her eyes on Catherine's Audi ahead of them, her mind growing still and cold. "Let's go earn our pay."

CHAPTER THIRTY-ONE

Catherine made steady progress across town in the late rush-hour traffic. She searched her rearview mirror several times for signs of Rebecca and Watts, but she could see no trace of them. She put it from her mind, reassuring herself with the knowledge that they *were* there somewhere.

It was precisely 7:00 p.m. when she pulled over next to the solitary statue of the woman warrior and found the message from the killer in the spot he had described. She was surprised to find her hands were shaking as she lifted the damp envelope from its hiding place. She brought it to the car, as Rebecca had instructed her, before opening it.

"Walk north on the path along the water," she read out loud, wondering if the police could really hear her. She reread the single sentence several times, thinking it was odd that he had chosen that path. The hard-packed dirt path had been nearly abandoned after a wider, paved path had been built nearer to the highway. *Of course.* She smiled at her own naïveté. *This route is perfect for someone who doesn't want to be noticed.*

Rebecca, however, didn't miss the significance for a second. "Hell," she groaned. "That trail is four miles long, and a lot of it is overgrown with brush. He could be anywhere."

"Well, at least you'll have good cover," Watts replied with uncharacteristic optimism.

"There she goes. Coordinate the teams to move in, Watts," Rebecca said, reaching for the door handle. She was surprised by Watts's restraining grip on her arm.

"Give her a few minutes, Sarge. You know where she's headed. If he's watching and sees you now, the deal's off. And I say the lady is safer now than she would be if we *didn't* know when he was coming."

Rebecca forced herself to watch Catherine's figure blur into the trees at the water's edge before she left the car. Watts pulled away at the same time, planning to drive slowly along the road that meandered through the park, hoping to stay in the same vicinity by the bearings Rebecca transmitted to him by radio. It left Catherine and Rebecca fairly isolated, but it was the best they could do.

"There's a runner coming this way," Catherine's voice announced in her ear, startling Rebecca with its clarity. She couldn't see Catherine, who was probably only a hundred yards ahead of her. The dense foliage near the water made for poor visibility, especially in the rapidly deepening darkness.

"I have contact with her, Watts," Rebecca relayed into her own tiny microphone. "We're about a half mile in along the trail. Nothing yet."

"He's passing," Catherine continued, a touch of relief in her voice.

A male cyclist passed Rebecca from behind. She noted his general description, but he was the wrong age and didn't appear suspicious. She relayed their general location to Watts again, knowing that he would direct the other officers staked out in the park in tandem with them as much as possible.

"A woman with a dog approaching. Cute dog," Catherine noted.

That, Rebecca knew, would be Valerie Thompson and Cleo. Cleo was a narc dog. They had decided to risk putting one officer on Catherine's direct route if they could, and the tiny Yorkshire terrier seemed like the perfect cover.

Val shook her head almost imperceptibly as she passed Rebecca a minute later. "Nothing," she whispered with disappointment.

Rebecca hadn't expected much. Obviously, he wasn't going to reveal himself. What she couldn't figure out was how he intended to get away, especially with Catherine. Could he be so psychotic that he didn't believe they would be following him? He had set this up so well, and this glaring flaw perplexed her.

"There are some fallen trees up ahead," Catherine reported. "I'm going to have to leave the path for a little ways to go around them."

"No!" Rebecca ordered frantically, although only Watts could hear her. She broke into a run, one hand pressing the small earphone against her ear, straining to hear Catherine's voice.

If Catherine was off the trail, not only was she more vulnerable, but also she was easier to lose. Seconds later, Rebecca heard Catherine's cry transmitted with agonizing sharpness and then recognized the harsh voice that froze her heart.

"Where is the wire? Tell me!"

Rebecca heard the rending of cloth followed by total silence as Catherine's transmitter went dead.

"Jesus, Watts! He's got her! Move, move!" Rebecca screamed into her mike as she raced along the trail. She saw the downed trees ahead and slowed as she approached, gun in hand. Carefully, she stepped off the path toward the water, scanning right and left for some sign of Catherine and her attacker. It was evident from several trampled bushes where he had waited for Catherine's approach. *They can't be far ahead!*

Rebecca's eye caught a faint flash of color in the grass. She reached down for the object, stifling a moan as her fingers closed over one of the cream-colored buttons from Catherine's blouse. Moving automatically, the tiny connection to Catherine clenched in her hand, she continued to search; her vision narrowed as her panic began to rise. Through the trees, not fifteen yards away, she could see the ever-present panoply of boats on the river, while the setting sun cast deep purple shadows across the water. Life went on normally around her, while her own reality collapsed into the sensation of a tiny button pressed into her palm. She heard footsteps behind her and turned, her gun poised. It was Watts, red faced and sweating.

"What happened?" he asked breathlessly.

"He was waiting here, just like we knew he would be. I was only a minute behind, but they're gone. He's got her," Rebecca recounted in a flat, empty voice.

Watts would almost rather she panicked. Her eyes were eerie—wild and feverish. She looked like a loose grenade with the pin pulled, ready to go off at any second. "They can't get out of the park, Sarge," he said as steadily as he could. "That's one thing we did right."

"What if he doesn't take her out of the park? What if he just rapes her and murders her, fifty yards from us, just like the others?" Her voice had an edge to it now, a desperate note of anguish.

"Too dangerous. We've got people all over here now. And besides, this guy is not stupid. He got her here for a reason, and it wasn't just to hump her."

Rebecca lunged at him. "Shut your fucking mouth!" She had her hands on his throat before she realized what she was doing. His lack of resistance as well as the absence of anger in his eyes penetrated her pain-filled mind. Just as quickly, she let him go.

"God...I lost it," she said, stepping back, shocked. She stared at her hands, then at him, her mind clearing. "I'm sorry, Watts."

He regarded her impassively, waving away her apology. Then he relaxed somewhat when he saw that color had returned to her face and her expression had again become sharp and intent. "Your call, Sarge. What next?"

"They're not here, Watts," she said, turning in a full circle and seeing nothing in the way of a trail to follow. "Which means they went somewhere, right?"

Watts nodded in puzzled agreement.

"So where the hell did they go? For that matter, how does he *always* disappear so easily? They didn't go up that path because two of them would have left quite a trail and we've got people up ahead. And they didn't go back past me. So, Watts, where did they go?"

They both turned at the same time—toward the river.

"Son of a bitch," Watts said, hurrying after Rebecca, who was pushing quickly through the shrubs and bushes. "Are we dumb fucks or what? It's been right in front of our noses the whole time. The goddamned water!"

Their eyes scanned the crew teams and solitary rowers on the river. It was a sight so familiar it had failed to register in anyone's mind.

"Janet Ryan stopped to watch the regatta," Rebecca exclaimed, "and I bet if we checked the dates of the other attacks, we'd find there was a regatta each time. Perfect cover." She rounded on Watts, her voice sharp with purpose.

"He's got to be headed for the boathouses. He can't stay on the water with her." She started back along toward the path they had just descended. "Get the car and meet me there. And for God's sake, keep this quiet. I don't want Catherine to end up a hostage with the SWAT team breathing down our necks. He won't be expecting anyone to come after him. He thinks he's outsmarted us. But if we get there quickly, we can catch him off guard and take him."

"I'll keep a lid on it for as long as I can, Sarge," Watts said, his tone cautious. "That means I'm your only backup, and it could get pretty hairy when we find him."

She met his eyes. His never wavered.

"That's good enough," she said, and then she ran. She'd find them, and if he'd laid one finger on Catherine, she'd kill him where he stood.

CHAPTER THIRTY-TWO

The first thing Catherine noticed was the pounding pain in her jaw. The second was the rhythmic sound of water rushing past. She tried to turn and found herself wedged uncomfortably into a narrow space at the front of a boat, face up, something pressing uncomfortably into the small of her back. Much more disturbing than her physical discomfort, however, was the man seated above her, rowing quickly and efficiently through the deepening dusk.

"We're almost there, Catherine," he reported softly in a surprisingly affable tone. "May I call you Catherine?"

She tried to focus on his face in the near darkness. She wanted to put a face to the voice; she needed that connection to quiet the rising panic that was making it hard for her to breathe. She needed to be able to think; she needed her senses and her intuition. If she froze now, she had a feeling that she would die. She very much did not want to die.

"Yes. I'm Catherine. What may I call you?" she asked, her voice sounding odd to her own ears. She ran her tongue experimentally over the inside of her mouth. Swollen, but nothing broken, all teeth intact.

"Raymond."

Her heart raced at this small triumph. "Where are we going, Raymond?"

"To a private place, where no one will disturb us."

"All right. Will you tell me why?" Catherine made no attempt to sit up. She couldn't go anywhere, and it was pointless to antagonize him.

Abruptly aware of the cold wind on her chest, she realized her blouse was open. She remembered him tearing it to pull off the tiny microphone wires that had been taped there, and she hadn't been wearing a bra to make the wire fit easier. He had not touched her breasts; she remembered that now. Then he had struck her. She tentatively reached up to pull the damaged material closed.

"What's the matter? Does your jaw hurt?" His voice was harsh now. "I didn't want to hit you, but I couldn't let you make any noise. You shouldn't have told them about us, Catherine."

"My jaw does hurt. I'm cold, Raymond," she replied, hoping to make him feel responsible for her. The more human she became for him, the less likely he was to harm her.

"You'll be warm soon."

She couldn't judge how long she had been in the boat, but she could tell that they were moving quickly. She closed her eyes and worked to calm the racing of her heart and quell the thin scream rising in the back of her mind. She wondered if Rebecca would find her in time.

There were fifteen boathouses on the river—some privately owned by universities, some city property, and some closed and boarded up, no longer in use. Rebecca was betting that he would take Catherine to one of the half dozen unoccupied structures. He couldn't risk bringing Catherine into the park, even at a distance from the abduction point. He had to know that there were police everywhere. But he could bring her here, unnoticed, and then leave alone at his leisure. The police couldn't possibly stop every single male in the park, not with a regatta just ending. There were thousands of people around. But if she bet wrong, it could mean Catherine's life.

It seemed to take forever for her to reach the first building. Watts, puffing from his jog from the car, joined her in the shadows cast by the first boathouse in a block-long row of them. She would need to check the entire perimeter of each one, possibly even the interiors, and she had to do it quietly. She was racing against the clock.

"Let's start with the ones that are dark, Watts. You take the street side, and I'll take the river side. When I move to the next house, I'll signal you."

"Right, Sarge," he grunted.

She melted quickly into the darkness, praying that she would be in time.

❖

"I can't turn on the lights, Catherine, but we have candles. Candles will be nicer, don't you think?"

He held her facing away from him with her right arm twisted behind her back and his other hand fisted in the hair at the base of her neck. He was strong, and the intense pressure on her elbow brought her up on her toes in an effort to lessen the pain. She might have been able to startle him with a kick to his shins, but she was quite sure he would break her arm if she tried. Overpowering him was out of the question; she was going to have to talk her way out of this.

"I have to tie your hands, Catherine. You can't be trusted, and I don't want you to spoil anything." He pushed her to the floor, and, before she could roll away, he pulled both wrists together behind her back. He wrapped them tightly with some kind of cord and hauled her to her feet by pulling on her bound arms.

She gasped with the acute pain in her hands and shoulders but forced herself to meet his gaze. He was an average-looking man, sandy hair, of medium height, with a slender build. It was the voice that captured Catherine's attention, and what she heard in it chilled her blood. There was a dreamy quality, almost as if he were reciting well-practiced lines. She had heard that tone before, and she knew what it meant. He was listening to other voices in his head. She needed him to listen to her.

"What might I spoil, Raymond?" she asked as he dragged her to a long bench that ran along one wall. "What are we doing here?"

"I brought you here to show you the truth. I don't want you to move while I'm fucking you. You have to pay attention to what I'm doing." He shoved her down on the bench and pulled a large zippered bag from underneath. Then he moved quickly and lit several candles, which he placed around them in a semicircle on the floor. "Just me. I want you to see."

"What? What is it you want me to see?" Catherine urged softly, desperately casting about for some way to interrupt his thinking. She was aware that her breasts were exposed, but he didn't seem to notice. He was obviously playing out a script already written in his mind, and if she couldn't distract him from it, she had no hope. Right now she was just a symbol to him, and she needed to be real. She needed to break the pattern.

"Raymond," she said again, "what do you want me to understand? You brought me here to tell me. I'm listening. I want to know."

"I want to show you how well I can fuck," he said through his teeth, suddenly sounding angry and defensive. "I want you to see how special it is with me. More than with any of the others."

"What others, Raymond? Who?" *Specifics, I need specifics. Reality is in the details.*

"Don't you think I know you've had others? You're a whore. You should have been happy it was me. You shouldn't have complained. You'll be happy now."

He was kneeling a few feet away, rapidly emptying the contents of a sports bag onto the floor. There were several pairs of women's shorts, more rope, and an automatic handgun.

"Raymond," she insisted steadily, trying not to look at the gun, trying not to think about what he might actually do to her as she lay helpless on the dirty floor. "I'm Dr. Rawlings. You called me, remember? Why did you call me, Raymond? Remember you wanted to talk?"

"What?" he stared at her as if he couldn't quite make out her words. He hesitated, still crouched over the items he had arrayed in front of him, his expression perplexed. Cocking his head, he listened in the silence. "So you can explain to them. Why would anyone complain when it's so good with me? So special. You can tell them all they were wrong to punish me. They'll believe you."

"Who, Raymond? Who doesn't understand?" He was very deep into his psychosis, and she was beginning to despair that she could reason with him. Her only hope was to keep him talking—about anything. "They were wrong...I understand. We'll fix that, but you need to explain it to me. What would you like them to know?"

"Just tell them you liked it," he snarled, reaching for the nylon shorts.

"Yes, all right," she said quickly. *I'm losing him.* "What would you like me to say? Tell me exactly what you want them to know."

He stood up abruptly and pulled her head back roughly by the hair. His face, previously unnaturally calm, was suddenly contorted with rage. "I'll do much better than tell you, *Dr. Rawlings*. I'll show you. And when I'm done, you'll know just how special I am. Then you can tell them all how very wrong they were."

Rebecca had about given up hope when she spied the dim flicker of light through the shutters of the last boathouse in the row. The building obviously hadn't been used in a long time, and she had to push vines and overgrown shrubbery away to get close to the window. To her own ears, her breathing sounded loud enough to wake the dead. She carefully, and noiselessly as possible, pried one piece of wood off the boarded up window and peered inside.

She turned her face to the small microphone clipped to the collar of her blazer and spoke in a hoarse whisper. "I've got them—rear of the last boathouse, ground floor. I'm going in. I need you *now*, Watts."

"Wait for me, Sarge! You'll get yourself killed!" Her voice had sounded strangely hollow in his ear—unnaturally calm. It spooked him.

Rebecca didn't hear his message as she moved carefully toward the half-open door a few feet away. Didn't matter. It wouldn't have changed her mind.

CHAPTER THIRTY-THREE

Hello, Catherine," Rebecca said deliberately as she stepped inside. She could barely make out the shapes at the far end of the room, but she could see Catherine and the man who stood beside her in the glow of the candles well enough. He was staring back at her, a look of confusion on his face. "Who is your friend?" she asked, walking forward slowly, her jacket unbuttoned, the strap that held her automatic released.

"This is Raymond, Rebecca," Catherine answered in a steady voice, astonished to see her but knowing better than to show it. *She looks so calm. Why does she look so calm?*

He moved quickly, pulling Catherine to her feet and stepping behind her, partially shielding himself with her body. He pressed the automatic to her temple.

"You shouldn't have come here," he said petulantly. "You've spoiled everything. I wanted her to tell them about me. Now I have to kill her."

"I don't think so," Rebecca said evenly, her eyes never straying from his face. She couldn't look at Catherine, couldn't think about her at all. There had to be only her and him—just the two of them—one on one. "I won't let you do that, Raymond."

"You have no idea who I am. You don't know my power." He laughed, sneering at her stupidity. "You can't stop me."

"*You* don't know how powerful *I* am!" she responded, stopping fifteen feet from him. She knew precisely how accurate she was from this range. She hoped he wasn't as good a marksman, but it really didn't matter. She didn't have any choice. "You can't have *this* woman, Raymond. I've come for her."

"You're a fool. I'll kill you both."

"No, you won't," she scoffed arrogantly, fervently hoping that

Watts was in position, and that he could still shoot straight. She was counting on him to save Catherine's life when she drew fire. "You can't kill me. Go ahead and try, you puny…pathetic…pervert. If you *were* any kind of man, you wouldn't have to pull women into the bushes and rape them." She raised her right hand carefully to waist level, her gaze locked on his. "I bet you can't even get it up if a woman is looking you in the face. I bet you're afraid to let her see just how weak you really are. I bet you don't have the balls to shoot—"

His eyes flickered in the instant he moved the gun from Catherine's temple. Rebecca rolled left, drawing and firing in one motion. She thought she saw Catherine pull away, but the impact of the bullet that tore into her chest pitched her backward. She was unconscious before she hit the floor.

She opened her eyes and immediately began struggling. Someone was holding her down, and she hurt. Jesus, she hurt. She tried to lift her arms, but she couldn't muster any strength. She cursed, but she couldn't seem to make any sound. Dimly, she recognized a voice, and her panic lessened.

"Rebecca, Rebecca," Catherine murmured soothingly, watching the monitor rocking crazily above the stretcher as the ambulance careened around corners. *God, her blood pressure is falling.* She pressed her palm to Rebecca's cheek. *She's cold; she's so cold.*

"It's all right, love," she said, brushing the hair from Rebecca's eyes, trying to calm her with her touch. The endotracheal tube in Rebecca's throat prevented her from speaking, and Catherine wasn't certain that the wounded woman even knew she was there. "You're going to be fine."

Rebecca was very tired, but the pain seemed farther away now. That was good. She wanted to tell Catherine not to worry, but it was so hard to talk. She fixed on Catherine's face; she was beautiful, and she was safe. Everything was all right now. Now she could rest.

Catherine met the eyes of the EMT who was frantically hanging bags of IV fluid as blood poured from under the compression bandage on Rebecca's chest. She saw her own fear reflected in his face, and her stomach lurched with sudden nausea.

"You should tell the driver to hurry," she urged, struggling to maintain her composure as she watched Rebecca's eyes close and her color fade to gray. She clutched Rebecca's limp hand to her chest, and gasped, "We're going to lose her. Oh, God…"

The rear doors were flung open, and a flurry of activity followed as people pulled the stretcher from the van and pushed it at breakneck speed into the trauma unit. Catherine followed as far as she could, and then abruptly found herself alone, strangely adrift in the now empty corridor. She turned slowly, disoriented, and saw a familiar figure hurrying toward her.

"She in there?" William Watts demanded, craning his neck to see beyond the heavy gray doors with the tiny windows set too high up for easy visibility.

"Yes," Catherine said dully. "She's in there." *She's in there, and she's alone, and she's dying. Please, please don't let this happen.*

"But she's gonna make it, right?"

"I…I don't know."

Watts peered at her, shocked more by her tone than her words. She sounded like *she* was bleeding to death. Her hair was disheveled, her torn blouse was held closed precariously with two buttons, and she was shaking. He slipped off his jacket and put it around her shoulders. "Come on and sit down, Doc. The Sarge is steel. She ain't gonna give up."

Catherine followed him because she couldn't think of what else to do. All she could do was wait. It was an agony worse than anything she could have imagined. She leaned her head back and closed her eyes, feeling as if her own life were steadily seeping away.

Catherine stood in the doorway, listening. It was comforting, somehow, to hear Watts's deep, hesitant voice in the near darkness of the deathly still room and to see him, a hulk of a man, leaning over the thin, sharp line of Rebecca's motionless body. She supposed she should have left, but she just couldn't bear to be that far away in case… in case…She closed her eyes, inwardly running from the unbearable thought of losing Rebecca. Trying to ignore her fears, she concentrated on Watts's words.

"So, like I was saying, Sarge," Watts continued conversationally, despite the fact that the woman in the bed gave no sign that she could hear him, "nobody can say for sure, not even Her Royal Highness Dee Flanagan, whose bullet actually killed the scumbag—yours or mine. But Mister Raymond Blake—that's his name—is dead meat. Two shots, dead center, right between the eyes. Too bad the prick died right away; I'd like to have had a chance to kick him in the balls a few times."

He rubbed his face, remembering what a fucking mess it had been with the Sarge lying on the floor bleeding like a river, the doc on her knees next to her screaming at him to untie her hands so she could help her, and him trying to call for backup and make sure the perp was dead. He eased into a chair next to the bed, thinking how much he hated hospitals.

"We don't have the whole story yet, but I got the highlights. Raymond Nutcase Blake was some has-been, wannabe Olympic rower. Seems he almost made the team a few years back except he raped an assistant coach of the women's squad first. He blamed her, I guess, for losin' his spot. What he's been doing is pinning a number on his T-shirt so he looked like one of the competitors during the regattas and using the water to come and go. That's probably the ninety-seven that Ryan remembers seeing when she tangled with him. I'll lay you twenty to one that Flanagan finds blood traces on his oars, too. I bet that's what the bastard used to knock out the vics, which is why we never found any sign of a weapon. The shrinks will probably come up with some fancy reason why the gym shorts reminded him of the coach he raped, or why he liked to jump women when the river was filled with rowers, but who cares? Bottom line is—he was a scumbag asshole, and he got what he deserved. Thanks to you." He blew out a breath, wishing he could be anywhere else, but afraid if he left, she'd…

"Detective Watts," Catherine said gently. "Why don't you go get some coffee? I'll be here if she wakes up."

He looked up at her, astonished, and wondered if she had read his mind. He pushed himself to his feet and replied gratefully, "Thanks, Doc. You might want to go home and get some sleep soon, too. They said it might be tomorrow before she comes around."

"In a little while," she murmured as she took Rebecca's hand and folded her fingers into her palm. It had been all she could do to go down to the cafeteria for something to eat. She wouldn't have, or even thought to change her ripped blouse for a scrub shirt, if Hazel hadn't appeared and led her away by the hand. The entire time she had been gone from Rebecca's side, she'd been terrified that something would happen to her or that she would awaken alone.

When Watts returned an hour later, Catherine had fallen asleep, still holding Rebecca's hand. He backed away, embarrassed, and left them to each other's care.

❖

Rebecca watched Catherine sleep. She was more thankful to awaken and find Catherine by her side than to discover that she herself was still alive. Dying wouldn't have been so bad, but losing Catherine would have been unbearable.

Catherine opened her eyes, sensing the gaze feather-light upon her skin. Rebecca's blue eyes were clear and bright and, astonishingly, pain free. "How are you?" she said softly, leaning forward to stroke Rebecca's face with her fingertips. *Thank you, thank you for coming back. I couldn't have borne losing you...*

"Okay. You?" Rebecca replied hoarsely, turning her head enough to brush her lips over Catherine's fingers.

"Much better now," she answered, trembling with relief. "Much, much better now."

"I'm sorry he hurt you," Rebecca said with fierce intent, but her voice was barely a whisper.

"No. He didn't." Catherine brushed her hand over Rebecca's cheek. "He didn't take you. That's the only way he could have hurt me."

Rebecca closed her eyes briefly, struggling to dispel the image of her lover bound and helpless, with a madman's hands on her. *God, if I had been a minute later.* She shuddered.

"Rebecca? Are you in pain?" Catherine asked anxiously. *You came so close to dying, and you're still so pale.*

"No. Just a nightmare," she murmured, smiling faintly. "I dreamed Watts was here."

"He has been." Catherine smiled in return. "Often."

"Told you I was having nightmares."

Catherine laughed, then leaned to kiss her. Her heart was beginning to beat normally as she finally let herself believe that she had not lost the woman who had claimed her soul. "You should get some sleep now."

"Don't go yet."

"Ah, my love, I'm not going anywhere." She couldn't contain the tremor in her voice as she added, "I just need you to get well. I love you, and I want to continue loving you for a very long time. Promise me that I'll have that chance."

Rebecca lifted her hand and cupped Catherine's jaw, caressing her softly. "I promise."

Catherine smiled and her heart rejoiced. Rebecca Frye always kept her promises.

About the Author

Radclyffe is the author of numerous lesbian romances (*Safe Harbor* and its sequels *Beyond the Breakwater* and *Distant Shores, Silent Thunder, Innocent Hearts, Love's Melody Lost, Love's Tender Warriors, Tomorrow's Promise, Passion's Bright Fury, Love's Masquerade, shadowland*, and *Fated Love*), as well as two romance/intrigue series: the Honor series (*Above All, Honor, Honor Bound, Love & Honor, Honor Guards*) and the Justice series (*Shield of Justice*, the prequel *A Matter of Trust, In Pursuit of Justice, Justice in the Shadows*, and *Justice Served*).

A 2003/2004 recipient of the Alice B. award for her body of work as well as a member of the Golden Crown Literary Society, Pink Ink, and the Romance Writers of America, she lives with her partner, Lee, in Philadelphia, PA, where she both writes and heads Bold Strokes Books, a lesbian publishing company. She states, "As an author, I know how much more it takes to 'make a book' than just adding a cover to a manuscript. Done with respect and love for the craft, creating a book is a never-ending joy. As a publisher, my mission is to provide that experience to every author at Bold Strokes Books."

Her upcoming works include selections in *Stolen Moments: Erotic Interludes 2* from Bold Strokes Books, *After Dark* from Bella Books, *Hot Lesbian Erotica* from Cleis, and the next in the Honor series, *Honor Reclaimed*, to be released in 2005.

Look for information about these works at www.boldstrokesbooks. com.

Other Books Available From Bold Strokes Books

Course of Action by Gun Brooke. Actress Carolyn Black desperately wants the starring role in an upcoming film produced by Annelie Peterson, a wealthy publisher with a mysterious past. How far is Carolyn prepared to go for the dream part of a lifetime? And just how far will Annelie bend her principles in the name of desire? (1-933110-22-8)

Justice Served by Radclyffe. The hunt for an informant in the ranks draws Lieutenant Rebecca Frye, her lover Dr. Catherine Rawlings, and Officer Dellon Mitchell into a deadly game of hide-and-seek with an underworld kingpin who traffics in human souls. (1-933110-15-5)

Rangers at Roadsend by Jane Fletcher. After nine years in the Rangers, dealing with thugs and wild predators, Sergeant Chip Coppelli has learned to spot trouble coming, and that is exactly what she sees in her new recruit, Katryn Nagata. But even so, Chip was not expecting murder. The Celaeno series. (1-933110-28-7)

Distant Shores, Silent Thunder by Radclyffe. Ex-lovers, would-be lovers, and old rivals find their paths unwillingly entwined when Drs. KT O'Bannon and Tory King—and the women who love them—are forced to examine the boundaries of love, friendship, and the ties that transcend time. (1-933110-08-2)

Hunter's Pursuit by Kim Baldwin. A raging blizzard, a remote mountain hideaway, and more than one killer for hire set a scene for disaster—or desire—when reluctant assassin Katarzyna Demetrious rescues a stranger and unwittingly exposes her heart.
(1-933110-09-0)

The Walls of Westernfort by Jane Fletcher. All Temple Guard Natasha Ionadis wants is to serve the Goddess, and she volunteers eagerly for a dangerous mission to infiltrate a band of rebels. But once she is away from the temple, the issues are no longer so simple, especially in light of her attraction to one of the rebels. Is it too late to work out what she really wants from life? (1-933110-24-4)

Change Of Pace: *Erotic Interludes* by Radclyffe. Twenty-five hot-wired encounters guaranteed to spark more than just your imagination. Erotica as you've always dreamed of it. (1-933110-07-4)

Fated Love by Radclyffe. Amidst the chaos and drama of a busy emergency room, two women must contend not only with the fragile nature of life, but also with the mysteries of the heart and the irresistible forces of fate. (1-933110-05-8)

Justice in the Shadows by Radclyffe. In a shadow world of secrets, lies, and hidden agendas, Detective Sergeant Rebecca Frye and her lover, Dr. Catherine Rawlings, join forces once again in the elusive search for justice. (1-933110-03-1)

shadowland by Radclyffe. In a world on the far edge of desire, two women are drawn together by power, passion, and dark pleasures. An erotic romance. (1-933110-11-2)

Love's Masquerade by Radclyffe. Plunged into the often indistinguishable realms of fiction, fantasy, and hidden desires, Auden Frost discovers a shifting landscape that will force her to question everything she has believed to be true about herself and the nature of love. (1-933110-14-7)

Beyond the Breakwater by Radclyffe. One Provincetown summer three women learn the true meaning of love, friendship, and family. Second in the Provincetown Tales. (1-933110-06-6)

Tomorrow's Promise by Radclyffe. One timeless summer, two very different women discover the power of passion to heal and the promise of hope that only love can bestow. (1-933110-12-0)

Love's Tender Warriors by Radclyffe. Two women who have accepted loneliness as a way of life learn that love is worth fighting for and a battle they cannot afford to lose. (1-933110-02-3)

Love's Melody Lost by Radclyffe. A secretive artist with a haunted past and a young woman escaping a life that proved to be a lie find their destinies entwined. (1-933110-00-7)

Safe Harbor by Radclyffe. A mysterious newcomer, a reclusive doctor, and a troubled gay teenager learn about love, friendship, and trust during one tumultuous summer in Provincetown. First in the Provincetown Tales. (1-933110-13-9)

Above All, Honor by Radclyffe. The first in the Honor series introduces single-minded Secret Service Agent Cameron Roberts and the woman she is sworn to protect—Blair Powell, the daughter of the president of the United States. First in the Honor series.
(1-933110-04-X)

Love & Honor by Radclyffe. The president's daughter and her security chief are faced with difficult choices as they battle a tangled web of Washington intrigue for...love and honor. Third in the Honor series. (1-933110-10-4)

Honor Guards by Radclyffe. In a journey that begins on the streets of Paris's Left Bank and culminates in a wild flight for their lives, the president's daughter and those who are sworn to protect her wage a desperate struggle for survival. Fourth in the Honor series.
(1-933110-01-5)